# CROSSING
# OVER

## ANN MORGAN

Windsor and Maidenhead

## RENARD PRESS LTD

124 City Road
London EC1V 2NX
United Kingdom
info@renardpress.com
020 8050 2928

www.renardpress.com

*Crossing Over* first published in audio format by Audible in 2019
First published in print by Renard Press Ltd in 2023

Text © Ann Morgan, 2023
Cover design by Will Dady

Printed in the United Kingdom by Severn

ISBN: 978-1-80447-022-0

9 8 7 6 5 4 3 2 1

FOR THOSE WHO DIDN'T MAKE IT

He creeps into the yard and freezes, back pressed against the gatepost.

Is it him, or is the house watching? Is that black shape in the window a person staring out? That, there, glinting in the shadows beside the drainpipe – is that some kind of camera lens?

The urge to run wrenches at him. What if this is a trap? What if they have waited until now because they know he will be too wrung out to put up a fight? What if they plan to corner him like a rat? They may have been trailing him, piecing together reports, tracking him from the air, sharing intelligence with the police.

The night sky is peaceful, the stars glistening, but that means nothing. He has seen beauty birth ugliness too many times to be taken in. He knows how life can hide hideousness behind a smile. He has seen, ah, he has seen...

He shakes the thoughts away – his head playing tricks. Probably.

For now, he is too knotted with need to care. He aches. He is cold. He is hungry. He has to hide. These things crowd out all else.

So. The wooden door. His hand on the bolt.

The creak of it opening rakes his brain. He glances back, alarmed, at the house. The place stays silent and still.

Then he is inside, trembling in the mousey gloom. Moonlight shines through the knotholes like torch beams and something flits above his head, making him gasp and duck.

The floor heaves and he is back on the boat, roiling with a nausea that has nothing to do with the pitch and plunge of the waves.

He grips a pillar to steady himself, the wood rough in his hand. Its solidity unlatches a door inside him, breathing in a kind of calm. Fluttering in the rafters flaps into stillness, slowing his heart with it.

It is all right. It is all right. It is all right. He has made it. As long as he stays quiet, he is safe. They will not find him here.

# ONE

She notices that it's open for the first time when Jean drops her home on Tuesday afternoon. They are in the car coming back from the thing at the village hall. Reckoning? No. Reckoning's what you do when you – you know – tot up numbers. Meeting. The word is meeting. They are in the car coming back from the meeting.

Jean swings the old Morris Minor into the yard, narrowly missing the gatepost, as always, and there it is: standing ajar, the padlock askew.

Luckily, Jean is too busy talking to realise. Her topic of choice at the moment is the U3A and the outing they had to that artist's house in Dungeness the other week – the name of which escapes her, but don't worry: it'll come. Really, shouldn't Edie think about joining, because it is such a good way of keeping the brain active and meeting interesting people and making new friends. Wouldn't she like to get out a bit more?

Edie nods and smiles. Coach trips with loads of blue-rinsers waffling on about holidays with their grandchildren to Centre Perks? She has no intention of doing anything of the sort.

'Mmn,' she says. 'Oh yes. What a great idea.'

Over Jean's shoulder the barn door gusts to and fro, opening and closing like a mouth muttering.

'Mmn,' she says again. 'If you say so.'

Silence. Jean is looking at her oddly. Edie blinks and redoubles her grin.

'I'm sorry. Got distracted there for a moment. You were saying?'

At all costs, she must keep the fact of the door being left open from Jean. She can't bear the thought of what will happen otherwise: the way the other woman'll smile and be kind about the oversight. Claim this sort of thing happens to the best of us. And afterwards the knowledge that will seep through the afternoon of how they'll whisper about it down in the village – Edie alone up in that big house on the cliff, struggling to cope. The plans they'll make to be helpful. The sour little pots of supper left on the step. Being kind to be cruel.

'…So I'll ask, shall I? Put in a good word?'

'Mmn,' says Edie once again, grinning. Her eyes stray to the wispy curls poking out from Jean's headscarf. She must dye her hair to get it that odd shade of… oh gosh, what would you call it? That tart fruit. The one they use as a fragrance in bathroom cleaners. Lemon. Yes, lemon.

An image comes to her of Jean bumbling into the chemist's in Totwith every eight weeks in search of a bottle of stuff in a box with a young woman's face on it. Funny, foolish Jean. Always anxious to fit in. Eager to copy the trends. So conventional in her little house with roses round the door and photographs on the mantelpiece of Graham, who shared it with her for more than sixty years, until the day he slumped to his knees in the post office clutching a value pack of masking tape to his heart.

'Right,' she says abruptly, grasping the handle and snapping the passenger door open. 'Thanks ever so for the lift. I'd drive myself, of course, only…'

They look towards the byre, where the Vauxhall Astra sits mouldering next to the rusted boat trailer, its wheels swathed in grass.

'Of course,' says Jean, so earnestly that Edie feels a rush of affection for this woman, her dear friend of more than eighty years.

'But you will be all right, won't you?' continues Jean, eyeing the string bag of bits from the Spar shop clutched in Edie's hand.

Impatience seizes her and she gets out faster than she meant to, making her head swim. 'Of course I'll be all right!' she shouts as the yard whirls merrily around her, byre, barn, house, gate and open door capering before her eyes.

Jean nods doubtfully. 'Only…'

And once more it is between them, piled on the passenger seat like a heap of… what horses do; the mistake in the WI accounts. She flushes hotly. Oh, why won't they let her forget about it? As if it hadn't been humiliating enough having to go round asking everyone for an extra five pounds to make up the shortfall for subscriptions. Forty years she's been doing those books, without a single hitch. And then she goes and makes one fluff – one schoolgirl error – and they are upon her like harpies, like hyenas scenting blood.

She glares at Jean, at this foolish woman with horrid yellow hair whom she has never liked, this busybody driving into her yard and peering around, hoping to catch her out. Really she ought to let rip and tell her what she's always thought of her. Now would be the ideal time. She could bring it all out magnificently if she said it now. Every last scrap of truth. How Graham was an oaf and a ditherer, whose fingernails were never clean. How she knew it from the first of the starry-eyed letters Jean wrote from the farm she was evacuated to in Somerset all those years ago during the war – pages and pages of hogwash pinched from the motion pictures.

But instead she smiles graciously, steadying herself on the top bit of the car. 'I'll be fine,' she insists. 'All present and correct.'

It is not quite the right word group, but it passes. Jean nods and turns her head to look through the windscreen.

'They've made a start, I see,' she says, indicating the field on the far side of the track where last week the diggers moved in to begin excavating the foundations.

'Yes.'

'Must be noisy for you.'

It is noisy. Much noisier than she had anticipated. And the workmen have a nasty habit of loitering by the fence on their breaks, gawping into the yard. One of them is a devil for whistling out of tune. 'Oh no. Not in the least bit.'

Jean regards her.

'Well that's something.' She turns the key in the ignition and the engine splutters into life. 'I'll pick you up at ten o'clock on Saturday,' she calls out over it.

Edie frowns. 'Saturday?'

'The charity cake sale. You said you'd make a walnut cake.'

She nods. 'Right-oh! Walnut cake. Ten o'clock. Jolly good.' She shuts the car door. 'Mind how you go!' she calls as Jean puts it in gear.

When the sound of the engine has died away, she goes to the back door and lets herself in. It is unlocked, but she won't mind about that. After all, this is hardly a thieves' paradise. They never used to lock it. Besides, no one comes here these days. Hardly at all. Since Father died, it has just been her. And that is how she likes it. Simpler that way. No mess.

In the kitchen, she puts the string bag on the table and is surprised by a pair of her sensible lace-up shoes placed on its surface. Silly old thing. What was she thinking putting those there?

She attempts a laugh. 'Ha!'

But the sound is thin and the kitchen seems to frown at it. A gull outside the window above the sink taps its beak on the glass like a school conductor, as if to bring her back in line.

Suddenly she can't bear it. She picks up one of the shoes and hurls it at the window, smashing a circle in the pane and sending the bird flapping seawards with an indignant squawk.

Oh, why did Jean have to go and ask if she'd be all right? She'd been doing so well up until that moment. She'd been feeling so happy. Even with all the business over the subscriptions, she had held her own. Not a single fluff, no wrong words, nothing. And then that silly idiot had to go and spoil it with her concern. Nasty, twittish, vulgar little woman. Remorseless, humourless, foolish old boot.

'Ugh!' she expels. Out in the yard, as if stirred by the vibration, or perhaps caught by a breeze, the gaping barn door creaks to and fro.

# TWO

She first notices that the barn is unlocked on the Wednesday morning. She is sitting at the kitchen table with the jotter and the back door is ajar, letting in an early spring breeze.

Writing in the jotter is something she does to calm herself. It has things in it like this: 'When I out the bath, I like to stand with the towel about me first please then drying', and 'I prefer my boiled eggs runny. Two minutes and fifty seconds' cooking time is quite efficient.' And some of the notings-down are in jaggeder writing and run along the lines of this: 'Please, I beg you, don't ever give me tea in one of the mugs from the back cupboard. It might seem a small thing, but the thickness of the ~~stuff they're made from~~ china. It makes me want to gag.'

She can't remember exactly when she started keeping these efforts. She saw the jotter one day in the Spar shop on one of those round-you-gos of stationery intended for children going back to school and bought it without knowing why. For months she didn't use it. Then, about the time they swapped to selling that nasty, rough paper in the post office – the stuff that set words jumping around and paragraphs mismangling themselves, obliging her to put the letter-writing on hold – she found the little ring-bound volume in the drawer in the back bedroom and started to write down her thoughts.

She finds the process soothing. She likes to be able to collect her domestic opinions in one place, and being able to hold them in her hands is a relief, so that, should confusion gust up, she can seek out the jotter and see in it aspects of herself set down: logical, definite and changeless. Just as the diary used to do all those years ago, when she still believed life would grant her a story worth recording, the little ring-bound volume with its floral cover calms her. That is why she works at it – for that and no other reason.

This morning she is particularly in need of the notebook's comfort. She has come downstairs to a most distressing sight: the milk bottle left out on the table, its contents souring in the sun. It is the sort of fluff of which she would never have believed herself capable – the kind of transgression out of which Aunt Susan would have made great moment in the days when they kept milkers and every drop represented labour and expense. Not to mention rationing.

She is so irritated about it that she feels almost resentful and keeps catching herself looking around for someone to blame. But of course there is no one in the house these days, only she. Just as has been the case for fifty years. The spoilt milk is her fault, the result of her carelessness, her failure to pay attention. Stupid, idiotic girl that she is. Silly billy. Worthless—

'Morning, Mrs M!'

She starts up from the table, banging the bone bit that links the leg parts together.

'Not Mrs,' she hisses, rubbing the sore – the knee – through her corduroys. There will be a bruise. 'I'm not m—'

'No need to get up,' says the man, barging into the room. 'I can see you're busy. Writing your memoirs, are you?'

Their eyes converge on the notebook, which has flipped closed on the table between them, revealing its pink, floral cover. She wants to reach out and snatch it from view. But the spindrift of a question is in the air and she can't think how she should respond. In a blast of scared it comes to her that she has no idea who he is, this man standing in her kitchen, and she grips the back of her chair, barely holding in a scream.

'Terrible news this morning,' continues the fellow companionably, reaching up to adjust his glasses. 'Three drowned off Hedley Point.'

'Mmn,' she says, eyes frisking him for clues. He is wearing some sort of uniform. Is it a uniform? That blue shirt and those trousers, the bag with the strap going across his chest. A telegram boy, could it be? Bicycling around the countryside, dispensing bad news with a wink and a wave?

But no – there is something wrong with this notion. Her brain throbs and she puts a hand to her forehead to try to soothe it. Oh dear.

'You wonder why they do it,' the man is saying. 'Risk everything in those flimsy boats with the waves in the Channel being what they are. Chances are they'll only be sent straight back where they came from if they do manage to make it across.'

He looks at her expectantly. She casts about in her mind, fumbling for a suitable card to play.

'Just goes to show,' she ventures.

He nods and points a finger at her. 'It most certainly does.'

She expels with relief. But the test is not over: now the man is looking out of the door at the section of field visible beyond the track where someone has seen fit to dig a big, ugly trench in the earth.

'Made a start, I see,' he says.

'Mmmn.'

'Must be noisy for you.'

She narrows her eyes, suspecting a trap. Hasn't she heard this somewhere before? 'I shall be quite adequate, thank you. Don't you worry about me.'

The man nods.

'Well, I won't keep you. I just brought this,' he says, placing an envelope on the table next to the jotter.

With a surge of relief, she remembers exactly who he is. The realisation makes her jut her chin and harden her voice. 'All right, thank you, Roger. You've delivered your message. You can go now.'

He laughs. 'Ha! Roger. That's a good one. You're thinking of Granddad, that's what you're doing. I'm not Roger. I'm Dave. Same eyebrows. Sixty years' difference.'

She blinks. 'Yes. Of course. That's what I meant. Dave.'

He seems to accept this and nods at the table.

'Red letter day, is it?'

She looks at the envelope, a crisp, cream affair written out in a swirling hand. It is not red. She frowns. The suspicion blows into her mind that he might be being impertinent, alluding to something indecent. She wouldn't put it past him, coming from such a family.

'I shouldn't expect so,' she says, with as much haughtiness as she can muster. It seems to do the trick.

'Right-oh. Best be off.'

As he turns and makes for the door, she slumps a little in relief. Good riddance. They are so uncouth, these telegram boys, coming into one's kitchen without so much as a by-your-leave, not even pausing to wipe their feet. Really, she ought to write to the MP about it, get him to urge Churchill to draft a law enforcing better conduct from such types. Or no, not Churchill – silly. Harold Wilson.

On the step, the knave hesitates, looks back over his shoulder. 'Not sure if you've clocked it, but the barn door's open. Might want to get the key and lock it up. Can't be too careful these days.'

It takes her a moment to sift his meaning. At first his choice of words sends her thoughts giggling off down the wrong track and all she can call to mind is the grandfather clock in the hallway with its hands stopped so long their top edges are heaped with dust. But then she realises that this is not the point at issue, that he is referring to something else, something she has forgotten to do. Across the yard, the barn door stands slantwise, a mouth grinning crookedly. She wants to smack it in its woody teeth. It would be today, of course, that she forgets to lock it. And now this will be reported all over the village. And they will laugh and say she is not good enough, that she ought to be banned. She knows how it will be: the eagle-eyed visitors arriving unannounced. The plans they'll make to be helpful. The sour little pots of supper left on the step.

'Yes, thank you,' she says smiling furiously at the telegram boy, at treacherous Roger who destroys people's happiness out of spite, who stands there, itching to betray.

When at last he has wheeled his bicycle out of the yard, she storms inside and slams the back door. It crashes to with a terrific thud, and for a moment she is afraid that the glass has shattered. A vision comes to her of Aunt Susan's face, pinched with disapproval, and she glances behind her anxiously, half expecting to find her there. But it is all right: the room is empty and the panes are intact. There is no need to explain herself.

Instead, she hurries through to the drawing room, wrenches up the lid of the piano and slams her hands down on the keys. The noise reverberates through the house, setting a pair of gulls flapping up off the hedge outside the window and away over the grey sea below the cliff.

She rams down another chord, lower on the keyboard, bringing out the instrument's thunder. Out in the yard, as if stirred by the vibration, or perhaps caught by a breeze, the gaping door creaks to and fro.

# THREE

Thursday morning brings an unwelcome discovery: the barn is unlocked.

She has woken in a good mood, ready to achieve things. In this, the sun assists her, streaming through the faded curtains as though summer were already here. Her head helps her too. Gone is the fog of yesterday – that terrible vagueness that swept in to confound her like the mists that blow in off the Channel now and then to swathe the house.

She feels vigorous, sturdy, equal to anything. If they sent a delegation up from the village now, armed with well-meaning suggestions and the threat of her best interests, she'd be ready for them. She'd know how to deal with their prying eyes and the way they'd inquire into all the corners when they thought she wasn't looking, seeking evidence of how she has spent the money, trying to discern the worth of anything that looks new or costly in an effort to calculate a definitive figure that they can relay to the regulars at the Ship Inn.

Ha! As if she'd fritter such a sum away on bits of furniture! She almost wishes that they would come so that she can watch their faces. Perhaps throw them a red herring or two for fun. For a bubble bath, as Michael might have said.

But no. It is better that they stay away. All she asks is to be left alone. Given everything she has endured, that is the least she deserves.

After breakfast, she goes out to inspect the work. Shrugging on a woolly, she crosses the yard and peers over the fence on the far side of the track. Two men in bright-yellow jackets offer her a wave, but she ignores them, wary of being drawn into conversation that might be riddled with confusion and foolishness, which could tremble her good mood.

They have made considerable headway. Already great heaps of earth rear up around the field, flanking a series of trenches criss-crossing the land like scars from a whipping. Already she can see that the village committee was right: the development is going to be huge and vulgar and too close to the yard. It will ruin the tranquillity of the spot and make it impossible to interest anyone in buying the farmhouse and outbuildings after she's gone.

Good. Perhaps she will leave instructions for the rest of the place to be sold to the same organisation so that they can smash it to the ground and build something truly ghastly there after she's gone. A place with no memory.

She starts to walk back to the house. As she passes the gatepost she sees it: the barn door creaking back and forth in the breeze. She halts and time does the same, a frame flickering on the cinema screen of her mind in the instant before the heat from the bulb burns it. Another image splices itself in: the same door in better repair and she in her jodhpurs, clutching bridle and bit.

The years fall away, unhusking her from now. She is there. Twelve years old and striding across the yard to tack up Dobbin for a day on the cliffs, cocking a snook at Aunt Susan and her pronouncement over breakfast that she intends Edith to spend the morning beating the rugs. And there is the door, swaying gently, beckoning like a hand. She goes over to peer in.

Ah, the familiar smell of hay, dust and wood. The active shadows, rustled by field mice, fluttered by sparrows and flitted by bats. The ladder leading up to the hayloft, and above that the roof and the rafters stretching across the space like the ribs of a great beast.

Time has moved slowly here, altering little. Seventy-five years have brought scarcely more than a note of damp in the air – that and a steely edge to the gloom, made keener by daylight streaming through the holes rot has punched in the roof. As her eyes adjust, Edie sees that the ladder now lacks a few rungs and several planks in the hayloft floor have splintered apart, as though Rumpelstiltskin has stamped his frustration there. Other than that, however, everything is as she remembers, pretty much just as it was that fateful day when she—

Only… hang on. What's that? There, against the back wall. Something glinting; a silver object flashing. Odd: she can't recall anything of the kind ever hanging there. She frowns and squints. Steps nearer, looks again. But can't for the life of her make it out. Goes closer still.

As she does so, it seems that all the mice and birds and bats about the place rise up as one and hurtle at her. She feels a rush of air and hears a whistling sound and as she turns to look in its direction, a hard thing catches her on the side of her head. She has time to register a voice – hers or someone else's? – calling out in alarm and a flash of pain, but not the falling that comes after and certainly not the thud.

# FUG

She wakes in the cupboard under the stairs with Aunt Susan's appalled face staring down at her.

Instinctively, she flinches and tries to wriggle to a seated position. 'I'm sorry,' she mutters. 'It wasn't me. I didn't mean it. I promise I'll try harder to be good.'

But then the darkness thins and separates into shapes edged with silver and she sees that she is not in the cupboard but on a cobbled floor and that the face regarding her with such alarm belongs not to a person, but to the moon, which is peering in at an open door beside her.

In the barn, silly. That's where she is. Must have taken a tumble and banged her head. Why, yes, here is an egg on the side of her forehead, throbbing fit to burst. Just like her. Just like the clumsy girl she is, always getting into scrapes. If Mummy were here she would kiss it better. Only she's not, and that's that. No use crying over spilt milk. Edith's got to be the responsible one now, the grown-up girl. Not make any trouble, that's the point. Not make difficulties for Father, who works so hard with precious little reward. Anyone can see she's been indulged for far too long, running about like a mad thing, engaging in all manner of boyish pursuits. Thank goodness Aunt Susan arrived when she did and not a moment later to take Edith in hand.

Tell you what, though: it's lucky no one found her out here in the middle of the night. There'd have been hell to pay if they had.

Then it really might have been a question of the cupboard and the black beetles. Not that she minds black beetles, really. She's not a scaredy-cat like Jean. It's just the thought of being in the dark when they come that she doesn't like. The idea of their legs crawling, catching her unawares.

What's this, though? A cup of tea in a hulking great mug and a plate of custard creams beside her on the floor? Quick! Gobble them down before anyone sees.

Oh! Bleurgh! The tea's cold.

The biscuits are good, though: vanilla sweetness melting on her tongue. Before the first is finished, she is already reaching for the second. Jaws working overtime. Crumbs scattering. She'll have to make sure she doesn't leave any telltales round her mouth to avoid a dressing down in the morning. Still, she doesn't care: the biscuits are too scrumptious for that. She only wants to think about eating them.

She gives a naughty smile. Here's an idea. When she's older and Aunt Susan is dead and they're not doing rationing any more, she's going to have custard creams every day. She's going to go down to Davison's and buy up every last packet. Then she'll take them home and stuff them into cupboards all over the house, wherever there's space. She'll even put them in the grandfather clock if she has to. And if it means the mechanism goes wonky or she can't get at her clothes and has to fashion alternative things to wear out of paper bags, she won't mind because she'll be able to have biscuits whenever she wants – until she's sick if she likes – and that will be better than anything else.

She crams the third custard cream into her mouth and grins wickedly around the barn, wondering what else she can do. Perhaps if there is one of those nice game pies in the larder she could creep in and sliver off a slice without anyone noticing. She has got good at that on the nights when she isn't to have any supper – sloping down after the drawing-room door shuts, shearing off almost imperceptible portions from meat loafs, terrines and hams, rinsing the knife and returning it to the magnetic strip on the wall. Yes. Let her at the baked meats! Aunt Susan clearly isn't about (maybe she's away visiting her sister or off on one of her overnight trips to place orders with the haberdasher in Totwith) and Father wouldn't care – probably wouldn't even notice Edie was up if he walked in from the yard right this minute.

But when she lets herself in at the back door and opens the larder, things are not as she expects. There are no dishes covered with lace food umbrellas. There is no meat loaf, no pie. There is no tin painted with a scene of skaters whirling on a frozen lake waiting for the next Christmas cake. Instead, there are cans and packets arranged along the shelves in forbidding lines, like soldiers massed on sand dunes, waiting to board boats. What's more, there is some gurgling, humming white oddment standing to the left of the larder door, smooth to the touch and hot at the back.

She narrows her eyes. Someone has been in, clearly. Changing things, messing about, introducing nonsense for a joke.

Well, she'll show them. She'll make a telephone call and file a complaint with Constable Harris, have these scoundrels bang to rights. She strides out into the hallway and picks up the receiver. 'Totwith twenty-three,' she says. But there is no reply from the operator, only a rude, continuous beep.

She bangs the handset down in fury. More trickery?

But when she looks up, the hallway doesn't seem to think so. The furniture stands silvered in the moonlight that shines through the kitchen doorway – the grandfather clock, the hat stand, the barometer stuck on 'fair'. They watch her warily, soberly, these friends, as though it is she and not everything else who has stepped out of line.

She shrugs and just like that, her anger pulls loose and drifts away – a piece of netting snagged for a while on the rocks, only to be swept out to the Channel by the tide. The drawing room doorway gapes in welcome, so she wanders in. And there it is, standing in the curve of the bay window. That thing he sent. A Diana? No, not that. But something like. She smiles. Gracious, wasn't there a to-do about it when it arrived in the back of that van? Aunt Susan's face. She'd never seen the like.

And now here it is. Exactly where the removal men put it. Gleaming and beautiful. A Domingo? No. A Joanna? Perhaps that will do.

She goes to it and opens the bit at the front. Underneath is a row of black and a row of white. Yes: she thought she'd find something like this in here. Black and white, white and black, and all with lines between. Pretty. Like teeth. Like teeth with bits of liquorice between them – that cheeky party trick of Jean's.

There is a stool here and so she sits and runs her hands over the white and the black, feeling how it is all divided up into sections. Yes. There is something you do with this. A bit of business hovering on the edge of her memory.

She presses down and – whoops! – there is a sound from deep inside the Joanna. A bold plunk followed by a thrum. She looks around hurriedly, but it's all right: nobody minds.

Well, then. She puts her fingers more firmly over the black and white bits, the keys. Or no – isn't that what you lock doors with? Sausages, maybe. Sticks? Blocks? Whatever they are, she puts her fingers back on them and, closing her eyes, pushes down. A handsome sound fills the room.

She smiles, shifts position. Tries again. There. Also good. Only a bit more complicated this time. Not as happy. Something out of place. A broken piece.

Without her telling them to, her hands feel out another sound and then another, fumbling at first, then steady, assured, like Dobbin finding his footing on the path down to the bay. Now, here are more noises, dark and mysterious, rumbling out of the belly of the Joanna with ladders of tinklings strung between them. Above them, a tune appears – a single note hanging like the moon in the sky, its reflection shimmering on the sea of lower sounds.

She plays on, eyes shut, as the image thickens: the pitch and churn of the black water, the waves slapping the bow, the little boat of the melody ploughing bravely forward as masses plunge and arch with the bass line below it, sounding the depths.

She nods to herself. Yes. This is true. This is how life strikes the mind – exactly like this.

She opens her eyes and looks across the room and of course, as she knew he would be, he is sitting there, silhouetted in the armchair by the door, back to listen to her, just as he promised. She gives him a dreamy smile and the old knowing pulses between them, magnetic and strange. Then the music sweeps her onwards, tumbling her into vastness as shimmering and slick as the night sky.

# THREE

'Cooey!'

A voice. Aunt Susan's? No, too merry for that. A stab of hope. Mummy's? No, silly. Mummy's dead. Drowned. Sunk. We don't talk about that.

Someone else, then. That nice teacher who started last term at school when Mr Richards got called up? Miss Wright?

Footsteps, the creak of the stairs and then another call: 'Edie? Are you up there? Are you all right?'

Well, then, best get up. No point being a slugabed. Breakfast and then perhaps a day with Dobbin on the cliffs. It's a sunny morning, after all. If she can just get her act together to throw back the covers—

The bedroom door swings inwards and a face looks round it. The owner is an old woman in an enormous pair of spectacles and a floral headscarf from which tufts of yellow hair poke out.

'There you are,' she says. 'But why are you still in bed? You haven't forgotten what day it is, have you?'

Edie stares up at the old woman. Who can she be? An ARP warden? A recruiter for the FANYs? Some distant relative on Father's side? A wild, glad thought comes to her: what if Aunt Susan has had a motor accident and this person has been drafted in to look after things in her absence? People are always saying she oughtn't to take the Totwith turn at such a lick. Perhaps all those spells Edie used to creep off to perform in the ditch in Top Field when Aunt Susan first came to stay have finally paid off.

But no. Something is skew-whiff. The old woman is looking at her as though Edie ought to know exactly who she is. She delves deeper for the solution but her mind seems to be in chaos, as though goblins have got in and gone rummaging through the drawers, flinging thoughts every which way. There is nothing for it but to grasp hold of the old woman's last sentence and try to make something from that.

'Of course I haven't forgotten,' she says crossly. 'Only I…'

Goodness, her head does throb. She touches the side bit, the temple.

'But what have you done to yourself?' exclaims the old woman, hurrying forward. 'Oh, Edie, have you had a fall? Your poor face!'

Edie pats her head doubtfully. 'What? This old thing?'

The woman frowns. 'Here, let me see.' She leans in so that the knot of her headscarf comes level with Edie's eyes and a waft of scent engulfs her – lily of the valley. Floral and too strong.

Edie recoils. 'Absolutely not!' she says.

The woman leans in again, protesting. 'But Edie, you've hurt yourself. You need medical attention. You ought to be checked over by Dr Brewer, at the very least.'

'Absolutely not!' she insists, indignant at this stranger making free with her nickname. 'I won't hear of it. You let me alone.'

The woman starts backwards, uncertainty in her eyes. Edie feels a jolt of triumph. The sound of her voice talking so confidently has given her courage. She has a suspicion that not all the words were quite right, but the tone was handsome and it all flowed so well. Anyone could tell the old woman was impressed. Now she simply has to carry this forward. Press home her advantage. Show this old ninny with her silly scarf and her nasty smell that she, Edith, is not to be ordered about.

'You go about your business,' she says, flourishing her hand imperiously. 'I'll be along presently. I just need a moment to… mobilise things.'

The woman looks doubtful. 'Well, if you're sure.'

'Quite sure, thank you,' she says, and the words gather round her like friends, making her smile.

*

There is an old woman in the kitchen when she comes downstairs.

'You took your time,' the old woman says. 'We'll have to get a move on if we're to get there and get set up before they open the doors.'

Edie stares at her. Who can she be? Some distant relative on Father's side? A wild, glad thought comes to her: what if Aunt Susan has had a motor accident?

'Is that what you're wearing?'

Edie glances down at her outfit: cheerful, colourful, just the thing for a sunny day. And Father always likes it when she puts on her best sandals with the pretty snowflake-patterned socks.

'Yes. What of it?'

'Well, take a cardigan, at least. It's not even March.'

She submits to this, allowing the old woman to sling a dowdy, knitted thing about her shoulders. No point making a fuss over every small thing. The secret is to pick your battles.

Next the woman is fiddling about with some paper objects on the side. 'You've got some post here. Several days old, by the looks of it. Wonderful copperplate writing on this envelope!'

She tries to nod, but at the sound of the word 'post', an odd thing happens: she has a vision of a wooden bar swinging towards her, and she can't avoid giving a shriek.

The old woman rushes over. 'Oh, Edie! What's wrong?'

She blinks. She is in the kitchen. An old woman is standing in front of her. There is no wooden bar. 'I'm quite all right, really.' She musters a smile. 'Please. Have another cup of tea.'

An uneasy silence flows between them.

The old woman reaches out and touches her arm. 'Are you sure it's a good idea to go today, Edie? Why don't you stay here and put your feet up? I could just give Dr Brewer a bell and—'

An inexplicable urge to cry comes over her. She fights it, gritting her teeth and shaking her head. 'I really must insist that you stop going on about this!' she says furiously. 'I'm perfectly in order. Please. Let's get on.'

*

The car door clicks closed, shutting her inside time once again. All of a sudden, she knows where she is: Jean's old Morris Minor. It's mid-morning, judging by the quality of the light. Which must mean they are going to some sort of community event – a talk or discussion group. Something of that register.

'This thing we're going to...' she ventures as Jean gets in on the driver's side.

'The WI cake sale?'

'Yes.' Cake sale. That was it. In aid of those... well, those people in tents. Refusers? No.

Jean starts the engine. 'What about it?'

Referees? Not quite.

Then as they pull out of the yard, narrowly missing the gatepost, she remembers. She claps a hand to her eyes. 'Oh God. I was supposed to make a cake, wasn't I?'

Jean shrugs. 'I wouldn't worry about that. I'm sure there'll be plenty. You know what Ruth Parker's like. There'll be heaps of other ways you can help.' She reaches across to pat Edie's leg.

The touch is more immediate than Edie anticipates, as though Jean's fingers are on her bare skin. Alarmed, she looks down to see that in place of her usual slacks, she is wearing a garish tartan skirt that barely reaches her knees. Worse, apart from a pair of horrid, frilled white socks shoved into her old brown sandals, she is bare-legged, the marbled veins of her calves brazen. Drawing her gaze upwards, she sees her top half has hardly fared much better: under the grey cardigan Jean draped round her shoulders, Edie is wearing a thin orange blouse with roses embroidered between the buttons. The sad slouch of it raises an uncomfortable suspicion that she has neglected to put on undergarments.

She can't possibly allow those others to see her like this! Imagine the looks they'll give, the way they'll whisper. She must tell Jean she's changed her mind – that she's not feeling well after all and on balance it would be sensible to stay at home.

She opens her mouth to say as much, only as she does so Jean nods towards the field flashing past them on the right, where further heaps of earth have appeared, as if thrown up by giant moles.

'Making progress, I see.'

Edie clamps her mouth closed and regards her friend with narrowed eyes. Harping on about the building work again, is she? Unable to leave it alone. Just like the rest of them. Refusing to accept that the land was Edie's to do with as she chose; that she was under no obligation to take anyone's views into account but her own.

She sees at once that failing to attend the cake sale would be an unwise move. In her absence, they will talk about her. For all the decades they have known one another, Jean will have no compunction in broadcasting whatever strangeness she has witnessed this morning. Probably she will embellish it, putting the worst possible construction on everything and indulging that tendency she's always had to play to the gallery. Silly little Jean. And of course they will egg her on, those others. Greedy for details, they will pounce on anything that might be construed as evidence that Edith Morley is failing. Because if that is the case then their mealy-mouthed opposition to the development for which she has sold her land would be vindicated. They could tell themselves earnestly – as they told her repeatedly at the meetings and unofficial gatherings to which she was summoned last year – that they had her best interests at heart. And this time they could believe it.

Oh, how they'd love to put her on the rack of their sympathy! Nothing would please them more than to coddle her to distraction, just as they'd done with poor Dora Woodruff. She knew how it would go. They'd start by trading anecdotes, comparing notes on

28

little eccentricities they'd witnessed: an oddly worded birthday card, a smile she'd failed to return in the Spar shop. The matter of the miscalculated subscriptions would come up. From there they'd move to venturing suggestions, all the while congratulating themselves on their kindness when really they were plotting her destruction. Someone would float the idea of instigating a rota of people popping in throughout the week. A call to social services would be mooted. There would be talk of meals on wheels, maybe a live-in carer or – please God, no – a home. And before she knew it, her life would be crammed with strangers, alien routines and ugly what-have-yous and thingamabobs so that she could never forget what was happening to her, so that those blessed moments when everything felt as it always did and she could be her old self fled from her for good.

Well, no. No, thank you. Not today. She wouldn't give in so easily. Edith Morley wasn't going down without a fight. Not this time. And if it meant she had to turn up to the cake sale dressed like an overgrown schoolgirl, so be it. At least this way she could keep a lid on the gossip. So long as she avoided any more fluffs, she'd be able to head off the worst repercussions of this morning's funny turn.

Shuffling in her seat to do up the cardigan and hide the blouse, she feels her foot connect with something.

'Careful of my simnel cake!' Jean blurts out. 'I was up at five to make it.'

Peering down, Edie sees that her sandals are sharing the footwell with a cardboard box wrapped in cling-film and containing a large, round cake decorated with marzipan balls. She rolls her eyes. Trust Jean to make a simnel cake at the wrong time of the year. And – hold on a minute – what's this?

'You've done too many balls, Jean.'

'Mmmn?'

'On the cake. You've put thirteen. You're not supposed to do more than twelve. Eleven, ideally. The disciples or the disciples plus Jesus. You're supposed to leave Judas off.'

'Oh. Am I?'

Edie shakes her head. She hasn't set foot in a church for seventy years and even she knows that. But then of course it's just like Jean to commit such a blunder. It has always been a habit with her to hurtle blindly into things, oblivious to the wider implications. More times than Edie can remember over the years it has fallen to her to steer Jean away from disaster.

'Never mind,' she says. 'I'm sure no one will notice.'

Still, as the first houses of the village appear, she turns her head to the window and allows herself a smile. Yes, it will be all right, the sale. She is more than equal to it. And if the younger members find her attire strange, well, let them. She has always had a reputation for being odd. She used to be proud of it – to nurture it, even – stalking around in man's clothes, yomping up to the top of Wickham Heights to watch the road leading out of the village for a visitor everyone said would never come. With a bit of luck and a fair wind they'd put today's blip down to that historic eccentricity and—

'Edith?'

They are all standing round the open car door, the hall behind them.

'Right-oh!' She flicks on a smile and bounds from the vehicle, looking around defiantly – see how spritely she is, how able! 'What can I do?'

But no one answers. They stare at the lumpy cardigan with the nasty blouse peeping over its collar, the hideous skirt and the socks.

She turns her head so as not to have to watch their expressions and Elizabeth Marsh gasps. Now they are all looking at the side of her face.

'Good gracious, Edith,' says Martha Beasley. 'What on earth—'

'Beep beep! Excuse me! Coming through!'

It is Ruth Parker, clutching a stack of Tupperware to her formidable red-cashmere-with-plastic-diamonds-besweatered bosom.

'Ruth!' exclaims Edie gratefully. 'Here, let me help.'

And she snatches the top three boxes, almost upsetting the pile, and hurries up the path and into the hall, away from their stares.

Inside trestle tables dressed with paper tablecloths have been set up along two walls and in front of the stage at the far end, forming a giant U. A number of the WI members are here, casting surreptitious glances at their neighbours' efforts as they lay out their wares. On the noticeboards behind the tables, someone has pinned up pictures of distressed people in boats and standing by squalid tents, and above the stage there hangs a hand-painted banner: 'ROTHAM WI MIGRANT RELIEF FUND CHARITY CAKE SALE'.

It all looks very well organised and for a moment, standing by the door clutching Ruth's Tupperware, she is at a loss as to how to make herself useful.

Then the vicar appears from the back office carrying a small black box. 'Petty cash!' he proclaims.

Edie hurries over to him. 'I'll take that!' she says, with as much authority as she can muster, and, pretending she doesn't see the glance passing between Elizabeth and Martha, who have just walked through the door, she whisks the money away to a table in the corner where a notebook and pencil are waiting to record the day's takings.

She beams to herself as she pulls up a chair and sets the boxes down. Oh goodie. This is a job she can do standing on her head. Since she was a little girl, numbers have been her friends. She has always found them faithful and dependable. They do not change their value or slink away silently when you are not looking, leaving your page blank. She likes how it is possible to chase them up and down columns and across the bar of a division bracket with reliably predictable results. In school, she was always top of the class for mathematics. Didn't Miss Wright tell her the day they received their General Certificates that she had never in her five years of teaching awarded so many marks to one student? She rubs her hands together with glee: here is her chance to cancel out that niggling mistake with the subscriptions and prove to them all just how sharp the old bird still is.

She opens the box and the notebook and picks up the pencil to make a start. But somehow it is not as easy as it should be. Though she does her best to apportion the float sensibly and keep track of who's got what, nothing will stay put. The numbers tie themselves in knots. In the seconds between her handing the clear bags of coins to the stall holders and picking up the pencil to record the figures, they stretch and morph and scamper about her head. Six flirts with nine. Three thrusts out its chest to become eight. And the whole rabble whirls round and changes places as vigorously as the morris dancers who come to foot it on the village green every midsummer's day. What's more, people will keep wandering over, wanting more tens and fewer twenties, asking nonsensical questions about her head or offering to make her cups of tea just when she is about to get everything straight.

The hall doesn't help matters. It keeps swapping to different versions of itself every time she looks up, like the slides clicking round in the projector Father used to bring out to look at old photographs after a few glasses of porter on Christmas day.

Now it is dressed not for the cake sale but for the nativity play. Now it is sombre and hushed and they are hearing the vicar relay the news about the outbreak of war, and Roger Allen is lurching to his feet, flushed and self-important in his telegram boy's uniform, proposing that those not eligible to fight get up their own volunteer defence corps. And now, oh, now it is festooned with bunting for the VE Day dance and though the band is gathered on the stage, there is silence because the door has opened, everyone has turned to look, and he is standing there, returned at last, just as she always knew—

'Edith?'

'Mmmn?'

Several middle-aged women in garish, ill-fitting woollens are standing in front of the table, looking down at her over their folded arms.

'We're wondering what you've got to say about this,' says the fattest, her huge breasts heaving under a hairy red pull-me-up studded with glittering plastic.

Edie looks down at the table to try to identify the cause of the trouble. But no, it all seems to be there, all present and correct: the book, the pencil, the box of peevish cash.

She smiles graciously, putting on her best minding-her-Ps-and-Qs voice. 'I beg your pardon, ma'am?'

'My cakes!' bellows the woman, pointing a quivering arm towards a queer plastic tub at Edie's elbow, which is empty but for a smattering of crumbs on a paper napkin printed with primroses. 'You've eaten all my chocolate plumpies! You were meant to bring them to my stand, not sit here in the corner scoffing the lot!'

Edie frowns and peers into the tub, then back at the woman's jowly face. Can she really have eaten a whole box of treats? She has no memory of it. It is not like her to be a greedy pig. That is usually Jean. She runs her tongue along her teeth, searching for a hint of sweetness. Hard to be sure. But they are all glaring at her, and when she looks at her pencil hand, she sees that there are smudges of chocolate on two of her fingers.

She blushes, mortified. 'Oh dear! I am sorry. I can't think what came over me. I'll run along to Davison's straight away and buy you some more out of my pocket money.'

But the woman is not listening. She is swivelling her head and speaking loudly in an effort to broadcast her outrage to the room. 'I simply can't credit it! Two hours I spent piping those last night and you go and eat them all – it beggars belief!'

Edie stares glumly at the ugly plastic box. They will tell Aunt Susan, of course, and then it will be bed without supper and rough chores when she gets home from school every afternoon for a week, just as it was when Mrs Brewer reported that she had been observed laughing during the sermon on Advent Sunday. Oh, it's too bad! She tries so hard to be obedient and not to give trouble, and yet she is always getting into botheration. If she could only be a different sort of girl, everyone would be so much happier. Father needn't go about silent and sad all the time, and Aunt Susan would be nicer to her if she weren't forever having to worry about her contrariness. But Edie will persist in letting the side down and disappointing everybody. It must be as Aunt Susan says: she is flawed in her nature, rotten to the core. She will never be any good.

She puts her hands to her face as the tears start to fall. 'I'm sorry,' she sobs. 'I didn't mean it. I know it was very wrong of me. Please don't be angry!'

When she takes her hands away and looks up at the group, they are staring at her. Someone coughs. A man wearing a dog collar steps forward – some sort of visiting clergyman, presumably, for he is old and grizzled and nothing like young, energetic Father Paul who can't be sent to fight on account of his eyesight.

'Ah,' says the clergyman, reaching out and patting her shoulder. 'There. Oh dear… Could someone…?'

In another moment, they are around her. Hands on her arms, voices at her ears. They are taking her home, they say. She is not to worry. Not in the slightest. Everyone quite understands.

Next she is in some sort of new-fangled vehicle beside an old woman in a flower-patterned headscarf with yellow hair tufting out round the sides and they are sweeping out of the village and bouncing up the track. In at the gatepost and the yard swallows them whole. Gollop. But my! They do go fast these modern cars! She is surprised the old woman is able to get the petrol to drive about like this, rationing being what it is.

Now they are in the kitchen, the old woman looking round. 'Do you think you might like to have a lie down? Go to bed, perhaps?'

Edie stares at her. Who can she be? An ARP warden? A recruiter for the FANYs? Some distant relative on Father's side? If that's the case, she certainly can't let the old woman imagine that she does childish things like go to bed in the middle of the day. She is not a baby, after all. Not by a long chalk.

'No, thank you very much,' she says in the most grown-up voice she can manage. 'I shall sit in the drawing room as I always do about this time. I may read the newspaper. I shall be quite content.'

She nods, pleased. There. That was just like a real-life lady. Anyone overhearing from another room would assume that she must be at least twenty. Maybe twenty-five.

The old woman certainly looks impressed – cowed, even. 'Well, if you're sure. But at least let me make you a cup of tea, won't you?'

She accepts, biting back a smile at the earnestness she has inspired, and goes through to sit on the chaise longue in the drawing room. The tea when it comes is in a hulking great mug, not a cup at all. At the sight of it, something stirs in Edie's memory: an incident in the middle of the night, jarring as a false note in a piano piece. But she can't place it, and besides, the old woman is distracting her, fiddling about the room, tweaking cushions and fingering objects on the mantelpiece. At length, she comes to stand before Edie on the rug.

'Look, Edie, please don't take this the wrong way,' she says, 'but when I was making the tea, I couldn't help noticing that the fridge was rather empty. The cupboards, too, if I'm honest. Apart from lots of packets of biscuits, it was all rather bare. What's more, the place could do with a bit of a clean…'

A nursery rhyme begins to spool through Edie's mind – 'Old Mother Hubbard went to the cupboard…' She wants to giggle, but that would be naughty. It's rude to laugh at grown-ups, so instead she flaps a hand in the manner of Aunt Susan. 'Oh, don't trouble yourself about that! It's just the time of the week. Davison's deliver on Tuesdays. We'll be drowning in things after that.'

Jean gives her an odd stare. 'Davison's?'

The room sags. The moment cracks, letting in an odd sort of mist that fogs the walls behind the old woman and renders the fireplace a blur. Edie feels giddy and a little sick, as though she has had one toffee apple too many before going on the helter-skelter.

'You're tired, that's what it is,' says the old woman. 'Why don't I put the TV on and let you put your feet up for a bit? It's all been a bit much, hasn't it? The fall and then my dragging you off to that sale.'

Without waiting for a response, the old woman shuffles to a glazed box in the corner and flicks a switch. The thing blinks and then a coloured, moving picture appears: a green bird bobbing and cheeping on a leafy branch to the accompaniment of a husky male voice.

Most alarming. Most weird. Not the sort of thing she, Father and Aunt Susan usually entertain in the drawing room. Unless – the crack in the moment widens, letting whispers in – all is not what it seems. Unless something fishy is going on. Unless – now she is getting to it – the old woman is not what she appears, but instead is a troublemaker, a Judas, a spy sent by that lot down in the village because they none of them like her, because they want to do her harm.

Suspicion thickens into certainty, a fried egg firming in the pan. She looks up, trembling. 'Get out,' she murmurs.

The old woman frowns. 'I'm sorry?'

Edie jabs a finger at her. 'Get out! Get out of my house! Get out! Get out now!' Hot tea slops on to her lap. She doesn't care. She goes on shouting 'Get out! Get out! Get out!' until the words are emptied of sense and have become mere sounds bouncing between the walls.

The old woman stands flinching, her face contorting, red blotches mottling her cheeks. At last she turns and scuttles from the room. A moment later, the back door bangs and a car engine shudders into life.

Edie sits on the sofa, waiting for the shouting to fade from her ears and her breathing to quieten. 'All better,' she whispers to herself. 'All better now.'

Only it isn't better. There is something cracked and very wrong. Something broken. A hurt that only Mummy could mend, except she's been gone for ages and no one's telling Edie where she is. That is the ugly truth she sees staring at her out of the black grate of the fireplace in this grand room in this house that she is beginning to suspect is not her home at all, but a place where they have taken her as a mean trick: there are no friends here. There is no one with the patience to look at life through her eyes. She has been left alone.

# THREE

The kettle begins to whistle as the cars pull into the yard. She watches them through the back-door window – the vicar driving himself and Dr Brewer, and Jean bringing Martha Beasley and another woman who she is unable to make out hunched in the back of the Morris Minor. Good. The tea will be just right in five minutes – piping hot and fresh. There will be no opportunity for anyone to speculate on how long it has been brewing or whether she remembered to warm the pot.

She lifts the kettle off the Aga and – oh, bother! – something gives in her arm, cack-handing her so that she slews hot water all over the counter. The silly thing dangles useless for a moment before righting itself, feeling creeping back apologetically. An angry red mark blazes on her wrist, but she can cover that with the sleeve of her woolly, and luckily there's still enough water in the kettle for the tea, so no one should notice. That's the main thing.

She turns and surveys the objects set out on the table. Oh, this is going to be fun! Everything is in order: the cake and scones baked, the crusts cut off the cucumber sandwiches, the homemade lemonade keeping cool in the fridge. No need to make an effort, Jean had said when she stopped by to tell her, oh so casually, that she and a few friends from the village would be popping up to see how she was on Wednesday afternoon.

But of course there is every need. Four days on from her queer episode, it is vital that she demonstrates to them all, Jean's committee, that she is entirely recovered. Back on top of things. Right as rain.

Particularly as it is true. The last couple of days she has felt very much like her old self again. Not entirely restored, it has to be said – there is still a little fuzziness in her thinking and yesterday she had to pause in the middle of the kitchen and remind herself sternly how to make a cup of tea. But you have to expect such occasional fluffs as you get older. That is the reason she festooned the house with notes reminding her of the visit and all the things she had to buy and cook and clean. It is not that she doubted her ability to remember – it was more of a reassurance policy. Belt and braces, as Father used to say. Oh, look, here's one still Sellotaped to the fridge. Better take it down in case the visitors read anything into it.

Crumpling the piece of paper, she glances at the delegation assembling itself in the yard. Her heart sinks as she sees Ruth Parker clamber out of the back seat of Jean's car, but she shrugs off the shame of the chocolate plumpies episode and goes to greet her guests.

'Hello! Hello!' she cries merrily from the top step, flinging her arms wide and beaming as though it is she and not they who arranged the visit. 'So glad you could make it.'

They shuffle towards her, adjusting their clothes from where they have got rucked up during the car ride. She sees them noticing her neat slacks, carefully tonged bob, subtle make-up and the cameo brooch she has pinned at the throat of her favourite sky-blue blouse. Good. Another tick.

Inside, she settles them in the drawing room and brings through the tea – just brewed, just nice. She smiles as she watches them glancing round the walls and the furniture, hunting out slut's wool, dust and windows gone dingy with neglect. They won't find anything here. She has been over it all with a fine-tooth comb and everything is pristine. Indeed, she feels almost sorry for their disappointment; perhaps she should have left them a cobweb to exchange significant looks over.

When everyone has their tea – presented in the dear little anemone teacups that came down from Mummy's great aunt – she offers round the cake and, by virtue of an artfully posed question, sparks a debate on what makes the difference between a Victoria sponge and a Victoria sandwich. Of course, Ruth can't resist sticking her oar in – neither can Martha Beasley – and before you know it there is a lively dispute going. Even Dr Brewer finds himself moved to venture an opinion on the pivotal importance of raspberry versus strawberry jam.

Edie takes the opportunity to watch for clues among the visitors – the vicar and Dr Brewer perched either side of Ruth on the chaise longue, Martha Beasley, who has taken the armchair by the door, and Jean in the little wicker seat by the window. Jean is the giveaway. Though she is making a show of being pleased with the tea and cake, she can't keep from nibbling at the dry skin on her lips. It is a habit she has displayed ever since she was a child, usually when anxious she is going to be found out for doing something wrong. So this isn't just a visit to see how Edie is getting on, then. They have an objective in mind. Plans have been made.

When at last the babbling dies down, the vicar leans towards her. 'How are you, my dear?'

She blinks rapidly and offers a surprised grin, as though it has never occurred to her that anyone might ask such a question. 'Oh, I'm all right. Fit as a fiddle, really. Can't complain.'

She is not going to make this easy for them. Not in the least bit.

They shift in their seats, holding their plates on their laps, careful to contain the crumbs.

'Only…' the vicar puts his fist to his mouth and coughs '…we all thought that last weekend you didn't seem, er, quite right.'

She hesitates and blinks, as though struggling to place the reference, all the while smiling brightly as though – whatever it is – she is sure it can't be anything terribly serious. Then she laughs and bats a hand. 'Oh, the sale. Ha! Yes, I did make rather a… an idiot of myself, didn't I? Those hideous clothes and that ridiculous business about Ruth's cakes – awfully embarrassing! The truth is, I should never have come. Jean, you were quite right to try to stop me. I had the flu, you see – I was running a temperature of 106. But of course, like a fool, I would venture out anyway. Couldn't bear the thought of leaving you all in the lurch. You know me – trying to do too much, as usual. It's been a bad habit of mine all my life.'

She sits back and regards them, doing her best to keep the triumph from showing on her face. She has delivered the speech perfectly – exactly as she practised. Not a single fluff. Whatever they have up their sleeves can't help but seem heavy-handed and unnecessary in the light of such reasonable words.

The five of them look at one another, each hoping that some-one else in the circle will find the gumption to speak. She has stumped them.

Delighted, she gets up and crosses to the tea tray with a view to offering more cake, eager to capitalise on their con-fusion. As she steps on to the rug, a memory ambushes her and tries to take over – the day she stood trembling in front of Father and Aunt Susan insisting that they should offer their services with *Bessie's Delight* in response to the Admiralty's appeal on the BBC; that, in spite of what had happened to Mummy, it was their duty to help the war effort and the poor soldiers she'd seen straggling over in the boats from France; that if Father wouldn't come with her she'd go alone – but she elbows it sternly aside and stays there at the tea party, playing the perfect hostess.

'The thing is, Edith, it's not just last weekend, is it?' says Dr Brewer, looking up from the sofa, a crumb of Victoria sponge (or did they decide it was sandwich?) stuck to his chin. 'Things haven't been entirely settled with you for a while.'

'There was that business with the subscriptions,' chips in Ruth.

'And the time you couldn't remember that the post office had closed and moved to Totwith,' adds Martha.

'And this is such a big house to look after all on your own,' continues Dr Brewer, so seamlessly that it appears that they, too, must have been rehearsing their words. 'I'm sure cleaning and taking care of it must feel overwhelming at times.'

She passes round the plate of cucumber sandwiches while she thinks what to do, willing her arm not to betray her by going wonky again. They are coming to the crux of it now, the point where they home in on their objective: turfing her out of the house that she has looked after on her own since Father died more than fifty years ago so that they can swoop in and take it over for themselves. She wouldn't be surprised if they haven't already had meetings on the subject, floating ideas about holding community cookery classes in the kitchen and turning the drawing room into one of those awful physical-jerks places where men in vests grunt and sweat. Well, they will find she possesses a weapon or two of her own.

She turns to the wicker seat by the window, fixing its occupant with a stare. 'What do you say, Jean? Is all this really necessary? Do I seem... unsuitable to you?'

Jean turns red and waves a hand pointlessly at her mouth. 'I'm not...' she says. 'That is, no one's saying... What I mean is... Oh, Edie, you know that no one admires you more than I do—'

Edie takes a step closer. 'Because you've known me longer than anyone. If anyone can comment on whether I'm fit to manage this place on my own, it should be you.'

'Please, Edie. Don't... I can't... We only want the best... At least try to understand.'

She rounds triumphantly on the room. Surely they must see that there can be no comparison here between her and this little pipsqueak with only the loosest command over her sentences?

'The thing is,' says Dr Brewer, raising his voice to cut across Jean's witterings, 'geriatric care has come on in leaps and bounds in recent years. It's nothing like it was in your father's day. There are all sorts of options and packages that can be arranged to suit different people's needs, particularly if, uh, money is not such a concern.'

Money! That business again. Obsessed with it, the lot of them. Itching to know who paid what and when. As if the place wasn't hers to do with as she chose.

The vicar slides a leaflet out of his inside pocket and passes it down the line. 'We thought you might like to consider some of the suggestions outlined here. No rush, of course, just something to ponder for now. And, naturally, if you have any questions, I'm sure Dr Brewer would be more than happy to—'

She looks at the document. The picture on the front shows a hunched man with poor teeth and a brown-skinned girl girning at one another. In the background is some sort of Bob's-your-uncle with metal legs and a handle for gripping. The sight of it fills her with rage.

'Mmn,' she says, so angry that she can barely get the sound out.

'That reminds me,' says the vicar, stroking his chin. 'We were wondering about your family, Edith. Next of kin. Is there anyone it might be worth contacting to come and visit? There are some legal things – power of attorney and the like – that it might be as well to explore.'

'Not for now, of course,' says Ruth. 'But looking ahead. Further down the line.'

They nod at one another, smiling cattily. They are half her age, most of these so-and-sos. She has known Martha and Dr Brewer since they were children. And now they are out for her blood.

'Perhaps a cousin?' prods Martha, who used to sit snivelling under the hedge by the village hall and had to be tempted out with jelly babies. 'Or a relative on your mother's side?'

An image of Mary Watkins rises: a smelly little thing in woollen tights who used to arrive with a dirty carpet bag and stay for the summer before Aunt Susan's time. She was so dirty that after she left Edie always had to scrub out the tub to get rid of the tidemarks. She was dirty on the inside too: Edie had once caught her bending sideways in the byre, the better to watch Dobbin's willy protrude from its soft belly pouch. The thought of that person coming again to her house and having jurisdiction over her affairs is more than she can bear.

'I'm afraid not,' she says firmly. 'There's only me.'

The vicar opens his mouth to try another tack, and she readies herself to blindside him with an offer of homemade lemonade. But at that moment Martha squeals. Twisting, she pulls a glinting, stringy object from the gap between the cushion and the arm of her chair.

They gape as she holds it aloft. It is a large, foil-covered cross studded with imitation gems and hung on a tarnished chain.

'Good gracious!' exclaims Ruth with a guffaw of surprise. 'How hideous! Whoever can it belong to?'

Edie stares at the cross, the edges of which have started to peel, revealing the plastic beneath. It is a gaudy thing, and she has an odd feeling about it. She is certain that it has nothing to do with her, and yet instinct whispers that she has seen it before – but of course these things can't both be true. She must be mistaken. Either that or this is the start of one of those terrible, foggy absences that descend on her now and then. And they are all here, watching.

'There it is!' she exclaims enthusiastically. 'I've been wondering where that got to.'

And though it is hideous and it doesn't go in the slightest with the cameo brooch, she grabs it and slips the chain over her head.

'Sentimental value,' she observes to Martha. 'A gift from an old friend.' And she pats the nasty trinket to her breastbone with a smile.

She can see by their expressions that she has got away with it – just. Nevertheless, her victory feels hollow. She is suddenly awfully tired. She has no stomach for bringing out the lemonade now. Let them do without it. She'll take the pot round for one last circuit instead. Hopefully the sight of it trickling dry will prompt them into thinking they ought to go.

And so it is that she is passing the piano on the way to attend to Jean's outstretched cup when the unpleasant thing happens. Framed in the far window pane she seems to see a dark-skinned man looking her full in the face. The vision lasts only a second or two – when she shakes her head and looks again he is gone and there is only the cliff edge, the sea and the sky. Still, it is enough to make her gasp and set the teapot trembling in her hand.

'Are you all right, Edie?' says Jean quietly as the others talk on.

'Hmmn?'

'You made a funny noise.'

Out of the corner of her eye Edie scans the bay window. There is no one there. She blinks, collects herself, smiles. 'Oh, it was nothing,' she says amiably. 'A touch of heartburn. I'm not used to all this sugar!'

The teapot's lid continues to rattle, so she claps her other hand down on top of it to still it and pours the last of its contents into Jean's cup with a flourish. The window stays empty all the while. Good.

She walks back to the table and sets the pot down on the tray firmly. Then she goes to her chair and sits down, surveying the room as they all sip their tea. She is doing it. She is managing in spite of everything. The afternoon has been a great success. There is nothing they can use to catch her out.

But oh, the tiredness is hitting her hard now. Though the conversation continues around her – touching on a one-way scheme for the high street, news of another boatload of migrants picked up at Dover and plans for a fundraising concert at St Stephen's – everyone's voices unravel and become harder and harder to follow, separating into phrases, then words, then senseless sounds. A bobbing feeling begins, as though the house has slipped down the cliff and is drifting away from the mainland, rendering all conversation distant and irrelevant as sleep laps the edges of her thoughts. If only they would leave. Why can't they leave, the wretches? Leave and let her rest in peace.

At length, they seem to get the hint. There are sighing noises. Dr Brewer glances at his watch. Martha pushes back her chair.

Edie starts upright. She looks round at them to see whether she has been napping, but is unable to read the answer in their eyes. Well, so what if she did doze? Falling asleep in an armchair at the age of eighty-seven is perfectly reasonable – even the most vigorous among them must give her that. She is not going to allow herself to feel sorry about it. She juts her chin defiantly and folds her arms.

'There we are,' says the vicar, rising to his feet and spreading his hands, as though he is about to invite them all to offer one another the sign of peace. 'Well this has been lovely. Splendid Victoria sponge, er, sandwich.'

They all murmur assent, shambling towards the door. She follows them along the corridor, crossing her fingers that no one will see fit to mention the earlier discussion, that they will grant her the dignity of pretending at least for the goodbyes that this was just a social visit, friends paying a call.

But of course, out in the yard, Dr Brewer can't resist returning to the topic, jumped-up boy scout that he's always been. 'You will think it over, won't you?' he says, clutching her hand as the others climb into the cars. 'The brochure. What we said. We have your best interests at heart, you know, Edith. And if there's anything you want to discuss, you mustn't hesitate to give me a ring.'

She nods, biting her lip, and stands back to wave. 'Goodbye! Thanks for coming!' she calls pluckily as the wheels start to roll and the cars pull out of the gate and away down the track. Then she hurries up the steps and slams the back door.

God, it seemed like they'd never go! Horrid, spiteful people, poking their noses into everything. Imposing their opinions. Presuming to know what's best for her. She hurls herself into a chair and puts her elbows on the table. The pamphlet stares up at her from a slick of sunlight – the bit of technical gubbins leering between the two faces. She crumples it furiously and hurls it across the room. She'll show them. Just as soon as she gets a bit of rest, she'll prove herself equal to anything. She'll do without it all. She'll manage by herself, just as she has done perfectly well for fifty years. She'll… She'll…

When she next looks up, the sun has dipped behind the hill leading up to St Stephen's. The dark-skinned man from the window is standing over her, his hands at her throat.

# FOUR

Jonah looks down and sees the old mzungu's face lolling above his hands. He steps back as the room swims into focus: the old woman's kitchen, the house on the cliffs, England.

The head rolls horribly. Eeeeh! Eeh eeh eeh! What has he done? Has he killed her? That wasn't what he intended. He only wanted to get what belonged to him. He thought he could unhook it easily from around her neck without waking her. Only she started screaming and he panicked that someone would hear and… then it is a blur.

Is she dead? The old woman's head seems to nod in reply. But then the eyes blink and the mouth gags. He sees her grimace, retch, look in terror.

He holds up his hands. Ah, ah, ah. Sorry, sorry, sorry! Can he get her anything? Water. Would she like that? Or some of those biscuits stored about the place?

No, no. Ah. Sorry! Sorry! Please. Don't scream. Don't tremble. There's no need to be frightened. It's gone now. It's past now. He knows where he is. It's all right. He is back inside the moment. Back in his skin. He means her no harm. He is a kind man. See? The son of a doctor, no less. Well, all right, a clinical officer, but it's effectively the same thing. Look. He's smiling. He has nothing but good intentions. Honestly.

It's just that his head these days is unreliable. It jumps about. It shows him things that aren't there. It sends him off down faulty paths and pulls him up short. Sometimes he thinks the border guards he met on the journey – those stony-faced men with guns and peaked caps – have marched into his head and erected barbed-wire fences and roadblocks, checking the free movement of thought. Also he hasn't been sleeping, because of the things that come when he does, and because he has to stay alert. So that's another – what is the word you might use? – factor. He is not making excuses. It is the truth.

It's like what happened the other day in the storeroom when he hit her. He is so sorry about that, by the way – her wounded head. He can still see the bruise. He felt so awful he watched until she came round and ate the biscuits, crouched in the corner of that big storeroom, praying to God she'd be OK. It sounds ridiculous now, but in that moment – can she believe it? – he thought someone had put juju on him and sent her to work his destruction. She looked so small, so scrawny that he thought she might have been a nyanga flown over in a winnowing basket to do him harm. And at the same time another part of his brain was telling him she was the police. Or one of those evil other ones. (Really, there is not much difference between the two – the police will sell you to those others for the right price. He has seen it happen many times.) And then, on top of that, some piece of him knew all the while that he was here, in England, in her storeroom, and that it was an old mzungu woman standing in front of him. So, you see, his head is not what it should be.

Here is another example: yesterday when he tried to leave for London, before he realised his precious cross was gone, he crept out of the storeroom and shut the door and the world was normal – fields, sky, those screeching grey-and-white birds. But when he rounded the corner – eeeh! Horrible! It was like someone had taken a scene from one of his nightmares and let it loose in the world. He seemed to see a crowd of azungu working with machines to excavate his grave. One of them was even whistling a badly tuned version of 'The World Is Not My Home'. No amount of knowing he was in England could help him then. His body was locked in that other happening, the vision spooling before his eyes. Terror banged in his chest. His limbs turned to stone. It was all he could do to drag himself to the storeroom and crouch there, quivering, muttering the Lord's Prayer over and over again.

But he's getting distracted. The point is, he didn't mean any of this to happen. In fact, he didn't know most of it *was* happening. He had no idea who the storeroom belonged to – or even, really, that it was a storeroom – when he staggered into it the other night, exhausted and soaked. He has no wish to intrude. He'll be on his way the very next minute, if she'll just give him—

'Oh, I see what's going on.'

The voice is so startling in its sharpness that at first Jonah is convinced it can't possibly have come from the frail little woman at the table and glances round the kitchen, seeking out another source. But no: the room is empty.

He looks back at the old woman, who has folded her arms and is nodding her head with narrowed eyes.

'Well, they don't let the grass grow, do they?'

Outside the window, a stretch of neglected pasture blows in the wind. But he has a suspicion that this is not what the old lady means.

He frowns. 'I'm very sorry, madam, but I don't think I understand—'

'Don't come the internet with me! They've sent you to do their bidding, haven't they? To get at me with metal and plastic. To go after me with deals on wheels! Don't think I don't know what you people get up to. I've read about it all in that… book!'

She waggles a hand at the far corner, but he can discern no book there, only a screwed-up piece of paper.

He passes a hand in front of his eyes. At times of stress or tiredness his English deserts him. Though he has spoken the language for as long as he can remember – chanting its nursery rhymes, copying down its irregular verbs from the blackboard, absorbing it from songs and films and printing it in block capitals on official forms – and though Amayi insisted he use it at every opportunity in preparation for the better life that would be theirs once Abambo got a proper position in Blantyre or Lilongwe – it has always had a slippery feel. He dislikes the way its words often turn out to conceal treacherous secondary meanings and how new terms frequently muscle in, barring his path while the sense wriggles out of reach. There are occasions when he wonders if such mechanisms aren't a deliberate trick on the part of the English to prevent speakers like him from ever conquering the language's core.

This is one of those times. The woman sitting in front of him in the stained blue shirt, with her hair going in all directions and mphangala-flower-red lipstick smeared around her mouth might as well be speaking an alien dialect for all he can make sense of what she's saying. Her anger is the only thing he can be certain of as she reels forth string after string of words.

When she pauses for breath, he makes another attempt at appeasing her.

'I'm horribly sorry, madam,' he says in his best English accent, working hard not to confuse his Rs and Ls, 'but I mean no harm. If you would simply give me my cross, the one you're wearing round your neck, I'll be on my way.'

She blinks up at him with an odd, childlike expression. Though he knows it is nonsense, he has the strange impression that the situation has reversed and that she is the one struggling to understand. Then the glint returns to her eye and he hurries on to get his words out before she starts to speak again.

'I dropped it, you see, the other night. I know I shouldn't have been in the house, but I wanted to check you were all right after what happened, that nasty bang on your head, and when I followed you into the house I heard your piano playing and—'

The old woman's eyes widen. 'My piano playing?'

'Yes, madam,' he says enthusiastically, relieved that he has got something across at last. 'Your piano playing. It was so beautiful.

I had to come in and listen. I think that must be where the necklace dropped out, in that chair by the door.'

The old woman leaps to her feet. 'How dare you!' she roars. 'I'll have you know I haven't touched a piano in sixty-five years!'

He flaps his mouth open and closed as though he is a freshly caught chambo wriggling in the basket. 'But you did! You were! I saw you!'

Her fury forces him backwards. 'Are you calling me a liar?'

'No! No! I didn't mean—'

'Because I'll have you know, young man, I won't stand for it. You might have been contracted to come here by people who think they know best, but this is my house. I'll have no hesitation in calling the calamities.'

A frown pleats his forehead. 'The calamities?'

'The police, dear heart. Don't think I won't do it!'

Panic wells up his throat like vomit. In all his dealings with officials back home and in the two years since, he has learnt one thing: the police are best avoided. He has seen what they do. How they are in league with the bad guys. How they will sell anything – and anyone – for the right price. He is sure it is no different here. Gilbert said as much, in fact, clapping him on the back as he accepted the last wad of 100-kwacha notes – money he had raised from the sale of the last of Abambo's Bruce Lee DVDs. 'And if you make it to England, brother, do your best to stay out of the way of the police. It's all above board, of course, everything I have arranged – but still, don't think there are no crocodiles just because the water's calm.'

'What do you mean, if I make it?' he'd said, blinking.

Gilbert's mouth had spread wide at that, his gold tooth glinting. 'That's the spirit, brother. Not if: when!'

Well, he is here now, standing in the old woman's kitchen, a few metres inside England. There's no way he is going to get slung in jail because he doesn't have the money to pay a bribe.

He hurls himself to his knees. 'Please, madam,' he says, clapping his hands in supplication. 'Don't call the police. I am urging you to listen to my words! I'll do anything. All I want is my cross and I'll be on my way.'

The old woman regards him. From where he kneels, she is a pair of watery eyes set either side of nostrils hairy as spider's legs. Yet she has a regal bearing that makes him think of the picture of Queen Elizabeth that hangs in Aunt Dudu's living room in Blantyre, above the sofa kept wrapped in its plastic delivery cover to save it from getting spoilt.

'You've got a hurt,' she says, reaching out and tracing the length of his forearm with a yellowed fingernail.

He looks. Sure enough, there is a slash in the skin, jewelling over with scabs. His eyes tell him it ought to be painful, yet his flesh is as numb as earth. The wound seems nothing to do with him, as though his real self has shrivelled away from his edges and is now little more than a knot of consciousness lodged deep inside his skull, leaving his body to fend for itself.

'That'll be from the boat crossing,' says the old woman. 'All that chaos on the beach and in the water.'

He stares at her wonderingly. How does she know that?

She holds a finger aloft. 'Don't worry. I've just the thing for it. I know what I'm doing. I went on a… an extravaganza run by the Red Cross.'

She hurries out. In her absence, he lowers himself into one of the chairs at the table and stares round the room. It is much better-equipped than he is used to – even the kitchen in the large white Victorian house they moved to for Abambo's last posting could not compete with this. It had been a hard blow for Amayi to lose it when they were obliged to vacate the house for the new clinical officer, taking up residency in the crumbling servants' quarters for a rent that, though small, was nevertheless a struggle to find each month.

But though that room seemed impossibly grand when they first arrived in the district, this place takes things to another level. It seems thronged with things. The ranks of cupboards running above and below the surface are formidable. The sink with its taps dispensing hot and cold water commands admiration. And even Aunt Dudu wouldn't be able to hide her envy at the sight of the refrigerator humming away by the door.

All the same, he has to admit to feeling unimpressed by the selection of foodstuffs the many cabinets contain. When he rifled through them the other night, in search of something he could leave beside the old woman to spur her recovery should she wake, he had turned up little more than packets of biscuits and faded cans of something calling itself Ambrosia. Even the ingredients to make a cup of tea – something he prided himself on remembering that the English liked before all things – were hard to assemble. Though the refrigerator was cold, the carton of milk inside it smelt evil and the teabags in the little pot on the side had a musty air. He was not at all sure that the resultant concoction wouldn't do the old woman, breathing raggedly on the storeroom floor, more harm than good.

Another thing that surprises him about the kitchen is how dirty it is. There is a gritty feel to all the surfaces, and in the daylight he can see that the tiles under his battered trainers are strewn with crumbs and dust. Cobwebs hang from the ceiling and the light fitting and the window panes are covered with a fine layer of grey fuzz, as though they are starting to grow fur.

Though the old servants' quarters can boast nothing so grand as a tiled floor, the rooms are always scrupulously clean. By the time they were seven, his sisters knew how to use a tsache, and they took it in turns to sweep every day. This rule stayed with them, even through the worst times. Though she would shake her head in wonder at the size of the kitchen and run her fingers enviously along the top of the great stove, Amayi would be appalled by the hygiene standards kept here. If this is a mark of the famous English eccentricity, it would leave her unimpressed.

Well, never mind. Soon Amayi will have her own modern kitchen to keep as spotless as she likes. He will see to that. He is here now, in England. The hard bit is behind him, and though there have been times over the past two years when he felt sure he'd never make it, he has survived. God has carried him through the trial, just as Pastor MacDonald promised He would. All that is left to Jonah now is to follow the last stage of the plan and make for London, the city of opportunity, which has an African barbershop on every street and a kanyenya stall on every corner just waiting to welcome new arrivals from back home. By nightfall tomorrow – who knows? – he might be strolling into that very same fried-chicken shop into which, so Gilbert told him, Roger's cousin had wandered four years previously, only to leave twenty minutes later clutching a bag of wings and an offer to start work as an administrator in the Tower of London the following morning. Ha! With luck and the Heavenly Father's blessing, he could have money on its way home by the end of the week.

Doubts begin to trespass on the edges of his vision, whispering that it may not be as easy all that, that the few web pages his phone credit had allowed him to browse in the weeks before he left home suggested that London, with its murders and homelessness problem and pollution, may not be as welcoming as Gilbert had implied. He shoves them back. After all, why shouldn't he be the lucky one? Why shouldn't good things fall into place for him after all this badness? He has seen more than once how surprising events can occur if you truly believe. What about that YouTube clip from the Rwandan Premier League game where Rayon Sports striker Moussa Camara hit the crossbar repeatedly until, digging around in the goal mouth, he found the juju that had been blocking his shots and then put the ball straight into the back of the net? You wouldn't think that a little bundle of twigs could hinder a top athlete like that, and yet there was the evidence up on the internet for all to see. What about the curses that men going to work in South Africa paid the sing'anga to set on their girlfriends so they and any man they cheated with would stick together? That had really happened to Roger's cousin's friend. The story of how he and the married woman he'd slept with had been forced to shuffle down the road in view of the whole village to the sing'anga's hut to get the curse reversed had had them hooting with laughter down at the trading centre.

The point was, life was surprising. Unexpected things were possible. And if believing had the power to shape the course of events, then why shouldn't he allow himself to think the best of what was to come?

A vision comes to him of Amayi's face when she opens the envelope he will send her and pulls out a wad of banknotes bearing the Queen of England's face. He grins at the thought of how she will stagger backwards, her hand to her mouth and amazement in her eyes; how she'll look across to his picture taped on the wall and smile to herself about the cleverness of her eldest son and how she always knew he would save them. Of course, he realises it won't really happen like that. It is all done by transfer these days. You queue up at a kiosk inside one of the shops in town and fill in forms and answer impertinent questions about your business. But the image of Amayi beaming and holding an envelope bulging with banknotes is hard to resist, particularly when he remembers all those guys who sit around WhatsApping each other nonsense behind the trading centre, grooving through life with their cartons of Chibuku Shake Shake and their chat about the Africa Cup of Nations. One head cannot lift up the roof, they'd told him, when he dared to share his plan. And they'd laughed and said he was a fool for going the long back way to England when South Africa was only a minibus ride distant. Well, he'll show them, won't he? On the day when he comes back a big man to sweep Amayi and his sisters and brothers off in a 4x4 VX.

He chuckles to himself. He is being silly now, he knows it. But, ah, it is good to know hope again. It has been such a long time that he had begun to wonder if that feeling had gone from him for ever. It is a relief to think that that part of him might not have died, but is sleeping instead, that being in England might wake it up.

All the same, he is starting to get anxious. The old woman has been gone a long time. Unease is burrowing up through him and nibbling his innards like a bilharzia worm. What if she has tricked him? What if even now she is on the phone to the calamities in some part of this vast, creaking house, whispering that they ought to collect him and take him away? What if they are climbing into their police vans this second and coming for him with their metal cuffs and…

A face appears at the window. It is the square-faced guard who jabbed him in the ribs with his baton on the Italian border, stamping his entrance to France with a bruise. He has come back to find him, to drag him, screaming, away! Before he knows what he is doing, Jonah grabs the nearest thing – a teapot standing at the edge of the table – and hurls it, smashing the glass.

The room snags, sags and wobbles about him. He closes his eyes, his breath surging in waves and the blood thundering in his ears. Aaa kuno! Save him, Jesus! Don't let him die now! Don't let him die like this!

When he looks again the room is calm. There is no one at the window. There is only a hole in the bottom pane where something – the teapot – passed through. He is miles from the Italian border. No one is coming to get him. Not immediately, anyhow. He is in England. He has made it. He is safe.

All the same, he better not hang around. Perhaps he would be better leaving right now, while the old woman is safely out of the way, taking advantage of the darkness beginning to seep up now from the hollows in the field outside to shield him from unwelcome attention. He could creep along the roads, keeping the sea at his back. He is sure to find his way to London if he does that. He remembers what Gilbert told him, leaning over the counter of his stall at the trading centre where people come to charge their phones for five kwacha a time: London is in the middle of England and all roads lead there. He would find it easily. And if for some reason he doesn't, he can always make for one of those other world-famous British towns: Leeds, Liverpool, Manchester City. What could be simpler?

He takes a step towards the door and stops. It is no good: he cannot leave without the cross. That is what has held him back these last few days, watching the house for an opportunity when he could creep in to retrieve it. Though he knows it is foolish to imagine that God lives in a piece of jewellery – and though he is well aware that Gilbert probably got it cheaply from the woman who comes through the trading centre every Tuesday selling trinkets and beads – he can't shake the thought that it has significance. Through all the trials of the last two years, when everything else fell away bit by bit, the cross has stayed with him, slung round his neck, lodged in his pocket or clutched in his hand. Indeed, there have been times when he truly believed it made the difference between him and the sinister, still forms left to be buried by the desert's sands or sinking through the waves. And if a voice whispered to him now and then that that was what he needed to believe because the alternatives were too harsh to bear, he stifled it. No, the cross had been his good omen. His protection on the journey. A thousand times more powerful than the charms sold by the sing'anga because it was imbued with the authority of Jesus Christ. It was what had got him here when so many others had failed. The thought of setting out on this final stretch without it was unsettling. Worse, it was arrogant. And he remembered all too well what Pastor MacDonald had to say about arrogance, grimacing and quivering on his upturned orange crate until it looked as though he might be sick. Any suffering in human lives was not down to God's limitations but people's flaws, arrogance being one of the worst. The good things of life were there for the taking. God was willing each and every person to reach out and fatten him or herself on His love. It only required faith and humility, which you could demonstrate by way of regular donations to the pastor's divine ministries fund (if you didn't have a bank account cash was fine). Wise choices – that was the key point. The good things of life were there for anyone to enjoy. You simply had to allow God to work through you and keep your mind fixed on Him.

So he has to have the cross. Even if he has to snatch it from round the old woman's neck, as he probably should have done when she was in the room and he had the chance. There is nothing for it but to wait until she—

The sound of footsteps interrupts his thoughts. The old woman rounds the doorpost. She shuffles into the room clutching a notebook and pen, and walks to the table without looking in his direction. The cross is nowhere to be seen.

She sits down and begins to write in the notebook, muttering to herself as she does so. There is quiet for a moment, during which one of the white-and-grey seabirds that used to strut through the camps across the water sets up a raucous cackling. At length, like a schoolboy waiting before the headmaster's desk, he coughs.

The old woman looks up, squinting through the gloom. 'Who's there?'

He blinks, bewildered. 'It's me, madam. From before. You said you were going to get something for my arm.'

The old woman's eyes narrow. 'A likely story. You're a burglar, aren't you? A braggart. Come to murder me in my bed as soon as look at me.'

'No, madam! Nothing of the sort, I assure you. I was only looking for my cross. And then you said—'

Her face hardens. 'Oh, I see what's going on.' She has folded her arms and is nodding her head with narrowed eyes. 'Well, they don't let the grass grow, do they?'

Outside the window, the pasture blows in the wind. But he has a suspicion that this is not what the old lady means.

He frowns. 'I'm sorry, madam, but I don't think I understand.'

He passes a hand in front of his eyes. He has an odd feeling of being trapped. Surely they have had this conversation before? Or maybe he is just tired? All those hours of sitting quivering in the dark, hiding from sleep and the nightmares it will bring, have pulled his thinking out of shape. Perhaps his English is slipping, making him miss something. Like a bad student sweating in front of the blackboard long after the others have been let out to play football, he is being forced to go over his lessons again. It is not inconceivable. His head is swimming like he has been smoking chamba and he does not trust it. His bones ache. He can't remember when he last ate properly. The biscuits he crammed into his mouth the other night as he searched the old woman's cupboards for something to revive her were not enough to make an impression. Before that it must have been at least five days since he tasted the slop they brought them in that last place, when a hatch in the bottom of the container door was unlocked and bowls slid through. And of course he can count more than two years, from the day he last saw Amayi, since he had his fill of real food, nsima. What he wouldn't give now for a taste of that.

'Don't come the internet with me!' the old woman is saying. 'They've sent you to do their bidding, haven't they? To get at me with metal and plastic. To go after me with deals on wheels! Don't think I don't know what you people get up to. I've read about it all in that… book!'

She waggles a hand at the far corner, but he can discern no book there, only a piece of paper.

He is almost convinced: this has all been said. If he opens his lips and tries to speak, he will find the words he used before waiting there, congealing like a half-chewed mouthful of food.

He frowns, uncertain what to do. Is this a trick? Or some sort of test? Has someone back home used the soil that he has walked on to reach across the miles and curse him so that he is trapped in a conversation that goes round and round in circles, dooming him to go over the same ground until death? Or maybe his mind has been taken over by one of the ancestors. Possessed. Then an image comes to him of the etiquette book Mr Mapanje used to pass around the classroom. The English, he had explained, were sticklers for politeness and using the correct rituals and wordings.

It could be that this odd circular talking was one such example. The only thing he can think to do is proceed with the steps he knows.

'I'm terribly sorry, madam,' he says in his best English accent, working hard not to confuse his Rs and Ls, 'but I mean no harm. If you would simply give me my cross I'll be on my way.'

She blinks up at him with an odd, childlike expression. With her bruise-purpled eye and scrawny neck, she makes him think of the cuckoo chick he found under a mlombwa tree on his way to school years before.

'I dropped it, you see, the other night,' he continues. 'I know I shouldn't have been in the house, but I wanted to check you were all right and then I heard your piano playing—'

The old woman's eyes widen. 'My piano playing?'

'Yes, madam,' he says impatiently. 'Your piano playing. It was so beautiful. I had to come in and listen. I think that must be where the necklace dropped out of my pocket, in that chair by the door.'

The old woman leaps to her feet. 'How dare you!' she roars. 'I'll have you know I haven't touched a piano in sixty-five years!'

His mouth flaps open. It is astounding how she manages to fill each word with exactly the emphasis it carried before. Anyone listening would be convinced that she was speaking these sentences for the first time. Perhaps she is?

He touches a hand to the side of his head. What if some new thing has gone wrong in there, a cog come loose in the workings making time jump and buck like a young ox under the drover's stick? Could it be that he has become like Musaiwale, who used to appear in the trading centre every now and then with feathers in his hair, scrounging mandasi and spouting odd stories about what he had seen out there, over that hill, in the bush. Is he now so mad that he cannot even realise it?

She is coming at him, forcing him backwards, purpled eye flickering. 'Are you calling me a liar?'

'No. I didn't mean—'

'Because I'll have you know, young man, I won't stand for it. You might have been contracted to come here by people who think they know best, but this is my house. I'll have no hesitation in calling the calamities.'

Calamities. Again, that odd word that blares out at him like a wrong note in a line of music. Only this time he doesn't need to ask what it means. So he has heard it before. This has happened. He is not mad. He is not turning into Musaiwale – not yet, anyway. He must try to hold on to that.

A thought comes to him that perhaps it is the old woman who is broken instead. Perhaps she is a victim of the forgetting sickness that affected some of the old people who used to come and consult Abambo, but he cannot afford to assume this. If his experience of the last two years has taught him anything, it is that what he imagines about azungu is usually wrong.

He shakes his head. 'Please madam. Don't summon the police. There's surely no need for that. All I want is my cross and I'll be on my way.'

But it is clear that this time his supplication is not earnest enough to thwart her intentions.

'Cross! I'll give you cross!' she mutters as she pushes past him.

The seriousness of the situation descends on him. She might really do it this time, this old woman tottering down the musty hallway, between the stacks of newspapers and cardboard boxes. She might call the police and have them come and take him away. Tomorrow, instead of strolling down the streets of London a free man with opportunities spread out before him, he might be hunched in a cell or juddering in a police van on his way to the airport to catch a flight all the way back to where he started with nothing to show for his grand promises and struggles.

Panic wells up his throat like vomit. In all his dealings with officials back home and over the two years since, he has learnt one thing: the police are best avoided. He has seen what they do. How they are in league with the bad guys. How they will sell anything – and anyone – for the right price. He is sure it is no different here. Gilbert said as much, in fact, clapping him on the back as he accepted the last wad of 100-kwacha notes – money he had raised from the sale of the last of Abambo's Bruce Lee DVDs. 'And if you make it to England, do your best to stay out of the way of the police. It's all above board, of course, everything I have arranged – but still, don't think there are no crocodiles just because the water's calm.'

'What do you mean, if I make it?' he'd said, blinking.

Gilbert's mouth had spread wide at that, his gold tooth glinting. 'That's the spirit, brother.'

No. His thinking has gone circular again. He smacks the side of his head in an effort to dislodge his mind from its lunatic wheel and focus it on the matter in front of him. The old woman has reached the hall table now and is fiddling with an odd, black contraption fronted by a big perforated circle. When she lifts the bar resting along the top, he sees it is a strange kind of telephone. She is about to do it. She is going to make the call!

Fear seizes him. He ought to rush forward and snatch the handset from her – knock her to the floor if he has to! Why not? He did it before in the storeroom without thinking. And she wasn't the first. There have been others whom necessity has forced him to elbow, shove and even kick aside over the last two years. Such actions have come to mean little: he has witnessed much worse in the ruined streets and tarpaulin slums through which life has dragged him. Sometimes he can almost feel God willing him to do these things in answer to His calling to survive.

A vision of the boy's eyes – Amanuel's eyes – at that last instant when they grabbed him swims up from the depths of his mind. Guilt squeezes his guts, but he pushes the image roughly away. He does not have the luxury of being sentimental. Not then. Not now.

So. The old mzungu. Power surges through him, urging violence. He lurches forward, arm raised.

But at that moment, the woman shakes her head and sets the handset down on the table. Her shoulders slump and the momentum of the conversation seems to drain from her.

Oblivious to him looking down on her from only a foot away, she turns and shuffles off through the doorway into the piano room.

'Coming here, moving things around,' he hears her say.

He follows warily, trying to keep his feet from making the floorboards creak. Perhaps she has a mobile phone in here that she plans to use instead?

The calamities seem to be forgotten, however: after standing for a moment in the middle of the tattered rug next to the low table scattered with crumb-covered plates and the remains of a burnt cake, the old woman walks to the piano and seats herself on the faded, plush stool. Lifting the lid, she stares for a moment at the keys. Then she raises her hands and begins to play.

It is different from the dark piece of the other night. Jaunty and cheeky. Surprising in places. Its happy feel reminds him a little of the songs of Robert Fumulani that Abambo and Uncle Godfrey used to listen to on the radio in between broadcasts of Shadreck Wame's sermons on Sunday afternoons.

But there is someone the music brings to mind more strongly than that, and when he thinks of her he is unable to resist sinking down into the armchair nearest the door – the one with the rip in the back where the stuffing is poking through – and letting the strings of notes lead him away.

She comes into focus in his memory: Hattie. The ginger-haired gap-year student with the odd, flat way of talking who had come to the district three winters previously to take part in a project to build a school for the children in the nearby village. The undertaking had not been a success. For a start, the NGO workers had looked at the map upside down and consequently sited the building on the wrong side of the village, out of the shade, so that the sun beating down on its corrugated-iron roof would render it unusable on all but the coolest days. Then there was a delay in getting the materials. Finally, when it became clear that the school would not be finished until the summer, the chief had suggested that the gap-year girl might start teaching in a temporary shelter close by. Only for another problem to emerge: it turned out that the young woman was not a teacher at all, but a pianist. She was going to Oxford University to study music, and in the heavy suitcase that the NGO had expended precious petrol driving to the airport to collect, she had brought not books and pencils and useful things like that, but a box of plastic recorders, two dented trumpets and a Yamaha keyboard that had got cracked in transit and would soon need new batteries. Most of the villagers lost interest after that, swatting the whole silly business away and wandering off to tend to their own concerns. He, however, had stuck around. He liked the girl – her awkwardness, the ridiculous floppy hat she wore, the way she flapped at her pink-blotched face in an effort to stay cool – and he felt sorry for her sitting in the shade of the shelter morning after morning, waiting for children who didn't appear.

Slowly, a friendship developed between them. On the days when he wasn't needed to help on Amayi's stall selling whatever baked goods she was able to muster to try to see them through another month, he would saunter over to the shelter and spend time with the young woman. Sometimes, to make her feel better, he would try the instruments. The shrill sound of the recorders embarrassed him and he couldn't get his mouth into the right shape to play the trumpets, but he found he liked the keyboard. Hattie – her name always made him want to chuckle but he did his best to keep serious – showed him how to pick out tunes. Pretty soon he was able to play four or five melodies fairly nimbly with his right hand.

When the batteries ran out, they talked instead. Hattie told him about herself, and about Hull, where she and her funny flat accent were from. She was enjoying her time in Africa, she said, even if the project hadn't exactly gone to plan. When she got to Oxford, she was confident that she would have an advantage over people who had come to the university straight from school because of the months she had spent away from home, seeing life. He nodded, staring out across the bush. When she talked like this, it reminded him of the look Abambo used to get when he stared up at the black-and-white photograph of St Bartholomew's Medical School in London that hung in his consulting room – those grand buildings where Abambo would have gone to study medicine had he not got expelled for standing up to a bullying teacher and been forced to settle for training as a clinical officer in Blantyre instead.

All the same, Hattie would continue, oblivious to the mistiness in Jonah's eyes, though she didn't mind living mostly on nsima, she could murder some biscuits for dunking. She had been relieved to find that they drank tea here; she hadn't been expecting that. And she was pleasantly surprised to discover that it was almost as good as what they had back home. But it seemed the practice of dangling a biscuit in the hot liquid until it went – what was that word she'd used? – mushy was not something Africans did. It sounded like a repulsive habit to him, but that was the thing she missed most. And so, the next day, instead of going to the shelter, he took his bicycle and a handful of ten-kwacha coins from the plastic Evian bottle tucked behind the washing tub and cycled the five miles to the trading centre and the God Is Able grocery store. There, with the help of Mr Banda, he found it: a box of Universal vanilla creams on the back shelf. He even remembered to get a carton of long-life milk to go in the tea and, to top it all, by the cash register he discovered a box of Tiger Head batteries that he hoped might fit the keyboard. He paid for the items and cycled home humming the tunes his new friend had taught him and jumping the potholes with a spiritedness he hadn't felt since school.

The batteries turned out to be the wrong size, but it didn't matter: Hattie was ecstatic when she saw the box of vanilla creams. Even though he'd hesitated over it, worrying that they might not be the right kind, she threw her arms round him in delight. The sensation of her lips on his cheek surprised him, and when he turned his head to search her face for signs that it had been a mistake, he was shocked to find her mouth waiting for him, pressing against his, and introducing the lascivious sliver of her tongue.

He was no stranger to kissing, of course. No stranger to much when it came to girls. Away from the watchful eyes of Amayi, round the back of the trading centre and off in the hollows and dips of the bush, he Gilbert, Roger and those other groovers had experienced many things. By the time he was fourteen Jonah had had numerous encounters, and he and Gladness had been a couple for nearly a year on and off. Still, somehow he had never associated such possibilities with Hattie. There was an awkward innocence to their relationship that came at least partly from the fact that he was always doubting whether he truly understood what she meant – not just in terms of the English phrases she used, but in the sense of the deeper underlying meaning, a way of looking that seemed not to align between them, as though even the landscape she saw was softer, lusher and more forgiving than the harsh, dusty reality that met his gaze. As a result, whenever Gilbert and the others raised the idea of a physical relationship with the mzungu, laughing and giving him sly glances, he dismissed it immediately as something far too complex to contemplate.

Hattie, however, appeared to have no such reservations. No sooner had they broken apart to breathe from that first biscuit-flavoured kiss than she was taking his hand and leading him off to the hut the NGO had designated for her use.

There followed a strange, intense period. The strongest image he retains from it is the shards of sunlight poking through holes in the walls and ceiling of Hattie's hut. Down at the trading centre he was a big man during these days, made for life now he had his rich mzungu girlfriend. He smiled and joined in the joking where he could, but underneath it all he found the whole thing embarrassing. Hattie had a hungriness about her that made him uneasy. When they were together she would writhe and moan, making such loud noises that there were times when he had no choice but to cover her mouth for fear those passing would hear. Though he suggested many times that they might go to the shelter once again and talk and play with the keyboard as they used to do, she seemed to have no interest in anything other than being together in the hut. It got so that—

'Oh, I see what's going on.' He is back in the piano room in the house at the edge of the mountain by the sea. The old woman has stopped playing and is sitting with folded arms, looking straight at him and nodding her head with narrowed eyes. 'Well, they don't let the grass grow, do they?'

This window does not look out on to pasture, but to the narrow strip of garden that he blundered into earlier in the day when the visitors came, where he had to throw himself to the ground when the old woman's gaze met his. Beyond it is the grey sea, calm today and glimmering with light. And there – the dark strip along the horizon: that must be France.

He stares at the view and its deceptive beauty as certainty seeps through him. There is no doubt: they have been through this conversation before. The old woman is repeating herself, drawing him round and round the same track of words. He casts about for a way to respond that won't have her hurrying to the telephone in search of the calamities once more. But it seems whether he answers or not she is determined to rehearse the scene again.

'Don't come the internet with me!' she is saying. 'They've sent you to do their bidding, haven't they? To get at me with metal and plastic. To go after me with deals on wheels! Don't think I don't know what you people get up to. I've read about it all in that… book!'

Indignation burns in her eyes, putting him in mind of the enthusiasm that used to blaze through Musaiwale at the height of one of his stories. He remembers how the madman's body would throb with the conviction of what he was saying, and how contradicting him put you at risk of being attacked.

An idea occurs to Jonah.

'Yes,' he says slowly. 'You're right. They did send me. I'm sorry. I didn't realise it would be so upsetting for you.'

She considers this, then nods. 'I thought as much,' she says. 'People think because I'm... crumpled that I don't know what's going on. They forget how long I've been around. There are secrets I know about things that took place here before most of them were even born – that vicar and Martha Beasley. That Dr Brewer. He forgets that I've known him since he was in... garters. He didn't get into medical school the first time round, but I'll bet he didn't mention anything of the sort when he called you on the apparatus, did he? Oh no. Too proud for that. Thick, they thought he was. A cowardy custard.'

He nods in return. 'It must be very frustrating.'

'Oh, it is! You've no idea. Rubber hoses, the lot of them. And all because they want to get their hands on my money, when it's their fault in the first place that I'm on my own like this. Roger Allen's, especially. He was the worst. But he's dead now, so serve him right.'

Outside the window behind her, one of the grey-and-white seabirds is strutting up and down the sill, like a general inspecting its troops. It pauses and throws its head back to utter a harsh cackle.

The old woman gives a grunt of approval. 'Anyway, dear heart. I'm sure you see now that there's no call for you to stay. We have no need of your services here. We are quite sufficient.'

He opens his mouth to say that he understands completely. He'll be on his way, post-haste, if only she'll give him what he is looking for – the cross that...

But she is still speaking: 'Oh, but of course you'll be wanting your committance... your fanfare... your... money to get you from A to B.' She glances out of the window at the thickening evening. 'I expect we've missed the mark with that. But in the morning I'll give you your train money back to London, or wherever your... conservatoire is based, and you can explain the situation to them. I hope that's acceptable.'

He shrugs. Why not? Money for the train cannot hurt. In fact, the thought is exciting: it will be his first taste of travelling by rail. He beams at the image of himself gliding along the tracks into

London, beneath the shadow of Big Ben. What a great picture that would be to WhatsApp to Gilbert and all those guys grooving through life down at the trading centre while time trickles by. Wouldn't that knock their mockery on the head once and for all! If only he still had his phone.

She answers his smile with a grin. 'Good. That's… planned, then.'

And she turns back to the piano and unleashes another cascade of notes, washing him once more into the open waters of reverie.

# THREE

'Cooey!'

A voice. Aunt Dudu's? No, not quite strident enough for that. A stab of hope. Amayi's? Iwe! But no, he hasn't seen Amayi in years.

Someone else, then. Hattie, the nice girl who came to the village with the cracked keyboard?

Footsteps, the creak of the boards and then another call: 'ET? Are you all right?'

He frowns. ET? Why would the girl be calling for that? She wasn't planning to resurrect film club in that school of hers, was she? A wave of nostalgia washes over him. Film club! Those evenings sitting on the wooden bench next to Gilbert and Roger with little Daniel playing in the dirt beside them. How hard he'd had to beg to persuade Amayi to let them go, but it had been worth it. Excitement and shoving. Jostling to get the best view. A sea of heads massed in the little thatched hut at the far end of the trading centre, and in front of them a small, flickering television loaned by Mr Banda who owned the God Is Able grocery store. The screen was so small and fuzzy that it was almost impossible to make out the picture from any further back than the third row, but that didn't stop a penalty-shootout hush descending when the title sequences began to play. The supply of videos was patchy – dependent on who was passing through and what the traders had picked up cheap in Tanzania – but in the time before the television blinked off for good in the middle of *Jumanji* they had worked their way through an impressive selection of American cinema's big hits. They had jeered at the pirates in *Hook*, shouted instructions to help Macaulay Culkin outwit the baddies in *Home Alone* and sung along to 'Hakuna Matata' in *The Lion King* – even if the colours were ridiculous and everyone knew that the only place you saw lions these days was in the wildlife reserves that the azungu paid mega money to drive through in their jeeps. Sometimes Gilbert and Roger argued about their favourites, but for him there was no contest. It was always *ET*, the one about the boy who finds an alien from outer space and hides it in his house and becomes its friend. He loved the scene in which the boy, Elliott, and his neighbours ride their bikes and the ET makes them fly. For weeks after seeing it he had spent every spare moment cycling up and down the road past the village, trying to make it soar.

Today, however, this isn't the bit that sticks in his mind. Instead, with his head full of the tinny sound of the television, he thinks of the part about the ET wanting to contact his family, the way he'd said it over and over: 'ET phone home.'

His heart twists. How long has it been since he spoke to them – to Amayi, Daniel, Elijah and the twins? Six months? A year? After his cheap Chinese mobile dropped over the side of the dinghy during the crossing from Libya he had taken to paying people to borrow their phones so that he could call the number he'd memorised for Gilbert and get him to arrange a time to speak to Amayi. Now and then he'd bought a phonecard from one of the makeshift shops people ran out of their shelters at stops along the way.

As the months went by, however, the calls got less frequent. He found it harder to find the will to make the arrangements. The queues were too long and he lost track of the requirements for dialling internationally from the different countries he passed through. When he thought of the eager voices that would greet him on the line, clamouring over one another in their excitement, he felt a terrible heaviness. What could he tell them? Though he had been

away far longer than the three months he had confidently pro-
nounced it would take to reach his destination – three at the very
most (this said with a jaunty thrust of his chest that had made
his siblings clap their hands in delight) – there was still no news.
The situation remained unchanged: he had no clearer idea of
when he might reach England and start making the money to pay
secondary-school fees for his brothers and sisters and give Amayi
the comfort and security she deserved. Really, he had told himself,
shivering inside the black plastic sack he used on the worst days
to try to keep some heat in his arms, it was better that he didn't
call but conserved his energy for pushing forward and getting to
his destination all the faster. There were times when he almost
believed this, when the things he repeated to himself seemed like
genuine reasons not to call his family. At these moments, he was
able to forget the fact that it was no more difficult to phone them
than it had been when he first arrived in Europe and that – beyond
the hustling for food and water, and whispered inquiries to see if
anyone had news of transport options or borders opening or other
more covert opportunities to move on – life in the camps was about
waiting, which he could do just as easily in a queue for a phonecard
as he could lying on sheets of cardboard, watching tarpaulin ripple
and flap above his head.

On these occasions, he was able to ignore the truth that such
excuses were as meaningless as the scraps of paper that the
Sudanese man who shared his shelter for a few weeks in the camp
near the Alps collected and scrutinised, insisting that they would
spell out something of greater significance if only he looked hard
enough. But such times never lasted. For the truth his objections
obscured rather than illuminated was that he was frightened;
frightened of what his relatives might hear in his voice if he made
the connection. The bright, hopeful young man who had swung
out of the village on the back of Gilbert's uncle's pick-up, full of
dreams of making a big success, had got lost somewhere along the
way – sunk beneath the waves of the Mediterranean or trampled

in the mud of the camps. He wasn't sure if that person would ever resurface. But at least if he didn't call home that young man could live on in Amayi, Daniel, Elijah and the twins' minds. This way, he still existed somewhere in the world.

Yet today, with that voice putting ET in his mind, he can't help but think of them and dream of the day when he can at last call them and tell them… But wait a minute. He is forgetting something. Wasn't there… hasn't there been a change? His thoughts flutter and jerk like birds in a trap. He isn't in the camps any more, is he? And those people who kept him and the others in the container in that last terrible place and muscled him down to the shore – they are nowhere to be seen. An image drifts towards him: rocks on the horizon scissored out of the darkness by moonlight; mobile-phone torch beams flashing over the side of a boat, darting over the surface of the water; and the flare of despair in Amanuel's eyes. Jonah feels again the heaving of his chest, the burn of the muscles in his limbs, and at last jags of stone razoring his fingers. He is – dare he believe it? – in England. Yes, he is almost convinced that this time the urgings of his brain are true. In which case, everything has changed, and he ought to call Amayi right away to report the happy news. That he has made it. That he is well. That her boy, her clever boy, has succeeded, and will shortly be tasting the success that England vouchsafes to all those who come to her shores with a genuine appetite to work for their own betterment, particularly people like him. For he is not just another immigrant. Iwe! He is an English speaker and a citizen of a Commonwealth country. That means he is streets ahead of all those he saw hunched over English phrasebooks in the camps. Although he is pretty sure Gilbert was joking when he said that his name is on a list kept by the Queen in Buckingham Palace (the boy is given to exaggeration now and then), it seems logical that he will get preferential treatment. How could it be otherwise? After all, his nation is linked to the United Kingdom by history. That has to count for something. Otherwise what is the point of international agreements and the portrait of HRH Princess Anne Abambo used to pass whenever he went into the district hospital to perform caesarean sections, and dignitaries flying back and forth to deliver impressive speeches? Yes, he is surely on his way now. All the trouble is behind him. The first chance he gets, he must call Amayi and tell her—

'Good gracious! Who on earth…?'

He jerks upright, banging his head on a hard surface. He is sitting on a stained armchair with yellow stuffing oozing like pus from one of its cushions in a dusty living room. An old mzungu woman he does not recognise is standing in the doorway with a bright, flower-patterned scarf tied round her head.

'I—'

'ET! Are you there?' She turns her head to project her voice up the stairs and her profile gives her away: she is one of the people who were sitting in the piano room drinking tea yesterday. He remembers catching a glimpse of her spitting a burnt morsel of cake into a handkerchief in the instant before he dropped to the ground and out of the other old woman's – ET's – field of view.

There is no such delicacy about her now, though. Now her voice is shrill, betraying an edge of fear. As he spots a muscle pulsing in her jaw, it strikes him that he is once more at risk of being reported to the calamities and he holds up his hands, gawping like a nestling, as if in hopes that the right words might fall from the ceiling into his mouth.

Before he can attempt any talking of his own, however, there is the sound of footsteps on the stairs. They both turn to witness ET descending, dressed in a pair of grey trousers and what looks to be a man's shirt, the untucked back of which dangles behind her like strange bird's tail.

'Ah, Jeans,' says ET, rounding the wooden post at the bottom of the steps. 'Good of you to call in.'

'Oh, ET! Thank God. I was so worried something terrible had happened.'

ET regards her with her head on one side. 'What's the flap, Jeans?'

The visitor jerks her head in his direction and contorts her mouth to deliver an elaborate whisper that turns out to be no quieter than her full voice. 'Who on Earth is he?'

ET looks coldly at him, then back at Jeans. 'Well,' she says at length. 'I see you've met my… associate.'

The skin between Jeans's eyes puckers, making her spectacles shrug. 'Your associate?' She stares at him and her mouth forms a circle as a thought dawns. 'Oh, ET! You don't mean to say you've taken our advice and called the agency?'

ET blinks. 'What else could you have imagined?'

Jeans claps her hands together, cheeks pinking to match her scarf. 'Oh, but that's wonderful news! I'm so pleased. Really I am.' Then she frowns. 'But I say, ET, isn't that awfully quick for them to have sent someone over? We had to wait a week to get anyone organised for poor old Dora Woodruff.'

At the change in tone, ET draws herself up. 'Are you casting aspersions, Jeans Roper?'

'Roper? Goodness, ET, I haven't been a Roper in nearly seventy—'

'Because I tell you, I won't stand for it. It's one thing to come here as a guest. It's quite another to go prodding into things uninvited. If you can't think of anything nice, I suggest you keep mum before we both say things we regret.'

At that, Jeans twitches and hunches in upon herself. She is like an elephant shrew, he decides, always watching for threats and poised to scurry off at the slightest danger. Afraid she is going to be caught.

'Yes, ET. Sorry, ET. Of course, you're right. I'm just so delighted, that's all. So very, very pleased that you've made the sensible choice.'

ET gives a grunt. 'Good. Well, now. Won't you have another cup of tea?'

The other woman smiles and reaches out to pat her hand. 'No, that's very kind of you, but I can't stop. Maisie's coming to stay for half-term and I simply must make it to Tesco's before her train gets in at Totwith. I just wanted to pop by to see you were all right after all the effort of yesterday – oh, and to drop this off.' She slides a leaflet out of her handbag and passes it over. 'It's for a recital at St Stephen's in aid of the Migrants' Relief Fund.'

'Yes, I can see that, thank you.'

'Well, I just thought that you might like to come along. It should be a lovely evening. Martha Beasley is laying on some cheese and biscuits for the interval. And she's supposed to be frightfully good, this young girl. Daphne said she heard them playing a recording of hers on Classic FM only the other week. So I thought you might fancy it. If you're feeling up to it, of course.'

The steel flashes again. 'Up to it? Why wouldn't I be up to it?'

The woman called Jeans steps backwards. 'I wasn't suggesting—'

'I'll be champing at the bit to attend,' says ET fiercely.

'Good. Great. That's settled then. I'll pick you up beforehand.' Jeans heaves a sigh and knots her scarf more tightly around her head. 'Well, better get on. Don't want to hold you up. You've still got some tidying up from yesterday to do, I see,' she says, nodding at the table, where the remains of the burnt cake sit hardening. She flourishes a hand in the doorway. 'Nice to meet you, um…' Then she seems to remember something and leans towards him, talking once more in her full-voice whisper. 'By the way, just thought I'd mention that there seems to be some unopened post on the windowsill in the kitchen. When you have a moment, I'm sure Miss Morley would appreciate some help going through it and getting organised. I suspect it's been a while since that side of things has been addressed, if you see what I mean.' She steps back, offers them both a nod and a smile, and with that, she is gone.

ET stands listening until there is the sound of a car engine starting up in the yard. Then she turns to him, her face cracked into a wicked grin. 'There!' she exclaims, advancing with a minxish wiggle. 'Didn't that go like a dream? She barely suspected a thing!

And you played your part brilliantly, my darling. Just like I knew you would. I'll bet she hardly even knew you were here.'

She reaches out and curls her finger round his ear, stroking the soft skin. He jolts at the touch, but she appears oblivious to his alarm and smiles warmly.

'And now you've come back to me. It's been ages and you've kept your poor kiddo waiting far longer than she deserved, you naughty darling. You ought to have seen the letters she wrote and wrote on your behalf. But it doesn't count for a bean now, because you're here, and that's all that matters. No one can take you away from me now. And it's all going to be exactly as it was before.'

Incredulous, he watches the spittle-flecked lips tremble towards him as her eyes close to slits. At the last minute, he leaps up, sending her tottering backwards to sit abruptly on the strange sofa with one arm that stands by the door.

Her eyes and mouth snap open, and it looks as though she is going to scream, but instead her face crumbles and shoulders start to heave.

'Oh dear,' she sobs. 'Oh dear. I've got it wrong again, haven't I? This isn't what I thought.'

She points to her head. 'It's this silly thing. It goes wonky and I can't stop it. Like the... vision box in the corner. Only worse, because that you can hit to make it work again; this just has to go on as it is.'

She wanders over to the television on the wooden cabinet with the wicker doors that remind him of the patterned back of the headmaster's chair at St Andrew's. She runs a hand over the fretwork and for a moment she seems to have forgotten his presence. Then she turns, anxiety in her eyes.

'I don't tell them that – those down in the village... those customers. If I did they'd give me no peace. They'd be on at me every second. I know what they're like. I've seen them at their worst. They watch for a weakness and they swoop. Like those big black birds you see on the nature emissions. The ones with the bald heads...'

'Vultures.'

She looks at him approvingly. 'Vultures. Yes.' Then her gaze wanders away across the room and out to sea. 'It's mostly all right. If only people would give me time to think, I'd get there in the end. But they won't. It's all go, go, go these days. Take your eye off the oyster for a minute and you've had it. Before you know it, you're chasing the van down the track with your trousers round your toes.'

He coughs. He is having trouble keeping up. Though he was top of the English class on more than one occasion back in the days when there was still money to go to school – though his written response to *Great Expectations* earned him a commendation in assembly – he is finding his comprehension unequal to the task here. There is a term for what ET is doing (he strains his memory for a glimpse of Mr Mapanje's hand chalking it on the blackboard). Using idioms, that's it – employing words that, clubbed together, mean something other than what they signify on their own. He'd had a list of such phrases copied down in the exercise book he'd kept so carefully in the days when such things mattered – to be over the moon, to lose one's head, to put the cart before the horse – but none of those are any help here. Once again, he feels a stab of frustration at English with its relentless exceptions and contradictions that seem to stand like security guards at the entrance of a fancy hotel, briefed to keep all but the azungu out.

Enough of this. He needs to be on his way. He coughs once more. 'It must be very difficult.'

But she doesn't like that. She whirls round, eyes flashing. 'Difficult? Who said anything about difficult?' She regards him with eyes as cold as the sea. 'Oh, I see what's going on...'

He holds up his hands in desperation. 'Please, madam, please, ET. It's nothing like that. No one sent me. I do not know the people down in the village – those customers, as you say. I'm here entirely by chance. There was a... a boat accident. I survived. All I want is to travel to London to find work. If you'd only give me the necklace that I dropped somewhere in this room – it has a silver cross on that is, as far as I understand it, entirely worthless, but it has emotional value for me – I shall make tracks.'

He nods, pleased. That was good. He got all the words out just as he wanted – no mixing up of Rs and Ls. And the use of the idiom 'to make tracks' – that was excellent. Mr Mapanje would have been impressed if he could have heard it. He would have got an A+. Without question.

The old woman fiddles with the bottom of her shirt. 'A boat accident?'

'Yes madam. Out in the English Channel, the other night. Big waves. People drowning.'

The boy's eyes stare at him, blazing with reproach, as hands reach to pull him over the side.

The old woman's mouth twists. 'Well, then. You must stay here.'

'Oh no, madam. That's not what I—'

'Tush. We'll find you work on the farm. Father won't mind. Aunt Susan's gone now, anyway. And as for me, I won't tell a soul.'

'Really, that's very kind of you, but I—'

'I can pay you, if that's what you're worried about. I've got lots of money… look.' And, turning, she beckons for him to follow her out of the room.

They walk to the kitchen and she pulls open a drawer to reveal rolls of banknotes packed in rows. It is more money than he has ever dreamt of, and he is unable to stifle a gasp. His fingers itch to take it.

She rounds on him with a child's giggle. 'It's lashings, isn't it? And that's not even a quarter of it. There's more in the sideboard in the dining room, and the bathroom cabinet, and… other places hereabout. It's from that business out there – the mowers and such. The grubbing-up. I keep it like this to confuse them. You can bet your bottom dollar that they've been fishing around the banks, asking how much I got. As if I'd let them find out. Vultures, the lot of them. Call the police as soon as look at you. And that Roger Allen, he's the worst.'

Her expression darkens. 'But you're not one of them, are you? They didn't send you?'

He shakes his head, eyes still on the money. 'Honestly, madam, I am not.'

She snaps her fingers and gives him a wink. 'That's right! You were in the boat. Silly me. Now, then, where was I?' She considers the drawer with its contents like the inside of a briefcase in a gangster film. Reaching in, she selects a roll of notes and holds it out. 'Will this do?'

He has no idea how much it is. He knows that pounds are worth a lot more than kwacha. Back home a wad like that would be big news, so he can only imagine how much is in her hands. The thought comes to him again, circling his head like a mosquito, that he could take all of it. It is what others what do in his place.

Ah, the things he could spend it on! A smartphone to call home. School fees for his brothers and sisters. Shoes for the whole family. A generator and modern kitchen appliances for Amayi. Maybe the move back to Blantyre she was always urging Abambo to apply for. And of course, the odd luxury or two to put those groovers down at the trading centre in their place. The image of him cruising through the village in a 4x4 VX surfaces in his mind once more, bringing a smile to his lips.

Yes. He will take the money. He will wait until the old woman is out of the room and then he will help himself to the contents of the drawer and be out of there before she realises anything has happened. By this time tomorrow he will be in London, transferring thousands of pounds back home, just as Gilbert and Pastor MacDonald promised. Just as God intends.

God. All of a sudden, Jonah thinks of the cross necklace. He cannot leave without it. Not with his mind so unstable and his body as battered and feeble as it is – weak from lack of food, the gruelling swim and the scramble up the cliffs.

He considers. He had not intended to linger in the British countryside. He had meant to go straight to London and try his fortune there, like everyone he'd heard about and so many of the heroes in the stories they'd read at school: Dick Whittington, Pip, Oliver Twist. Still, farm work is familiar enough to him from living in the rural areas and the old woman's offer seems genuine. If he stays here for a little while, he will have time to regain his strength and find the cross. It might give his head a little time to quieten down, too, so that it stops rushing horrors at him every time he ventures outside. And it will mean that he doesn't have to take the risk of travelling while those bad guys from the boat might still be looking for him. Then, when he is recovered and they have long forgotten him, he can take the rest of the old mzungu's money, leave for London and really make the most of his chance. He can enter the British capital wearing his best face. That is a much better plan.

'Yes,' he says, nodding. 'That will be fine, thank you, ET.'

'Oh, goodie!' She gives a squeak and a bounce. 'Wonderful, Michael!'

Jonah opens his mouth to correct her as, outside on the window-sill, a seabird throws back its head to laugh.

# TWO

It takes him a while to get used to the house. It is so vast and full of things, and there is rotting paper everywhere he looks, suffusing the place with a sour, musty smell. The corridors and staircase are lined with boxes of it, and stacks of yellowing magazines run up both sides of the stairs. There are piles of newspaper clippings stretching back more than half a century in almost every corner, and when he examines them he discovers that many of them bear feverish scribbles in the margins and pencil circles scored around certain words. One – an article dating from 1953 reporting that Prime Minister Winston Churchill had announced the end of the police hunt for something called deserters – seems to be particularly popular, for it appears on several of the stacks, as well as fluttering out at him occasionally from drawers.

In addition to the newspaper cuttings, he is forever stumbling upon bundles of letters. Some of them are computer-generated, and a few are topped with red stripes and have words like 'final demand' stamped in bold, but many are handwritten and half-finished, riddled with crossings-out. The dates and intended recipients vary, and the writing hunches and withers as the paper gets newer, but the gist of them is the same: they are all requests for assistance in finding information on the whereabouts of someone – a soldier by the sound of it – to whom something terrible happened many years ago... but here the crossings-out get fierce and the lines of script wander and seem to lose their way. It is most perplexing, and he can't understand why ET has let so much good writing material go to waste. He can well remember Mr Mapanje's stern lectures about conserving paper and the preciousness of the trees sacrificed to make it, and yet here are reams and reams of the stuff spoilt and set aside. Some of it even bears the jagged marks of mice teeth.

If the half-finished letters and cuttings spewing out of cupboards and bulging from boxes aren't confusing enough, he is also obliged to contend with the objects. Nothing can be done simply in ET's house. It contains a huge number of trinkets designed to adorn – or, he is often more inclined to think, complicate – the most straight-forward of tasks. The soap on the sink in the bathroom must be set down on a special dish, the toothbrush returned to its holder. Cardboard matchboxes live inside silver cases with catches liable to stab fingers not used to the trick of them. Umbrellas inhabit a leather stand. What's more, the cupboards not stuffed with cuttings and letters are crammed with stacks of painted boxes, porcelain pots and glass jars – some containing oddments the uses of which he cannot begin to fathom, but many of them empty, as though the main business of the house is to store pockets of air. There is even a silver photograph frame on the chest of drawers in the room next to ET's – to which she directs him with a wink and the perplexing idiomatic observation that Father is away on farm business – containing nothing but a square of yellow paper. As for the bed, it is so festooned with frilled blankets, cushions and decorations of every type that he cannot begin to see how to get into it. When he finally strips all the layers off, the underpart is lumpy and squidgy, and he knows there is no hope of him managing to sleep there. He opts instead for the rug on the floor, which, though prickly and furred with dust, affords him a similar level of firmness to the floors and groundsheets to which he has become accustomed. On his second evening inside the house, he sinks down on to it bewildered and exhausted, listening to creaks and groans that sound almost human and more than once make him think that someone is standing over him lamenting a great disaster. All the same, oblivion claims him quickly, and instead of their usual dark sharps, shocks and explosions, his dreams bring repeated visions of the contents of yet another cabinet teetering, tipping and raining things down on his head. He wakes gasping, with a strong yearning to find himself back home on the edge of the village, surrounded by nothing more challenging than the cooking hut with its stone stove, the sleep mats kept rolled in the corner during the day and the family's little stack of bowls and plates.

Not everything seems determined to frustrate him, however. In the wardrobe in the bedroom beside ET's own, he finds a stash of woollen tops and some rugged trousers that prove invaluable against the cold breezes that rattle through the windows and snake around corners inside the house. They are strange, rough, thick garments – not the fine, sleek items he might have imagined the English to wear – and at first they feel itchy and heavy against his skin. When he catches sight of himself in a mirror, he sees that they make his limbs look thin and spindly, as though he is not substantial enough to fill the role that such an outfit requires. He looks like an impostor, and it comes to him that he ought to leave the house and steal away, that he is doing something ridiculous and even indecent by lingering there.

ET does not appear to share his misgivings, however. She nods approvingly when she sees him in the heavy trousers and jumpers, seeming so thrilled that he wonders for a moment if he hasn't forgotten a conversation in which she instructed him to use the clothes – whether this is in fact what the odd phrase about Father being away on farm business means – and whether he ought to thank her for her thoughtfulness in the time-honoured tradition of British politeness. But by the time this occurs to him she has already wandered away and started muttering about something else.

Another useful object is a notebook with a floral cover, which he finds next to a stack of envelopes in the kitchen. At first he thinks the scraps of writing inside it are as rambling and inconsequential as the unfinished letters, but, after frowning at the jagged sentences for a while, he begins to see that there is more to them than that: they are instructions about how ET likes things to be done around the house, almost as if she knew he was coming before he arrived. As a guide, the notebook is very clear. It demystifies many of the objects in the kitchen and bathroom and makes him much more confident in his interactions with the old woman. For her part, ET seems to appreciate its influence too. She is much calmer when he follows her directions meticulously, watering the plants on the windowsill in the piano room from left to right, for example, and dragging the wheezing vacuum cleaner through the pathways weaving between the stacks of paper in the morning rather than the afternoon.

For this, it turns out, is his main duty: keeping the house as clean as possible and attending to whatever domestic matters arise. The farm work ET mentioned when they agreed he would stay does not materialise and, on balance, he is glad. Looking out of the kitchen door at the diggers groaning and creaking in the neighbouring field, he feels he would rather not be working among them. There is something sinister in the monotonous way they gouge the land. Furthermore, when the workmen clamber out of them and stand around near the track, smoking cigarettes and drinking from flasks, they are hard-faced and their voices sound harsher even than the cackles of the grey-and-white seabirds. He suspects these men would not tolerate his presence with patience.

There is also the problem that he can't discern exactly what the land around ET's house is used for. From years of living near the village and helping out Roger's family during the harvest and planting seasons (in spite of Amayi's disapproval) he knows the rhythms of maize farming like the back of his hand: the early starts to clear the ground and stack the dried stalks ready for burning; the back-breaking hours digging new dirt rows from the previous year's ridges, all the while taking care that you didn't drive your hoe through your foot; the nervous wait for the rain and the rush to plant at its first approach; and then the weeks of watching until the stalks had grown higher than a man and they began to announce on the radio that the dowe was ready, heralding the end of the hungry season. At a pinch, he'd be a useful pair of hands on a tobacco farm, too – he had heard enough of Gilbert's accounts of working ganyu on the government plantations to know how the process was managed. But peering out of ET's grimy windows at the grasses swaying on the hills, he sees no evidence of either crop – or, indeed, of any other arable activity. Nor are there animals grazing, though the pasture is so rich and succulent that he is sure most oxen would have had no hesitation in trampling their masters for a chance to curl their tongues round it. It is most peculiar – almost as if the azungu don't need to grow food or earn money from their land. The sight of all that fertile space left fallow gives him an uneasy feeling, and he is grateful not to have to venture out into it.

Useful though the notebook is, however, it offers no advice on a concern that is gnawing his mind from its centre outward, fast destroying his capacity to focus on anything else. There is no real food in the house. No nsima, of course – he was expecting that – but nothing that can be considered an acceptable substitute, either. There is no rice, no bread, no margarine. There are no beans or leaves that could be used to make relish and, though the refrigerator is well set up to store it – blasting him with the memory of winter in the camps when he opens the door – there is no meat. He had assumed that, living in a wealthy country, the English would eat goat, mutton, chicken and beef every day – several times a day, in fact. Hadn't Gilbert promised him kanyenya stalls on every corner in London, alongside the ubiquitous African barbershops? And yet when he opens ET's refrigerator he finds nothing apart from a carton of yellowing milk and an evil smell. There are packets of biscuits tucked among the papers and trinkets in various cabinets, and even, oddly, inside the tall stopped clock in the hallway that seems to watch his comings and goings with disdain. For a glad half hour he thinks he's discovered an answer to the problem when he happens upon a row of tins in the tall cupboard by the kitchen door. But when he does finally get the lids off a couple of them, the contents are disappointing. The tins contain red and yellow sauces that are sour and sweet respectively and bear no discernible resemblance to any of the ingredients pictured on their labels. Although the old woman gobbles them down gamely enough, he can't bring himself to swallow more than a mouthful or two of the stuff, and he knows it won't be long before he has to find another solution.

On his third morning in the house he awakes to a sensation he has not felt so powerfully in years: hunger spilling out of his stomach to consume him, turning his arms and legs to hollow, aching shells. The crisis point has come.

He tries the old woman first. But as soon as he opens her bedroom door and sees her smiling muzzily up at him, he knows he will get nothing useful from her. Her expression tells him that it is a Michael morning – the name she insists on calling him when she is in one of her playful, dreamy moods where idioms roll in like waves of mist, obscuring her meaning from him utterly so that he can do nothing but concur and hope the sense catches up later.

'Come to see me, have you, darling?'

He nods.

'Well, be sure not to let on to Aunt Susan. Or that awful, snivelling telegram boy, for that matter. We can't have people spreading gossip.'

He nods again and withdraws, his stomach growling furiously. Clearly he is on his own with this one.

Downstairs, he stares around the kitchen hoping for a hitherto unforeseen solution to present itself. But there is nothing. The cupboards regard him haughtily – so many places to put things, and yet precious little he can eat inside.

He cannot avoid it any longer: he is going to have to go out and find food. He opens the kitchen door, braced for what might be out there, and peeps across the yard. But God is smiling on him: his head is quiet and the present holds. No one seems to be watching.

Though it is early – the sun still toiling its way up the slope of the sky, the dew glittering on leaves and cobblestones – the workmen have already appeared in the field beyond the hedge. Perhaps he could ask them where he should go to get provisions?

But at the thought of approaching the boundary and hollering his requests over the roar of the machines, his English scatters. Besides, how can he be sure that these men in their bright-yellow jackets are not in the pay of the authorities or part of that network those bad ones told them stretched everywhere they turned? If they realise he is a foreigner, perhaps it will prompt them to make a phone call that will lead to him being captured all over again.

The track stretches off round the corner from the yard and disappears. Somewhere out there, perhaps only beyond the crest of the next hill, lies the answer to his problem. He has only to find the will to go and seek it.

Still, his mind recoils at the thought of what terrors – real or imagined – might erupt from the bushes or descend from the clouds. Wouldn't it be easier, it whispers to him, to fall back on some of the bird-trapping skills Roger taught him back home? He could fashion a little noose and use the hardened crumbs from the burnt cake as bait. It would only require one of those monstrous seabirds to fall for the ruse and they'd have meat for several days.

He considers this seriously for a while as he stands on the threshold, remembering a ball of string he saw sitting beside a pile of boxes in the hall and talking himself through the knots he would use. Then Gilbert's face appears in his mind and he realises the ludicrousness of the train of thought.

What is he doing? Isn't this exactly what he left home to escape – that hand-to-mouth existence, that reliance on nature and chance and the favour of God and sing'angas? He is in England now, a rich, prosperous country where people have no need to scrabble in the dirt to survive. Here no one sets traps for birds – or if they do, it is only for entertainment. Instead they get in their Rolls-Royces and Aston Martins, James Bond-style, and drive to big, luxurious shopping facilities where everything you could ever want is piled up as high as the eye can see at all times of the year. That is what he ought to be doing. He has the money to buy provisions – the old woman has seen to that – and in case what she has paid him isn't sufficient, he can always take more out of the drawer. In fact, perhaps he'll do that. It is high time he was on his way.

It is harder going than he anticipates. Though the track leading out of the yard slopes downhill, he feels as though he is climbing with weights on his legs. Hunger fiddles with the dial of his senses, making the groan of the diggers alternately blare and recede to almost nothing, and sending waves of heat and chill through his limbs. For a moment it seems as though the lane is thronged with bodies, all trudging silently; then he blinks and it is empty again. He feels as though he is walking on the spot for days with the ruts of the lane stretching as far as he can see, and then all of a sudden he has arrived at the junction with the sealed road and has a decision to make: left down the hill and round the bend or right up the hill past the old stone building that, judging by the cross on its top, is probably a church. He stands there a long time, swaying, waiting for his brain to supply the answer. But instead of presenting a choice, his thoughts flit through a wild array of alternatives. He could get a sing'anga to come and assess the merits of each direction; he could call Gilbert and ask for advice; he could lie down under that bush, in that soft patch of grass, and go to sleep.

It is only by a supreme effort of will that he eventually drags himself onwards, down the hill, round the bend, along the flat stretch and up the slope on the other side. By now he is trembling and dragging his feet. An image circles his brain like a mosquito: the people trudging out of the bush during the worst time, stick limbs gnarled with weeping sores, begging for casual work, for ganyu they would never find the strength to do, their eyes already looking off into the distance in anticipation of a refusal; the pain on

Abambo's face when he dismissed them. Jonah swats the memory away but it persists, landing again and again, sucking his thoughts dry until all that remains is the suspicion that he has become one of them and that the lush countryside he sees around him now exists nowhere but in his imagination – a hallucination conjured in consciousness's final burst of activity before his mind goes dark.

A car zips past and he whirls away in alarm, almost losing his footing and reaching out to steady himself against a tree. The jab of fear galvanises him and he hurries to the top of the slope to find buildings waiting on the other side. A strip of houses starts gradually before broadening out into a small town, with streets running off the main road, which is lined with more houses, with a few bigger buildings in the centre. From this distance he cannot make out the giant shopping facility he is expecting, but he is confident that somewhere in this cluster of buildings there will be a place he can find food.

He has to walk more than halfway through the town before he spots it: the glass-fronted store with fluorescent lights blazing beneath a red-and-white plastic sign. It is less impressive than he imagined, and its name – 'Spar' – confuses him. Surely this is something you do in boxing? He can't see how it relates to food at all. It seems ridiculous, and for a moment he grins to himself, thinking of how he will save the information up to tell Amanuel later, and how they will chuckle at this instance of British eccentricity. Since the pair of them met on the road out of Italy they have always made each other smile with the odd things they notice on their travels and comparisons of the girls who catch their eyes along the way. And though Jonah was frosty at first, having long learnt not to waste effort on engaging with people who would more than likely disappear round the next bend, something about the young Eritrean appealed to him. When Jonah glanced over the shoulder of the border guard who struck him and saw Amanuel doing an impression, pulling his chin back in an effort to replicate the man's jowls, he had to swallow a laugh – his first for months. After that they stayed together all the way up through France. And though neither of them could take the edge off the cold European wind, soften the tarmac on which they slept or improve the taste of the bland soups well-meaning people served them in the camps, somehow their companionship made the experience more bearable. Even in that last terrible place they had found things to roll their eyes at. Yes, he promises himself. He will tell his friend about the Spar shop, and they will chortle together at its strangeness. But then he remembers – the eyes, the waves, the darkness. The knowledge of what he did kicks him in the guts and his smile twists into a wince.

Luckily, the layout of the Spar shop's aisles is comprehensible enough. In fact, it is not dissimilar to the way Mr Banda organises his goods along the shelves in the God Is Able grocery store, although here the products are arranged more strictly in sections, complete with signs dangling from the ceiling proclaiming what customers can expect to find underneath. He can only imagine the chaos that would ensue if the shopkeepers in the trading centre back home attempted to adopt such a rigid system: the gaps that would open up on the shelves at certain points in the year or when the supply chains broke down, while the unexpected items that arrived now and then on the trucks from Tanzania accumulated in heaps on the floor.

He pushes his way in through the door, setting off an electronic fanfare, and helps himself to a basket from the pile just inside. A woman watches him from behind the desk, her jaws chewing mechanically. He offers her a smile, but she keeps her face blank and observes him coldly, as though he were not standing in front of her but happening instead on a television screen that she can switch off whenever she chooses.

He turns his attention to the aisles and tries to sift his thoughts for what he might need. 'Milk', a sign proclaims. He makes for it gratefully. Yes. The old woman likes that in her tea, just as Hattie did. A refrigerator looms, shelves bristling with different-coloured cartons bearing pictures of cows, goats, blades of grass. Luckily, he knows from the mouldering container in ET's kitchen which of the multitude to select. He drops it into the basket with a satisfying thud and feels a rush of pride. Here he is, shopping in an English supermarket and finding what he needs without assistance.

But when he turns, the rest of the store yawns in front of him and he staggers dizzily against the refrigerator. He thinks for a moment that the place is about to dissolve into something hideous, but luckily the shelves and fluorescent lights keep steady before his eyes.

'Careful,' calls the woman behind the counter. 'We had that serviced only last week.'

He holds up a hand in apology – sorry, sorry, sorry – straightens himself and looks the shop in the face once more. Though it had seemed smaller than expected from the outside, it now looks huge. He can't think where to begin.

A rack of magazines looms over him, azungu faces leering. 'Top Ten Diet Tips.' 'How *I'm a Celebrity* left me battling PTSD.' 'Dream Yourself Fabulous!'

At length, he catches sight of some sliced bread in see-through bags at the end of the aisle. It is an extravagance, he knows – back home they only have sliced bread as a treat on Christmas Day or when they used to visit Aunt Dudu, spread with Blue Band margarine and washed down with sweet Chombe tea. Still, he hopes the money from ET's drawer will stretch to it. Next to the milk there is a section of the chiller dedicated to spreads. He is surprised to note that there is no Blue Band – he had assumed that all the best-quality products would be represented on the shelves of British shops – but he finds something that looks similar and hopes it will do.

There follows a frustrating ten minutes, during which he wanders the aisles staring at the bright packages and trying to make sense of labels and logos that seem calculated to confuse. Look where he might, he cannot see a thing he recognises – no Maluwa soap, no Cowbell powdered milk, no Top Society lotions. When he happens upon some Fanta in the soft-drinks section, he almost weeps with relief and sets about loading the basket with as much as he can fit into it.

Once the frenzy has subsided and he has returned all but one of the packs of cans to the shelf, he stands in the aisle and tries to work out what to do. Eventually, out of the dust storm of his thoughts, a calm voice emerges. His head speaks to him like an adult talking to a child, as though it is Abambo taking him through the stages of learning to ride a bicycle once more. The main thing, it tells him, is that he must get enough things to stave off the hunger and enable him and ET to survive the coming days. It doesn't matter if it is not all entirely correct. What is important is that it is sufficient.

On the strength of this, he adds rice and eggs to the basket, along with some more of the tins ET seems to favour. He spends a while looking at the wilting collection of vegetables on the far wall and picks up a couple of tomatoes for good measure, but as there is little else he recognises, he leaves the rest undisturbed. Cooking is not a skill he has ever needed to master with Amayi and the twins to take care of it, but he suspects even they would struggle to find the ingredients to make a decent meal here. The shop makes him think of the jokey 'Changa' song they used to sing at primary school, trying to describe how to make bushbaby meat edible by mixing it with all sorts of unsuitable things.

At the checkout, the woman – 'Here For You Donna', according to a badge pinned to the front of her red top – scans and bags his purchases without comment. When he gets out the roll of notes to pay, however, her mouth drops open, and she looks so scandalised that he assumes he must have committed a terrible faux pas and hides the money away below the level of the counter while he peels off a note. Perhaps it is impolite to show your money in public in England – in the same way that eating with your female relatives or asking a woman about her pregnancy would be back home.

As he is reaching for the plastic bags, he catches sight of a string of cards hanging from the shelf behind Here For You Donna. 'International Calling Cards', reads a sign, and there is a picture of a mzungu woman with a phone receiver and very white teeth super-imposed over a map of the world. It occurs to him that with one of those cards he wouldn't need a mobile. He could phone Gilbert to arrange a call with Amayi from the landline in ET's home.

He gestures eagerly at the display. 'I would also like to purchase one of those international calling cards, please.'

Here For You leans across the counter and frowns. 'Come again?'

He eyes her warily. He would be happy to revisit the shop, of course, should he need supplies, but he has a feeling this is not what the woman means. Does buying a phonecard depend on promising repeat custom, then?

The woman rolls her eyes. 'Say what you said again.'

But now he is nervous. His palms are becoming clammy and his English is scattering. He stares at the woman's angular, chewing face, willing her to pluck the meaning from his eyes.

'Oh, for fuck's sake,' says the woman. 'I haven't got time for this.' And as though she has flicked a button that switches him off, she turns away, picks up her phone and begins to scrabble at the screen.

The sight of the device galvanises him. He points at it and then at the cards on the display. 'That! Please, madam. That!'

With a great effort, she brings her gaze back to him. 'Oh, you want a phonecard. Well I'm not sure if it'll work for Africa, but yeah, sure, all right.' She rips one off the strip. 'That'll be fifty pounds, please.'

It seems a lot, particularly as it says '£5' on the sign. Still, it's possible that he has misunderstood and that that is the price per unit. England is a wealthy country, after all. It's not surprising things cost more here.

He hands the money over and takes the precious card. He will go straight back to the house and prepare some food for him and ET, and once they have eaten he will waste no time in making that call. By God's good graces, he will be talking to his family within a few hours.

He hurries from the shop, giggling at the thought of the surprise and delight his news will cause after all this time. 'Iwe! You're not in England!' Ah, ah, ah! He can just hear them now: Amayi's soft tones, the chattering of the twins, Elijah babbling about his latest goal and Daniel trying to make his voice sound grown-up, gruff and serious. He cannot wait to talk to them!

But outside, terror is waiting, pawing the ground like an angry ox and putting its head down to charge. It barrels into him, shattering his strength. It is all he can do to stagger to a nearby bench. The world around him bobs and shimmers like water.

He has got to get food into his body. He rips into the bag of bread, cramming slice after slice into his mouth. And for a while, the taste and smell of it are all he can think about.

# ONE

They muddle along in the house for several days. He serves up meals as best he can, and if they don't conform to ET's usual standards she never troubles to say so. Indeed, she often eats them greedily, slopping the liquids on to her chin and chest in a most un-English manner.

'Lovely, darling. Lovely, Michael,' she tells him warmly, and seems so pleased that he doesn't bother to set her straight.

The stove is a concern. When he looks at it closely, he is surprised to find it is more primitive than he anticipated. Instead of the user-friendly gas or electric-powered modern convenience he imagined he would be able to operate at the touch of a button – much like the handsome Western oven in Aunt Dudu's kitchen – the thing requires naked flames to be kindled in it. Yet, although there is a hatch inside which fires have clearly burnt, he struggles to see how to fill or light it. In the end he gets it going with the help of a basket of logs by the back door and some matches he finds under the sink. All the same, the great metal bulk of it makes him uneasy, squatting in the kitchen, working grudgingly as if it knows he shouldn't be there, using it.

The phonecard turns out to be another frustration. Though he follows the instructions printed on the back in tiny letters, he cannot get the call to go through. There is only ever a long, continuous tone, which back home he would take as a sign that the line is not working. After repeated attempts, he gets so irritated that he is tempted to ask ET about it or see if she has a mobile phone he can borrow. Only the fear that she might take offence at the request stops him. She is paying him to be here and do a job, and he is keen to respect that. The last thing he wants is to get off on the wrong foot in this new country where he has hopes of achieving so many things.

It is for this reason that he continues to exercise restraint in the matter of the money in the kitchen drawer, only helping himself when he needs to go food shopping. He is also very careful to be attentive to ET and the dictates of the notebook. For the most part, and much to his relief, she resists any attempt to help her with things that concern her cleanliness or appearance. She slaps his hands away when he tries to put a cardigan round her and shuts him firmly outside the bathroom door. Nevertheless, the food preparation and the other household chores keep him busy enough. There is also the question of her safety. She wanders at night sometimes, mostly within the house and often to the piano.

One night, however, lying on the rug in the spare room, he hears the back door creaking open in the kitchen below. When he gets downstairs she is standing in the yard in her nightgown, strands of her silvered hair swirling in the breeze. She does not respond to her name, and when he looks into her eyes he sees the same absence he used to glimpse in his brother Daniel's expression during the night wanderings for which Roger said they should take him to the sing'anga. Knowing better than to interrupt her he follows a few steps behind as she makes her way to the storeroom and slips inside the door. She mutters there for a while, seeming to talk to someone in the dark, active space, as the straw rustles and bats flit about the rotting remains of the suspended platform, picked out by shafts of moonlight piercing the roof. Then, with a sigh and shrug, she turns and totters back past him into the house. By the time he peeps into her room she is in bed and fast asleep.

During the day, though she is often active and agitated, bustling from room to room, moving things from here to there, there are periods when they are quiet together, sitting side by side on the lop-sided sofa in the piano room. On these occasions, she often seems to be looking through the wall at something far away. At times the wistfulness he sees in her eyes reminds him of his grandmother and the stories she used to tell about the old days before the forests were cleared for the government plantations, when cobras still slithered between the trees and it was not unknown for lions to prowl into the villages in search of fresh meat.

Then, on what turns out to be their last afternoon together in the piano room, he sees an emotion he has not witnessed in her before: fear. It is a miserable day. The wind howls, spattering rain on to the window and seeming to quiver the air all through the house. Out over the English Channel, the clouds huddle together, crowding out the light and making the hour seem later than it is.

Perhaps it is this that brings the terror creeping up from the depths of ET's mind. He knows it the second he sees it: the paralysis, the tension, volition draining out of every limb. In an attempt to calm her, he goes to the corner and switches on the television. It turns out to have the opposite effect. When the screen blinks into life, it reveals a distressing picture: people clustered on a small boat in the middle of a churning expanse of water. There are noises, too: cries and the buzz of motors, the slapping and sucking of waves. Horror grips Jonah, forcing his hands to his face as the memories fly at him, sharp as shards of glass. For a moment he can do nothing but endure the onslaught of colours, sensations and sounds. Howls, a hand scrabbling, spilt petrol shimmering on waves.

When he is able to notice the room again, he realises that ET is pointing at the screen and gabbling, words tumbling over one another in their rush to leave her mouth. And as she speaks, she turns her head to look out of the window at the sullen sea. He follows her gaze and his memories slow and thicken. A day like this: bitter cold and unforgiving, bleeding into night. People herded down to the water's edge, cringing as those in the hooded jackets bark commands. One man scratching at his T-shirt with a biro,

99

trying to ink digits on to the fabric – the old trick so many had used on the crossing from Libya of writing a family member's phone number on your clothing in the hopes that if anything happened to you some kind stranger would see it floating in the water and make the grim call. Only this time, those others have told them, theirs will be the only boat. There won't be anyone to rescue them or take note of their corpses if they slip overboard.

People muttering. Some of the women moaning. But between him and Amanuel, silence. A solemn resolve. They have their plan. The time is approaching. There is nothing more to say.

In the distance, the light from the oil tankers out at sea—

'Oil tanks blazing,' mutters ET, and Jonah nods absent-mindedly, intent on the vision unfolding before him: harsh voices shouting in several languages. Hands shoving him in the small of his back.

'Shoving, shouting, the boat tipping—'

Overhead, a helicopter circling. People scattering in the glare of its searchlight.

'Planes swooping… Soldiers running for cover and Father and me left bobbing in *Bessie's Delight* like sitting ducks… Stukas screeching. The Germans attacking. Machine guns. Drrrrr-drrrrr.'

And then the screaming. The children first followed by the women as the boat leans—

'Drrrrr-drrrrr. Doof!'

—further and further until those on the outside edge totter and flail—

'Thrashing. Men gasping for air. Belongings strewn across the water. Limbs, too.'

But there is no chance of tipping out. Not this time. Not by accident. Those others have made sure of that. This is a bigger boat than the flimsy crafts they took from Libya. Its two large engines are packed inside black cases that gleam like beetles' shells. Money has been spent to ensure they make it to the other side. If nothing else, they are worth that effort. And so they sit hunched in the powerful boat. All of them desperate.

'Desperate.'

Desperate to get away from the nightmare—

'The hell on earth.'

And as they sweep away across the water, he looks back at the mean shapes on the shoreline, huddling as night descends. The place where every last shred of his faith in human goodness vanished.

'The hell on earth.'

He closes his eyes, but it isn't enough to shut it out. The dark shapes advance, growing in detail by the second, closing in. He hears again the doors of the container sliding open, sees once more the hard faces looking round, the hands beckoning that woman, this boy. Then the slams, the screams, the rhythmic thudding. The silence. The hunched figure limping back. And, eeeh, the hatred! The bitter resolve that burgeons in his chest that next time he will stand up and oppose it – that if he does so, others will join. That this is Europe, and such things cannot happen here. That people cannot be bought and sold like pieces of meat. And yet, on every occasion that the cruel eyes peer in, terror gags him, whispering that if he plays the hero now he will lose; that those same eyes will seek him out in future and summon him to worse things; that he might never get away, never be free. And so… nothing. Face turned to the wall. Yet never quite able to stop himself watching for that last, terrible glance back revealing the horrific discovery written anew on each victim's face: that they are not the exception; that the rules of the universe do not bend for them.

And so, unable to save others, they make a plan to save them-selves, he and Amanuel, whispering in the darkness while those around them sleep. When their turn comes to be transported they will make a break for it. They will wait until the shore of England comes in sight, and then they will tip over the side of the boat and swim. It won't be easy – Jonah has only once ventured into Lake Malawi and Amanuel has never been in deep water before. Still, you hear of people swimming the Channel all the time. Rumour has it that in the camp further along the French coast, where the sea narrows, people often do it. There are hustlers selling wet suits for those willing to take their chance. He and Amanuel are young and strong, and they won't be attempting the whole thing. When set against all the hardships they have endured, thrashing their way through a bit of water will surely present no challenge. And so they wait through the winter, kept warm by the knowledge of what they intend to do.

The first part of the plan goes perfectly. With a bit of subtle shuffling, they manage to secure two places at the side of the boat. As they skim away into the darkness and night descends over the French coastline, Jonah reaches back and pats his friend's arm in triumph. It won't be long now.

But eeh eeh eeh, it is cold on the water. The wind slices through their clothes and spits spray in their faces, leaving them drenched and shivering. When the lights of England begin to appear and he sees the ghostly shapes of the white mountains rising out of the sea – cliffs – it takes some moments before Jonah can bring himself to act. Only the knowledge that the engines will soon be dipping and the boat pulling in to deliver them to other cruel hands spurs him on. Taking a deep breath, he taps Amanuel's knee using the signal they have agreed and hurls himself over the side.

Bubbles. Cold. Salt in his mouth and eyes.

Only by a supreme effort does Jonah retain the focus to strike out away from the boat, driving his arms and legs to pull and kick, pull and kick. When at last he is confident he has made sufficient progress he stops and looks back, eyes scouring the surface of the water for his friend. At first, he sees nothing. Then the flashing of a mobile-phone torch draws his gaze. The boat is nearer than he supposed. The engines have been turned low and it is gliding to where Amanuel thrashes and gasps, eyes wide and glinting in the approaching glare. Hands reach over the side towards him. In another instant, they will have him by the shoulders. Kicking his legs beneath him to stay afloat, Jonah watches. He ought to shout. He ought to scream. If he can distract them for a moment it might buy Amanuel enough time to disappear into the darkness. But fear clogs his throat and he attempts nothing, does nothing, only looks on as they seize his friend and drag him upwards. In the last instant before he disappears inside the boat, the torchlight flashes on Amanuel's face. Though he knows it is impossible – that the beam must be blinding the Eritrean and turning all else black – it seems to Jonah that his friend is looking straight at him, eyes big with reproach. A new, terrible guilt lodges in the seabed of his consciousness as the engines fire and the craft roars away.

'Dunkirk.'

Her voice jolts him. He has forgotten she is there. He has forgotten he is there. He looks at her. 'What did you say?'

She jerks, her mouth strangely crooked. 'Dunkirk.'

And with that – with the name of that last terrible place – Jonah collapses, sobbing to his knees. He cries long and loud for the boy who set out beaming and waving on the back of a pick-up truck, clutching a rucksack and a parcel of Amayi's zigumu cakes. For the shadow who haunted crumbling doorways and bomb-shattered buildings in Tripoli, listening always for the click of guns and the tread of feet. For the shell that sat beneath the blue tarpaulin, watching dead-eyed as women scrabbled through bins, old people stumbled and children tottered tearfully from shelter to shelter, seeking arms that would never hold them again. For the sad figure stolen from himself and turned into a thing for others to sell. And for the being forced to look his fellow beings in the face and make over and over the same unforgiveable choice: my survival matters more than yours.

When at last his sobs subside and he looks up, the light has faded, the day dying in earnest now. ET is slumped at a weird angle against the wooden arm of the sofa, her mouth askew.

# BEEP

Sobbing and sobbing and sobbing sand bobbing sand bobbing sand bobbing – FLASH! FIRE! – sand bobbing sand bombing sand bombing sand bombing and bodies and bodies and bodies and bodies – JUDDER! DUCK! COVER! – and bodies and bodies…

They have been at sea for more than twelve hours, chuntering round Route Y behind the tug with its Lewis gun pointing the way. She was excited at first, caught up in the romance of it – the moon glittering on the water, the secret of her girl's hair tucked up under a flat cap so as to send the naval officer's gaze skimming past her at Ramsgate and the exhilaration of this adventure that she has instigated. She and Father setting out once more on the English Channel, this time with a naval rating assigned to them by the authorities and in response to a call from King and Country to come to the rescue of England's brave soldiers, with no Aunt Susan in sight.

But then the bombing started: the blasts that lit up the night, splicing a frame of day into the darkness. At first it was in the distance. Soon, however, their convoy came under attack, the little boats jerking and lurching on the ropes attaching them to the tug like bows on the tail of a kite.

Finally, the inevitable: a direct hit on the motor launch behind them. The face of the man at the wheel in the instant before it went down – a mild face better suited to reading the paper by the fire and strolls on Sunday afternoons, now wrenched by terror.

'Aiming for the tug,' grunts the rating as he shoves the tiller hard a-port in an effort to escape the worst of the wash. But the thought that Jerry had smashed that poor man's boat and sent him flailing to his death by mistake didn't help.

Grimly into the day beyond, then. Sleeplessness throbbing in her ears. She eats because it makes sense to, rather than out of any desire: one of the soggy cheese sandwiches with which Aunt Susan made a great show of presenting them before standing at the gatepost to wave them off with her handkerchief, all the while scanning the road and fields for anyone her performance might impress.

The afternoon bleeds out. The sun sinks. But then it seems to get stuck, orange remaining in the sky long after darkness should have fallen and reddening in the east, as though the Stukas wheeling above them and the mines bobbing beneath the waves have between them sent the world careening straight into the next morning.

The French coast looms, backlit by flame. The town is a set of jagged black shapes. To the left of it lie the beaches – long, sloping expanses of sand, thick with trees. Or no, those are not trees, Edie realises as they near the land and the tug's engines slow. They are people – lines of men shuffling towards the water, scattering and regrouping whenever a bomber threatens to swoop out of the clouds.

Dread drags at her. There are so many of them. How can there be so many? What difference can *Bessie's Delight* make in the face of need on such a scale? They can't manage more than twenty-five soldiers on any one trip – a mere thimbleful from this ocean of misery.

All at once, she is afraid that she has been an idiot. Aunt Susan was right to laugh at her: this is a fool's errand. She ought never to have suggested it. Father hadn't wanted to come. Left to him, *Bessie's Delight* would have continued to moulder in the outhouse, disintegrating like the photograph of Mother yellowing on the chest of drawers in Edie's room. But she had forced the issue. With her stubbornness and her ridiculous insistence that she would go by herself if she had to and tell the navy where to find the boat, she had dragged him into this, forcing him out once more on to the waters that had washed away the woman he loved.

Now there is nothing for it but to do what they can. Once the rating has detached the rope that linked them to the tug, they proceed through the shallows, following the 800-yard-wide deep-water channel that the naval officer told them runs along the coast. But even in a motor yacht as small as *Bessie's Delight* it's slow going. The water is clogged with all manner of oddments − kit bags, paddles and the wrecks of other boats. A half-submerged canoe drifts past as they near the shore, as does the head of a merry-go-round horse. At first, Edie assumes her tiredness is making her imagine things, but when she glances up at the seafront and sees the remains of a carousel standing behind what must in happier times have been the promenade, she is not so sure. There are also objects that bear less scrutiny: boots and caps and other bits of uniform, not all of which are empty. Edie is grateful for the excuse the smoke and cordite in the air give her to look away and cover her face with her sleeve.

As they come within a few feet of running aground, the men on the shore surge towards the boat. Ragged and battered, they look less like soldiers and more like gentlemen of the road, and Edie can see that many of them are only a few years older than she is. There is even one blond boy who seems to have forgotten himself completely and is standing in the surf, sucking his thumb. Weak and exhausted though they may be, the soldiers retain enough energy to jostle for their chance to escape the beach. It requires considerable forcefulness from the rating to make them board one at a time so that they don't swamp the boat. When they have taken on as many as they can, Father puts the engine into reverse and, with the help of a few smart jabs of an oar over the bow, they float backwards, turn and head out to the destroyers waiting in deeper water to take the troops home.

She loses count of how many times they make the trip as day dawns and thickens. The rhythm of loading, turning, weaving through the wreckage and holding the boat steady as the men clamber out and heave themselves up the rope ladder on to the deck above numbs her. The faces blend into one. Only occasionally do the scream of a Stuka or the blast of another vessel hitting a mine in the distance jolt her from her reverie and set her heart racing.

At length, as the sun begins to drift towards the horizon beyond which Britain's coastline lies, the rating suggests it is time for them to do the same. Their petrol is getting low and crossing back under cover of darkness will minimise the chances of a Stuka pilot trying to pick them off for fun. They'll make one last run to the shore and take the men they collect back with them.

The beach is as full as ever and the hours of waiting have done nothing to dampen the soldiers' eagerness to board: if anything, their attempts are more urgent, as though they sense their chance to flee is slipping away. When he scrambles over the side with his kit bag, causing his fellow passengers to mutter about pushing in and ignoring the order to abandon all personal belongings, she feels a flash of impatience. But then she looks at him and sees by the dying light of the day that his face is soot-stained and spattered with burn marks, and her irritation turns to sympathy. Clearly he must have got caught up in a blast or trapped in one of the burning buildings around the port. She ought not to judge him harshly. He is just like the rest of the men after all – one more scared and bewildered BEF private trying to make his way home.

With the coming of the morning on the way back, however, Edie's assessment changes. As dawn breaks, rousing her from a light doze, she looks back at Father sitting at the tiller, his face grey with tiredness. From there, her gaze slides over the soldiers hunched on either side of the boat and sprawled across the deck. That is when she notices. The third man along on the left – he isn't pale like the rest of them. Though he is shivering as much as the others, his hands aren't blue with cold. There is no green tint of seasickness about his lips. Instead, his skin is a deeper colour and stippled with freckles, some of them as big as farthings – the marks that in the half-light she had taken for injuries.

She stares until he looks at her, then ducks her head, blushing, wondering at herself for being so rude. The bumping of the boat against the dock at Ramsgate jolts the embarrassment from her mind. Suddenly everything is activity and noise, the men stirring and jumping out with a shout of thanks to Father – 'Cheers, squire!' 'Much obliged!' 'You're a gentleman and a scholar, sir!' – to be welcomed by banners and women pressing bread into their hands and military police watching for potential absconders with quick, mistrustful eyes. As Father and the rating busy themselves with making *Bessie's Delight* secure before going to report her safe return, Edie gets out and sidles off along the front, past the line of buses waiting to ferry troops to the station and the stall offering free postcards for soldiers to send to families fretting for their safety. There is a buzzing sound in her ears, and although she can see her feet walking beneath her, she cannot feel the pavement. Outside Kaufmann, the grocer's, with its sign in the window appealing to passers-by to 'Support this patriotic business run by British citizens', she sits down on a low wall with a sigh.

'Well, it seems as though I wasn't the only odd one out on that boat.'

Looking to her left, she discovers him sitting there, rolling a cigarette from a battered tin of Player's Navy Cut tobacco.

She smiles. 'You noticed, then.'

'Reckon I was the only one who did. You were impressive out there, kiddo. Every bit as good as a boy.'

She blushes. 'Thanks.' Although, thinking about it, she can't see that she really did much of use – certainly not by the time he'd joined them. It was Father and the naval rating who did most of the work on that final crossing: she'd been so exhausted she had no option but to sleep.

He holds out his hand. 'Michael.'

She takes it. 'Edie.'

And he shakes her hand firmly as though she really is a boy.

'You'll be off home now, then, I suppose,' he says, putting the cigarette to his lips and lighting it with a match. His eyes are a strange colour – such a light brown that they are almost gold and flecked with green.

'Uhuh. Just waiting for Father to notify the navy that we're back.'

He nods. 'And will you have far to go?'

'About twenty miles. We have a farm just round the coast near Rotham.'

His odd eyes widen. 'Well, isn't that a strange coincidence? My aunt lives in the nearby town. Now, what was its name again...'

'Totwith?'

He snaps his fingers. 'Totwith. Well, waddya know?'

He says the last bit in a thick American accent, like a character in a film, surprising her into a laugh. Then he leans towards her, the end of the cigarette glowing.

'Listen, kiddo, do you think it would be much trouble for me to get a lift with you and your dad?'

She frowns. 'Aren't you supposed to get on those buses?'

He makes a face. 'They're for infantry. Not for regular soldiers.'

'Oh.' She wasn't aware that there was a distinction. A prickly, cotton-wool feeling is creeping up her arms. Very soon her eyes will close. She blinks in an effort to focus.

He is still talking, his gestures with the cigarette leaving orange circles in the air like a sparkler's trail. 'Besides, they told us before we left France that if we had other means of transport from the ports we ought to use them. Save fuel and help the war effort and all that.'

She nods. This she understands. Since petrol rationing came in, Aunt Susan has had to limit her trips to the haberdasher in town to every other week. It has been the source of much discussion.

She smiles. The thought of helping this curious, funny man pleases her. In an odd way she can't explain, she has an idea that it will make up for the queer thoughts she had about him on the crossing. When Father appears, yawning into his sleeve, she rushes up to him to make the case.

And so it is that the three of them bounce back to Cliff's Edge in the old truck, the two men in the front seats and Edie and the kit bag in the back. As they pull into the yard, Aunt Susan emerges from the kitchen.

'Oh, thank goodness. I was imagining all sorts of horrors. I've made mutton hotpot specially to welcome you home.' Then she lays eyes on Michael and touches a hand to her hair. 'But I wasn't aware that we were expecting guests.'

'Oh, I'm not staying,' says Michael. 'Wonderful as mutton hotpot sounds. I was just cadging a lift.'

He swings his kit bag on to his shoulder. 'Thank you, sir. So long, kiddo.' And with that he strides out of the yard, away down the track and into Edie's life for good.

# BEEP

The sea has got into her head. The waters are overtopping the cliffs of her mind and have rampaged through the house of her, scattering thinks all around. Wade through the debris – galoshes on, careful – and what's this! Sodden papers telling words of other nows. First day at school and a visit to the Totwith Odeon with Roger Allen all clumped together – blackboard, chalk smells and sitting with her gas mask on your knee in case the future had a raid in it. The horrid feel of his hand on her waist, fingers making sweat sprout through rayon. Mother's funeral with all the eyes watching to see if Edie will be going to be brave or nonsense, good or cry, and then afterwards back to Cliff Edge to see Mary Watkins bending to gawp at Dobbin's willy and sell off the cows – what hasn't happened, in fact, for twenty years apart. The day of the Black Maria. All of them standing up the track. Jean's teeth worrying, worrying, worrying at that lip, watching him get taken without a word. Roger Allen cycling after on his tandem with Cynthia Beasley.

The waters well higher. Up the staircase into the bedrooms, the bathroom with its blushful contents. Things of the body. Rude suggestions. Aunt Susan with her porcelain contrivance and naughty rubber tube. Don't squeak unless you're spoken to. The bedroom where she will night all her days, its dormer goggling always towards an empty track. The waters topping level with the hayloft and the sighing business of darkness, that first sweet, searing

time. Letters swilling. Please, sir, if it's not too much trouble...
Dear madam, I write to ask... Reverend Brigadier, if you could
find it in your heart... Mulch. Mulch, all of it. But will be written
with such thrust, such certain, by head and hand that did not know
time can just go and go, littering up the new of you with false starts
and waitings. Because if there will be one such wrinkle, there could
always be more. Until the house of you was full of dry scribbles
and crossings-out. Nothing but scrap. An empty shell of who-ness.
Standing on the cliff of what might still come, waiting to be sluiced.

Here comes the water, surging up to the rafters now, lapping
the roof of you, smashing out the windows and letting in currents
carrying lost moments and queer ideas, tumbling everything into
now, so that your mind is pinioned like a body wired up to machines
in a hospital bed, trapped in a constant twilight where voices and
footsteps come and go.

# 12

Jonah sips at the cup of scalding brown liquid he's managed to coax from the machine along the corridor and watches her. She looks peaceful, lying back on the clean, white pillows – quite transformed from the contorted creature she'd been a few hours ago, slumped and dribbling over the side of the couch. There are a number of wires and machines that he doesn't like the look of and a rather unpleasant tube jabbed into the back of her hand (along with a bag filling with yellow liquid a little below the level of his knees), but these seem to be normal, judging by the state of the azungu lying in the other beds arranged at intervals down the sides of the ward. Overall, the place seems calm. Strain his ears as he might, he cannot hear any of the wailing or clamouring that echoed through the district hospital where Abambo used to perform operations. Here there is only the shush and beeping of the machines, the hum of the lights and the squeak of the footsteps of figures in blue overalls hurrying along the corridor outside.

'Cooey!' He looks up. It is the old white woman in the floral headscarf. The one with the name that sounds like trousers. Jeans. Beside her stands a mzungu girl with two rope-like plaits, slurping at a red ice lolly.

Jeans hurries forward. 'I came as soon as I could! They said about the ambulance in Spar and I knew it could mean only one thing. Oh, ET!'

She clasps her hands under her chin and regards the bed before rounding on him with a stricken face. 'How is she?'

He thinks about his answer for a moment. 'Quiet.'

She nods. 'What have the doctors said?'

There was a word that the woman with the clipboard used. Something like caress... 'They think it is a stroke.' He can tell by Jeans's nod of recognition that he has got it right. 'But they are waiting for a... someone they can give all the information.'

'Next of kin. Yes, of course. Well, luckily that's in hand. As soon as I heard something had happened I called Dr Brewer. ET was always very funny about details like that – she's a very private person, as you know – but luckily there was some form in her records she'd filled out donkeys' years ago and it had the details of her cousin, Mary Watkins, so at least there's someone to take the reins on the family side. The surgery is making contact, and it shouldn't be long before she's here. I met her several times when she came to stay with ET as a child. Nice girl. Fond of animals.'

There is no obvious response and he is wary about the meaning of 'donkeys' years', so he keeps quiet.

'Oh, it's so fortunate you were there!' exclaims Jeans after a minute or two of listening to the machines beep and whir. 'I dread to think what would have happened if she'd been on her own.'

They look at the bed. The girl slurps at the lolly.

'And they think she's going to pull through. That she'll be all right.'

At first Jonah assumes that Jeans is making a statement, that she must have talked to a doctor on the way in, or that perhaps there is some indication in the signs hanging over the bed that he is not equipped to appreciate. But then she continues to stare at him, and he realises that she is in fact asking a question.

He spread his hands in a gesture he sometimes saw Abambo use when a patient's chances were finely balanced. 'It is difficult to say.'

Another nod. 'Well, I can't tell you how grateful I am. It's quite clear that she wouldn't have stood a chance if you hadn't been there. The fact that she's here now is down to you and your excellent... qualifications.'

He stares at her. Has he heard her correctly? His qualifications, did she say? The word makes him want to laugh and shout and vomit all at once. Qualifications? Him? The boy who was forced to drop out? Who was obliged to leave school the day the head-master announced a rule that only those carrying receipts to show they were up to date with their fees would be admitted into the classrooms? Who had to walk away from the building feeling the eyes of his fellow students on his back? Who then had to listen to Amayi berating Abambo, telling him that he was a fool to stay in this dead-end post in the middle of nowhere, treating paupers for a pitiful salary that rarely arrived, that if he were in Blantyre in a properly respected position she wouldn't have to beg for favours while their children's futures withered to dust? (Never mind that most of the rest of Jonah's classmates followed his example within two months and that, three weeks after that, the school closed indefinitely when the teachers themselves stopped showing up.)

No, he has no qualifications. What he did the day ET collapsed – forcing himself out and running down the track to the sealed road to flag down a motorist and persuade him to let Jonah use his mobile phone to call the calamities, in spite of the eyes he was convinced must be watching from behind hedges – had come not out of books or exams or hours spent in lecture theatres. It had proceeded from nothing more sophisticated than the sickening knowledge of what grey spreading out from the mouth means.

It is a colour ingrained in his memory, and one that he saw several times during his travels, usually in the instant before he turned his head away. But even had the journey of the last two years not taken place, his brain would have retained the image of that ashen pallor as clearly as the first time he saw it fourteen years before.

It was the February of the year following the bad harvest and four months after he had been obliged to walk away from school. By then, life in the old white house near the village had entered what he naïvely imagined to be its most difficult phase – after keeping the family on two meals a day for as long as she could, Amayi had been obliged to abandon serving phala for breakfast and to limit them all to just one daily serving of nsima made from the last of the poor-quality maize she had managed to purchase for ten times its usual cost from the ADMARC fifteen kilometres away. Hunger had expanded to fill every moment, so that, even as Jonah ate his share of the sorry little grey lump that now came to the table in place of the proud, ivory mound that used to afford him seconds and thirds, his body ached like a wound that would not close. There was hope, however. The December rains had been good and, weak though they all were, most of the local farmers had managed to plant the next crop and even secure some of the starter packs of fertiliser the president in his boun- tifulness had seen fit to offer at a discounted price. The green shoots had grown into strong stalks as high as a man's chest. In a few weeks, the succulent dowe would be ready and, judging by the abundance of ears ripening in the fields, May's harvest would be a bumper one. There would be no question of the family of dear Dr Jeremiah, who had done so much for so many in the community, missing out.

With little to do but wait, the family spent the days conserving energy – sleeping as many hours as they could and venturing out only to draw water and collect the firewood needed to prepare the evening meal. They were not the only ones suffering. One afternoon, on his way back from gathering a spindly bundle of branches, he met Roger trudging along, glum-faced, with a battered sheet of corrugated iron strapped to his bicycle.

'Off to sell that for thousands at the trading centre, brother?' Jonah had joked as they drew level, his good humour awakened by the joy of seeing his friend.

'Ha!' Roger had replied. 'You know me. Always hustling.' But the words had sounded oddly flat, and they stood for an awkward moment feeling the breeze blowing down off the hills.

'What is it, anyway?' But as soon as he'd said the words, Jonah regretted them, for in that instant he recognised the pattern of the rust eating through the edge of the metal as the irregular shape that used to jut out above Roger's family's front door, and saw the dents where mangoes dropped off the adjacent tree and thudded on to the house each year.

Roger shrugged. 'Just some scrap metal I found by the side of the road.'

He'd nodded again, unable to meet Roger's sunken eyes, and instead called out cheerily as he pushed off on his bicycle, 'Well, I hope you get a good price!'

The next time he saw Roger in the distance, wheeling another sheet of corrugated iron, he kept his eyes on the ground.

But although most people were struggling, one member of Jonah's household seemed to be suffering the effects of the food shortage less than the rest. In the afternoons, when his wife and children lay down to doze, Abambo would set out in the direction of the trading centre and return several hours later with astonishing tales. One day it was that the kanyenya stall had had a surplus of meat and had given him a free portion; the next it was that he had found a bag of zigumu cakes by the side of the road and gorged himself on them (no, he was sorry, but he hadn't thought to bring any back with him: the cakes were so delicious that he hadn't been able to resist gobbling them all up); then there was the time he ran into Gilbert's father and got invited to share a meal with him; and the day when a mandasi vendor ran after him and gave him a bag of freshly fried donuts because – what are the chances? – their grandfathers had been childhood friends in Mangochi. All of these lucky adventures meant that when dinner time rolled around bringing Jonah slavering to the table, Abambo was far too full to manage any more food.

'No, no,' he proclaimed, holding up his hands in protest. 'You have my portion. There's no way I could eat another mouthful.'

Things went on like this for several weeks. Then came the afternoon on which Jonah ran into Gilbert. He was wheeling his bike along the road that led from the village to the forest five kilometres distant – too dizzy by this time to contemplate getting on and pumping the pedals – when he caught sight of his friend on the crest of the next hill. Believing himself to be unobserved, Gilbert made no effort to hide his misery. His arms and legs had shrunk to sticks so that the Manchester United T-shirt he had been so proud of getting the previous year hung off him as though it belonged to another, older boy. His teeth seemed to have grown huge in his face and he dragged his feet as though the energy to lift them from one step to the next was more than he could afford. Upon catching sight of Jonah Gilbert made an effort to rally, and a flicker of the old roguishness ignited in his eyes, but it was too late to conceal the truth.

When they got within speaking distancing, they both raised their hands and muttered 'moni'. No one bothered with 'muli bwanji' these days: asking someone how they were seemed like a joke. Even so, Jonah was shocked by the angles in Gilbert's face, and he cast about in his mind for something to lighten the mood and make his friend smile. Then he had it.

'Hey, brother! Wasn't it funny about our fathers meeting the other day? Man, I tell you, my Abambo couldn't believe his luck. He came home stuffed from that massive meal at your house.'

Gilbert put his head on one side and regarded him oddly. 'I don't know what you're thinking of, brother, but there hasn't been real food at our house since before the rains.'

There was an unpleasant smell coming from Gilbert's mouth – rot mixed with the sort of chemical odour that sometimes emanated from the God's Blessings barbershop. But it wasn't this that made Jonah start backwards. It was the impression that in that instant someone had ripped the sky away.

Still, he did his best to put a good face on the conversation, shrugging and offering a comical expression. 'Eeeh! Sorry, brother. I must have got confused. Perhaps it was Roger's house instead. Well, anyway, tionana, brother. See you later.'

The next day, when everyone else was asleep, Jonah followed his father on his afternoon walk. As usual, Abambo headed in the direction of the trading centre, but about a kilometre from the house, instead of joining the road and heading down the hill, he veered off the track and lay down under a bush. There, judging by the snores that started up a moment later, sending a gecko scuttling, he slept.

After several hours, when the sun was starting its descent, Abambo hauled himself out from under the bush, patted the dust from his trousers and strolled back to the house, tailed by his eldest son. It was good timing: Amayi was just bringing the bowls out of the kitchen and carrying them to the table where the male members of the family ate their evening meals. Before she could assign one to him, however, Abambo was holding up his hands. You know, it was the funniest thing, but he'd had another bit of good fortune that afternoon. Old Trywell down at the trading centre – did Amayi remember him? The one who used to earn his living selling wooden utensils to azungu tourists – well, he had come into possession of a crate of early ripe mangoes. There were too many for him alone – and anyway, they didn't agree with the old man's stomach – so Abambo and several others sat round and ate to their heart's content. He knew it sounded ridiculous to be sated on mangoes alone, but these were such juicy ones that they filled him right up. There was no way he could contemplate eating anything further that day.

Abambo continued to talk, but his eldest son was unable to make out what he said. Thunder was roaring in his ears, blotting out all other sound. He opened his mouth to shout that it wasn't true – that Abambo had been nowhere near the trading centre and couldn't have spoken to Old Trywell that day, that if Amayi went down the track that led to the road and peered under the mphangala bush by the penultimate bend, she would see the imprint from his body revealing the exact position where he had dozed all afternoon. But as Jonah was about to speak, the image of Roger carrying the corrugated-iron sheet from the roof of his house reared up in his mind. He shut his mouth and went to take his place with his brothers, who were already waiting for the evening meal.

The terrible thing came soon after that. Though many days of hunger still stood between them and the longed-for harvest, a feeling was beginning to drift over the family that the end of their sufferings was in sight. The maize stalks were tall now – higher than Jonah's head – and the fast-maturing dowe cobs were clearly visible with their wispy fronds like the tufts of hair on the end of donkeys' tails. It wouldn't be long before they got to taste their sweetness.

Emboldened by nature's promises, Father and the boys shrugged off their weakness and set about sweeping out the storeroom and sorting through the heaps of empty sacks that had lain in its corners for so long.

Jonah was just carrying out a bundle that needed mending when he looked down the track to see his father bending over with his hands on his knees, peering at the ground. This in itself was not unusual. Abambo was known locally as a bit of a dreamer. When he wasn't cycling around administering vaccines and seeing patients, he could happily while away an afternoon out in the bush wandering from plant to plant or watching the wheeling of swallows above his head. Indeed, it was not unusual for him to set out on an errand and return with nothing more than a vague smile on his face – much to Amayi's exasperation.

Yet something about his father's stance that afternoon made Jonah uneasy. Leaving Daniel and little Elijah playing near the sacks, he walked down the track to where Abambo stood hunched over. The older man seemed oblivious to his approach, but when his eldest son put a hand on his shoulder, he looked up, motioning for Jonah to be quiet.

'See how they're all going here and there,' he whispered. 'Isn't it amazing?'

Jonah looked, but could see nothing apart from the red dust of the track. There wasn't even a line of ants carrying off fragments of grain or blades of grass. The ground was empty of life.

'I think they have a plan,' continued his father. 'I think they're expecting a transformation.'

Jonah looked into the older man's eyes and saw an odd fire blazing there. 'Don't you think you'd better sit down for a bit, Abambo?' he said.

His father's brow creased. 'Sit down?' he erupted. 'Why on earth would I need to sit down? You don't know what you're saying, my son.' Yet when Jonah put his arm around his shoulders and led him to a patch of shade at the side of the track, he came without resisting.

'Rest there for a few moments while I get you some water,' said Jonah.

He was only gone a short while, but when he returned carrying half a cup of the water his sisters had drawn from the village well the previous day, it seemed as though Abambo had aged several years. He frowned when he tried to focus on Jonah, and spoke in an oddly formal, distant way, as though he was unsure who he was. The hand that reached out for the water trembled and he managed only a few gulps before the cup slipped from his grasp and tumbled to the ground, spreading a dark blot across the red earth. Yet instead of expressing the irritation he would normally feel in the face of such waste, the man blinked up at the sky, rubbing his mouth and muttering.

Thoughts buzzed around Jonah's mind like bees. He glanced towards the house to look for Amayi, before remembering that she had gone to a cousin's funeral and wouldn't be back until dark. His eye snagged on his brothers, carrying and sorting the maize sacks, but they were still children and couldn't be expected to know what to do. The same went for his twin sisters, bustling importantly about the kitchen but still running off into the bush to play when they thought no one was looking. It was down to him.

The district hospital was ten kilometres away. Nothing to Abambo when a WhatsApp came through that an emergency C-section or appendectomy was required – in normal times, he could cover that distance in twenty minutes. But Jonah could see that there would be no hope of speeding there on the bicycle today. Apart from the hospital, Abambo was the health-care services in this part of the district, and he was hardly in a position to treat himself.

For a while it seemed hopeless. Then a solution popped into Jonah's mind: a healer. That was what they needed. He dismissed the thought at first, remembering how Abambo would roll his eyes at the mention of the sing'anga with his charms and incantations. Yet the idea kept returning, persisting. After all, people still went to consult him, didn't they? Long before they came to Abambo, in many cases. There had to be some good in it, otherwise why would the traditions continue? If there was the slightest chance the sing'anga could save Abambo, it would be foolishness on Jonah's part not to take his father there.

The sing'anga's house was three kilometres distant on the far side of the nearest village. Roger had pointed it out on one of their bird-trapping expeditions, back when they had the energy for such things. Surely, with Jonah's help, Abambo could manage to walk there?

It proved not to be the case: when he helped him to his feet, his father staggered and slumped on to him, almost toppling them both to the ground. So Jonah fetched the bicycle and loaded him on to it, frightened anew at the lightness of this man who, only six months previously, thought nothing of cycling thirty or forty kilometres a day during a polio-vaccination campaign.

But though it was easy to get his father on to the bicycle saddle, keeping him there was another matter. He slumped and slipped about and his fingers would not grip the handlebars. It required all Jonah's strength to prevent him from falling, and before he had wheeled the bike half the distance, he was regretting not having helped himself to water from the plastic jerry can in the kitchen. By the time he pushed the bicycle up the slight incline to the hut set apart near a grove of blue-gum trees, his head was swimming and bright shapes were dancing before his eyes.

Unlike most of the dwellings in the village, the traditional healer's home had a door. Around this were hung a series of charms and magical items: a vulture's foot, a sheaf of feathers, a series of objects carved from bone.

'Odi, odi!' called Jonah, knocking on the iron sheet covering the entrance. 'Can I come in?'

He stood and listened. But there was no reply, only the feathers twisting in the wind and the breeze ruffling the dried straw of the roof, producing a sound like termites munching.

'Odi, odi!' He called again, his voice given a hard edge by the burning in his arms and his father's vacant stare.

Footsteps. But not from inside the house. Instead, the sound of someone walking out of the blue-gum grove at the back: a wiry man with one blind, white eye, clutching a cigar rolled from dried maize husks.

If Jonah was looking for the sing'anga he wouldn't find him here, he said, shaking his head. No, sir. The sing'anga had gone away into the forest. Nobody knew where. Perhaps he would be back in an hour. Perhaps never. In the mean time there was only him, Maliro. He had assisted the sing'anga a bit as a boy and learnt some of his arts. For a modest fee, a mere handful of kwacha, he would be happy to take a look at the boy's... uncle, was he? Eeeeh! Abambo. Sorry to hear that. That was bad.

He waited, Maliro, the tip of his tongue flickering in and out of his lips like a black mamba's. All the while, he watched Jonah intently with his one good eye.

Jonah stood, trembling with the bicycle as a heavy weight sank through him. Money. Of course. He had forgotten in his panic that he would have to pay for his father's treatment. Traditional healers were not like Abambo, giving away services to anyone in need, regardless of Amayi's muttering that his energy would be better spent applying for positions in the city or, failing that, turning his hand to a more profitable venture that would help them through the hungry season. Stupid to have come all this way without thinking of that. And yet, if he had remembered, it wouldn't have made a difference: the plastic Evian bottle where they kept the housekeeping money had been empty for weeks.

There was nothing for it but to make his best effort. He knew little was impossible in these situations. Hadn't Abambo himself made exception after exception, continuing to offer what treatment he could in the lean spells when first his salary and then medical supplies stopped coming through? Surely he was owed similar consideration himself, now, in his hour of need?

Flinging himself to his knees, he clapped his hands in appeal. Please, older brother. Ah, please, achimwene. Have pity. They had come so far. The old man, he could see, was gravely ill. Surely it would be possible to defer the debt on this occasion? He would undertake personally to repay it just as soon as his family was in better circumstances. It would not be long. Even now, the harvest was ripening, the dowe cobs getting fatter by the hour. Soon money would be flowing through the government coffers and out to the rural areas once again. If he would only grant the treatment it would be a matter of weeks – days! – until he received his payment. What's more – yes, he would really do this! – Jonah would promise to pay double in recognition of the man's kindness. Ah, please, achimwene! Please!

Maliro regarded him, sliding his gaze over Jonah's ragged Coca-Cola T-shirt and scrawny arms. He shook his head. Ah, no, sorry. He couldn't do it. These days it wasn't possible to put that sort of trust in people. It wasn't anybody's fault. It was simply that hunger had raided the future and carried off its materials, making it as flimsy and likely to collapse as a hut that hadn't been lived in for years. No one could say with any certainty who would make it through. It was nothing personal. The best thing would be if Jonah could think of someone who could give him money. It was so little when you were looking at it in the scope of life. Didn't the family have uncles? What about a wealthy relative living in the city?

Jonah's mind called forth an image of Aunt Dudu and the grudging way she had served them food the last time he and Abambo had made the trip to Blantyre, ladling helpings from the pot as though she were counting every mouthful. He shook his head sadly. No. He was afraid there was nobody of that sort.

The man nodded as though he had expected this answer and sucked on his cigar. In that case, the best thing he could suggest was the district hospital on the far side of the trading centre. It was azungu medicine, and so not as powerful as what he and the sing'anga could do, of course, but occasionally these white remedies were of some benefit.

Jonah turned and looked down the slope at the track zigzagging off through the bush. From here the journey to the trading centre was a good five kilometres and the district hospital was at least another six further on. Really, Jonah was a kape for letting hunger and exhaustion trick him into coming here: if they had set off directly for the hospital they would already be halfway. But there was no point saying any of this, no point wasting the energy that anger would require. And so, with a nod, he set off down the slope.

For a while, the going was easier. The incline helped and the wheels of the bicycle seemed to find their way over the ruts and stones without any effort on his part. Jonah began to feel hopeful.

'Don't worry, Abambo,' he said cheerfully. 'I'm going to get you to the help you need.' And although he was anxious and his father was making noises he had never heard before, he felt a surge of pride because here he was being the big man, taking control and saving his family.

As he walked, he grew in confidence. Abambo was known in the hospital, a familiar, well-respected figure; the staff would do all they could for him. Besides, hadn't his father always told him that the trick in medicine was never to give up hope? The human body was an extraordinarily resilient creation. There had been so many cases Abambo had treated that had looked as though they must end in disaster, only for a surprise reversal to happen and the patient to walk back into life again. Surely there was every chance of a similar miracle here? After all, hadn't his Abambo been having some extraordinarily good fortune with all those meals he'd found on his afternoon walks? He went for nearly half a kilometre before he remembered about Gilbert and the sleeping, and the fact that none of his father's stories about the food he'd found were true.

Then the bike hit a sharp stone. He heard the front tyre pop and the snake's hiss of the air rushing out. Within seconds the effort of wheeling the bicycle doubled, until he was forced to drag it with every step. It wasn't long before he could manage no more.

He stared at the path ahead, which climbed gently for a few hundred metres before disappearing out of sight. He was pretty certain that the hospital lay just beyond that incline. It couldn't be more than a couple of kilometres further on. In the days when he used to attend the village primary school, he had walked that distance without thinking. Even going slowly and supporting his father, he was sure they could make it within an hour.

After concealing the bicycle as best he could behind a thorn bush, he slung his father's arm about his shoulders and started to walk again. He had no idea what he would do if it was gone when they came back to look for it, but he couldn't think about that now. By this stage, Abambo was not responding beyond the occasional indecipherable mumble and half the time his feet were trailing rather than moving of their own accord. Nevertheless Jonah kept up a bright babble about how soon they would get to the hospital and how quickly Abambo's colleagues would sort everything out and then how they would be back home in a flash and preparing to taste those luscious dowe cobs. Couldn't they just imagine them now? Succulent and juicy. Fresh from the fire.

Eeeh, but it was tiring! Stars burst across his vision and thirst scrambled his brain. When he realised his father was no longer making sounds and saw that his eyes were closed and his face completely grey, Jonah dispensed with his patter and ploughed all his energy into keeping them moving, one step, then another along the road. And when it became impossible to pretend that he was taking steps independently, Jonah heaved Abambo over his shoulder and trudged on.

Night was falling by the time he staggered into the hospital forecourt. He had been worried that the medical staff might have gone home by now, so his heart leapt when he saw the lights blazing and he heard the generator's robust rumble. His joy, however, was quickly curbed by the sight of the long queue curling up to the entrance. His mind ran ahead, leaping up the steps and bursting through the double doors, clamouring, 'Please! Urgent! Clinical officer coming through!' over the commotion emanating in bursts from the place every time someone came or went. But his body was too exhausted to comply, and instead he sloped meekly to the back of the queue where a woman chattered mindlessly about the cholera epidemic that meant every clinic within a fifty-kilometre radius was overrun as Jonah laid his father down in the dust. He let the words wash over him and instead fixed his eyes on a nurse with a clipboard who was working her way down the line. Watching the brisk manner in which she noted down people's details and symptoms, he found himself caught up in an odd sort of wishing. Part of him yearned for her to be with him now, yet he also hoped she might never reach him, that her capable gaze might not fall on Abambo lying silent in the shadows behind him.

At last it was his turn. He stepped aside and gestured at his father. The woman leant down, her brow pleating in her effort to make the patient out in the gloom. Then her eyes widened and her lips pressed together, and Jonah saw that he would not have to worry about explaining the bicycle's disappearance after all.

He looked down at Abambo's body and a howl ripped through him. Even in the darkness he could make out the grey cast that lay across his father's features like a shroud. He had never forgotten it.

That was why, when ET slumped sideways on the couch that afternoon, he had known the matter was serious. It was not the dribbling or the odd sag on one side of her face. It was the greyness that seeped over her and all that it recalled.

He looks up at the woman in the headscarf, at Jeans. 'Qualifications,' he said slowly. 'Yes, I suppose you could say that.'

'And running down to the road to seek help as you did. Such quick thinking with the phone line cut off as it was – I had no idea she'd let things go so badly.'

She smiles and glances at the child who, having smeared her mouth with red stickiness, has laid the empty lolly packet on the end of ET's bed. 'Anyway, we're all very grateful. Not just me but the whole village – Maisie too, aren't you darling?' The child shrugs and pokes speculatively at her nostril. 'Even though she doesn't get out much these days and some of us haven't always seen eye to eye with her, ET's known to everyone. Quite a local character. It would have been awful to think of something happening to her all alone in that big house. We can all sleep much easier in our beds knowing you've got things under control.'

She stands up, unfastening and redoing the knot of her head-scarf. 'Well, we ought to be going. Maisie's favourite programme, *Blue Peter*, starts in half an hour—'

'It's not my favourite programme!'

'And we can't let her miss that.' They shuffle out of the cubicle.

At the end of the bed, Jeans turns and clasps her hands under her chin. 'Thank you again. You really are a saint.'

Jonah watches them go. He reaches for the plastic cup, but the tea has gone cold and there is an unpleasant scum floating on its surface. He looks back at the bed. Odd, but there seems to be more colour in the old woman's cheeks. What's more, her breathing has quickened and her hands, now arched into claws, are twitching and worrying at the sheets.

She is troubled, and he is troubled too. Something Jeans said is nagging at him, gnawing at the edge of his thoughts like a mouse at a maize sack. What was it? The thing about the whole village being grateful? No. Not that. The saint thing. Had that been it? No. Then—

'Time to go, I'm afraid. Visiting hours are over.'

Jonah looks up to find a tall, round-faced man in blue overalls standing at the end of the bed. Reality stutters like one of the VHSes at film club, and suddenly he is looking at the man from Burkina Faso who sat next to him on the back of the pick-up truck across the Sahara Desert, chattering and giggling about his plan to play for Real Madrid.

Jonah blinks and the man becomes a doctor once again. 'Ah, sorry, sir. I'm not a visitor. I'm the old woman's – Miss Morley's – carer. I brought her in.'

The doctor shrugs. 'Doesn't make a difference, I'm afraid. We can't accommodate people staying overnight here.'

'I'm not asking for accommodation—'

'I didn't say you were.'

Jonah frowns. But he had. The doctor had just said precisely that.

'I'm sorry,' the man continues, offering an apologetic smile. 'But I expect you could do with a break yourself, couldn't you? It can't be very comfortable sitting hour after hour in that chair. You're welcome back on the ward any time from 2 p.m. tomorrow. I'm sure Miss Morley will be glad to see you then.'

He stands aside and gestures towards the door with his arm, compelling Jonah to get out of the chair. As he passes him, the doctor points at the wound on Jonah's forearm, protruding from the sleeve of one of the thick shirts from the wardrobe in ET's spare room. 'Nasty gash you've got there,' he says. 'You ought to get that looked at.'

Jonah nods and goes out into the corridor. Fluorescent lights flickering, a trolley bearing a cardboard dish shaped like a bean, a poster about the dangers of failing to wash your hands. And then he sees it. There, beyond the painting of a field of flowers: a public telephone hanging inside a little plastic cabinet on the wall. All of a sudden, he knows what it was in Jeans's words that caught his attention – the idea of ET's cut-off telephone. Now at last he is in a place with working telephones. Here is his chance to use that card and make his call.

Glancing over his shoulder to check that the doctor isn't watching him all the way out of the building, Jonah goes to the plastic cabinet. When he puts the handset to his ear, he hears a long tone, quite unlike the aggressive beep that greeted him from the receiver in ET's house. Well, then. He dials the code followed by Gilbert's number. There is a moment of silence and then a persistent tone that sounds over and over again for a few seconds at a time. It is ringing. Gilbert's phone is ringing!

But there is no answer. The phone rings until it disconnects. Jonah tries again and again, becoming almost mesmerised by the process of keying in the number and listening to the trilling sound. He is just reaching out to start his sixth attempt when a fat mzungu taps him on the shoulder and asks in an aggressive voice: 'Are you going to be long?'

This is a piece of English he can dig the buried meaning out of: the man wants to use the phone.

So, shrugging, Jonah steps away from the cabinet and saunters in the direction of the exit. But the thought of the phone drags at him and slows his steps, almost as if he had picked up the receiver and carried it with him until the wire pulled taut. When the mzungu finishes his conversation, Jonah returns to the cabinet, resolved to try the number once more.

He does not get the chance. Just as he is stretching out his hand to pick up the receiver, the phone trills into life. It is ringing. He glances around, but there is no one nearby who seems to be waiting for a call. He is alone in the corridor apart from a small woman swirling a mop across the floor.

He picks up the receiver and speaks haltingly into the mouthpiece. 'Hello? Who is this, please?'

'I should be asking you that!' storms an angry voice at the other end of the line. 'Why do you keep flashing me? I've just had to spend 500 kwacha buying credit to call you back. This better be something good!'

Jonah is so surprised that he drops the receiver and runs from the corridor. Bursting through the doors at the end, he dodges a man in overalls pushing a trolley – 'Watch it!' – and jumps a yellow wet-floor sign. Spooked as an ox taking fright at a familiar object looming unexpectedly in its path, he hurtles past families with pushchairs and groaning, big-bellied women on their way to the labour ward, desperate for space and quiet, for somewhere he can think.

At last, they're in front of him, the electric doors of the main entrance. In another second he is through them and out in the car park under the sullen, English sky. But here worse awaits, for the car park is not a car park but a shattered marketplace strewn with debris. Before his eyes a large vehicle reveals itself to be a truck riddled with Asma Boys touting AK47s as they scour the ruined streets of Tripoli for any cowering, quivering figures they can haul out to ransom or sell.

With a squeal of terror, Jonah turns and hurls himself back through the see-through doors, forcing his way past a gaggle of mzungu bodies into the fluorescent space where at least, at last, he can breathe.

# 2

By the time he arrives on ET's ward at shortly after 2 p.m. the following afternoon, Jonah is exhausted and furious. He has passed an uncomfortable night on a row of three red plastic chairs just inside the hospital entrance, where the lights, frequent alarms and perpetual sounds of voices and hurrying feet ensured that he got no more than ten minutes' sleep at a time. When the sun hit his face and the bustle increased to intolerable levels, he took himself to a place boastfully described by the sign above its entrance as the Welcome Respite Cafeteria, where a range of beige sandwiches squatted behind scratched glass. The woman in charge of the cash register insisted on putting the thing he selected in an odd sort of press, heating its contents so aggressively that when he bit into it he burned his tongue. After twenty minutes of running his face and mouth under a tap in the toilets, he headed for another public telephone, only to encounter a further frustration. Although Gilbert's phone rang when he dialled the code and number, no one answered, regardless of how many times he tried.

At first, he passed this off as bad luck. Gilbert was busy, after all, and couldn't be expected to be at his beck and call every minute. However, after several hours of trying to reach his friend, he began to feel uneasy. Suppress it though he might, an image kept bobbing to the surface of his mind of Gilbert sitting with his feet propped on a crate and a bottle of beer in his hand, checking who was calling when his phone buzzed and laying it aside. How many times had Jonah sat at the charging stall in the trading centre and watched his friend do just that, often accompanying the dismissive gesture with a rude comment about whoever was on the other end – 'What? That kape? Why would I want to talk to him?' 'I swear, this idiot must think he's some kind of bwana, calling all the time.' 'Choka! Scram!' Many was the time Jonah had laughed at the spectacle of these hapless fools who were oblivious to the fact they were being roundly abused. How did he know that his friend wasn't doing the same to him? Although he was using a public telephone, he was pretty certain there couldn't be too many calls with a British dialling code showing up on Gilbert's mobile. Though his old friend liked to think of himself as an international businessman, the guy was hardly Simbi Phiri. Surely, he must have suspected it was Jonah on the line?

When Jonah enters ET's ward to find a sharp-faced white woman standing at the end of the bed, he is not in the mood to be polite.

'Who are you?' he says, folding his arms.

The woman turns and frowns at him, her prominent nose reminding him of the snout of a rat he surprised once in the storeroom, peering over the edge of a maize sack.

'I beg your pardon? I might very well ask you the same question.'

She might, but she doesn't, so Jonah says nothing, and continues to stand at the end of the bed. He looks at ET. Is it his imagination, or does there seem to be more colour in her cheeks and tension quivering in her jaw? Certainly she seems more agitated. The hand that was busy picking and worrying at the covers yesterday is hard at work this afternoon, scuttling across the blanket.

'Well?' says the ratty woman. 'I'm waiting.'

He turns his attention back to her. It is hard to tell the age of azungu, but he would put her at somewhere in her fifties – past childbearing but not yet wizened. From the way she is tapping her foot, he surmises that the question she might have asked has been posed while his attention was elsewhere.

'I'm ET's carer,' he says.

Something cracks in the woman's face and a smile breaks through. 'Oh, forgive me! I didn't realise. I thought you must have been some sort of porter. So you're the one we're all so grateful to! The one whose quick-thinking saved ET's life!'

He shrugs. 'It was nothing. I only—'

'What was your name again?'

He looks at her and finds he doesn't want to give his name to this person, so instead of Jonah, he says, 'Michael.' After all, he is Michael often enough to ET. Why not to this woman too?

The woman nods as though she approves. 'I'm Angela,' she says, holding out her hand. 'Mary's daughter. We've been so worried. Mum especially, of course. They were such great pals as children. Mum used to come to stay at Cliff's Edge all the time, and ET really took her under her wing. She'd be here herself, of course, but what with one thing and another – the sciatica and the ingrowing toenail – she's not been up to it. Being in your eighties is no joke. But of course you know all about that. Tell me, have you been caring long?'

He considers. 'You could say that.'

'So I should think – the sort of quick reactions you demonstrated with poor ET. The presence of mind. And I suppose you have been helping her get affairs in order too?'

He frowns and tries to think what she might mean. The word 'affairs' suggests something illicit between men and women to him. But surely that can't be what this woman, Angela, is suggesting?

'I only ask because we've been behindhand with thinking about such things, and it occurs to me that now might be the time to start giving the matter some consideration. Start the process for assuming power of attorney and suchlike – all those things I'm sure you've witnessed a million times before. For example, do you happen to know if ET keeps her money in a particular bank or—'

'Miss Watkins?'

They turn. The mzungu woman with the glasses and the clipboard from yesterday is back, offering them a businesslike smile.

'Yes,' says Angela.

'So glad you could make it. I'm Dr Bloom. I expect you'll be wanting the latest information about your... my apologies, what is she? Your aunt?'

'In a manner of speaking. At least, I've always thought of her that way. My mother is her first cousin, and the pair were great childhood friends. ET didn't have any children of her own, of course, so, really, I'm the closest thing she's got to a daughter. We speak on the phone almost every week. ET calls us whenever she needs anything. "Hello, Norfolk daughter," she says. (She calls me her Norfolk daughter.)'

The doctor flicks her smile on and off. 'Well, in that case I've no doubt you're anxious to hear what we've found. And I'm afraid it's not very good news. As I'm sure the nurses or Miss Morley's carer here—'

'Michael,' says Angela.

'Michael, has told you, Miss Morley suffered an ischaemic stroke yesterday. As is usual in such cases, we've carried out a number of tests, including an MRI scan, to ascertain the extent of the damage, which I am sorry to say is considerable. The left side of the brain has been compromised, which explains the sagging you see on the right side of her body. As Miss Morley is right-handed this means the speech and language areas have also been affected. We won't know for a few days – until the swelling has gone down – quite how permanent some of the symptoms are, but it's likely that she will be far less independent than she was prior to this episode, even though we hope physiotherapy may help with some of the worst physical effects in time.'

'Lucky we've got Michael to take care of things,' says Angela.

'Indeed,' says the doctor, throwing him a fragment of a smile. 'Although it's likely that Miss Morley will require substantially more care from now on. Social services will have to carry out a home assessment to see what support she might need. The basic state-funded package equates to four half-hour visits a day, but it's often the case that people in your aunt's situation need more care than that – possibly even a transfer to a nursing home.'

A line appears between Angela's eyebrows. 'And how would that be paid for?'

'That would depend on the patient's private means. I should also mention that the tests showed that although this is Miss Morley's first major stroke, it appears that she has experienced several similar minor episodes over the preceding months, or possibly even years, suggesting that she has been suffering from a condition called vascular dementia. I don't know whether you've noticed her becoming more confused or erratic at all…?'

Angela shakes her head vigorously. 'Oh no. Not ET. She's sharp as a button. Always has been. We were saying only the other day how well she manages for her age, weren't we, Michael?'

Jonah holds out his hands. 'I—'

'Well that's surprising, given what the scan showed,' continues the doctor. 'Although it is sometimes the case, particularly with very intelligent people, that those with this condition can compensate for a great deal before their impairment becomes apparent to those around them. Taken on their own, these little clots and bleeds are often negligible, but over time they can have a marked effect on a person's cognitive ability. You might notice that the person is struggling to remember words or to perform tasks such as cooking or cleaning. They might act strangely or get lost in familiar places sometimes, and they can sometimes make unusual or irresponsible financial decisions…'

Here Angela shoots Jonah an anxious look.

'The pattern is usually that there is deterioration immediately after an episode, which can be so minor as to be passed off as a funny turn, and then things remain stable for a while – a sort of stepped effect with long plateau periods. Over time, however, the damage has a cumulative effect, sometimes leading to global impairment.'

They are all quiet for a moment. Angela bites her lip. Out in the corridor someone breaks into a coughing fit.

Dr Bloom makes as if to continue, but then Angela cuts in: 'Sorry, doctor. Just going back to what you were saying about irresponsible financial decisions. Is this a common problem in people with this sort of affliction?'

The doctor puts her head on one side. 'It isn't unusual. Still,' she smiles brightly, 'I'm sure things like that are secondary concerns right now.'

'Oh yes, absolutely,' says Angela, nodding her head energetically so that the curtains of hair hanging either side of her face jiggle. 'Of course! Our first thought is for ET's health and comfort. By the way, doctor, what are the chances that she might suffer another of these terrible major strokes soon? I'm guessing from what you say that a second one might be terminal?'

They talk on for a while, the doctor and Angela, discussing plans to keep ET in for observation for the next few days and possible outcomes further down the line. When unpicking the technical language gets too much for him, Jonah tunes out and simply watches the women. Odd though it seems, there is something familiar about Angela. Not that he knows her – he is sure he has never met her before in his life. She was not one of the blank-eyed officials he encountered on his journey, nor was she one of the earnest azungu charity workers who came to the camps, bringing food in tins and soaps that made him gag with their strong, synthetic scents. Still, he has seen something of her before – the eyes glinting like bawo marbles, the quick clutching hands. At last, he has it: Angela is like the uncle who swept in after Roger's mother died and took control of the land that Roger was supposed to inherit, claiming he ought to manage it in his role as the keeper of the children of his sister. There is the same quickness and sharpness about them both – Roger's Uncle Mizeck and this mzungu, Angela – a hunger that has little to do with food.

Once the doctor leaves, Jonah expects that Angela will want to sit with ET a while, and he remains standing so as to allow her to use the single chair beside the bed. This proves unnecessary, however, for when Dr Bloom leaves the ward Angela seems more interested in talking to Jonah than to ET, and makes straight for him, staring up at him with glinting eyes.

'You don't need extra help, do you?' she says in a funny half-whisper that is at once spikey and soft. 'You're doing just fine as you are. It's a scam, anyway, all this home-assessment nonsense. It's just a way for private companies to get their mitts on vulnerable old people's savings. Really, it shouldn't be allowed.' She shuffles closer. 'What is she paying you, anyway, if you don't mind me asking? Minimum wage, is it? Or more than that?'

Jonah regards her. The conversation has a significant feel, as though disaster will descend if he gets something wrong. He is anxious about the meaning of the word 'mitts'.

Before he can attempt a reply, she steps back and flutters her hands. 'You don't want to say. Quite right, too. Worth every penny, of course, whatever it comes to. But you're all right on your own, aren't you? We don't want poor ET to waste any more money on unnecessary wages. No need for a great Hugh and cry.'

Hugh, he supposes, must be one of the visitors who came to have tea with ET – the fat man in the waistcoat he glimpsed through the window, perhaps. 'Mmmn.'

She gives him a smile. 'That's settled, then.'

Next, shifting her bag strap on to her shoulder, she says in a much louder voice, eyes looking around the ward as she speaks: 'Well, Michael, once again, thank you. We're so grateful to have dear ET in such excellent hands. Me, Mum, the whole family. You will keep us posted, won't you? And if there's anything you need – not money, obviously: I'm sure ET's got plenty to cover that – anything at all, please don't hesitate to call us.'

He nods.

She leans in and taps the side of her nose. 'I'll be in touch.'

And with that she is gone – hurrying off, her handbag clutched under the crook of one arm. When he turns back to the bed ET's expression has changed. The tension has seeped away, and there are the makings of a cheeky smile instead. Foolish though he knows it to be, he can't shake the idea that between them they have somehow played a joke.

# 13

Jonah spends the next few days drifting in and around the hospital. He keeps away from the windows to minimise the chances of the bad imaginings trying to possess him again – and on the off-chance that those others have tracked him to the hospital and are even now creeping towards the entrance between the parked vehicles of the car park, clutching iPhones with screensavers bearing his image.

During visitor hours he sits by ET's bed. No one comes, apart from Jeans, who blusters in on their penultimate afternoon in the place with the remains of a chocolate bar stuck to the underside of her bag.

'And has there been any progress?' she keeps saying, eyes straying repeatedly to ET, as though at once hopeful and afraid that she will find her old friend awake and chatting.

In the first few days ET hardly stirs at all. She wakes once or twice to offer him a smile and slur words that he doesn't catch. But over time, she starts to seem more alert, watching warily as various figures in overalls talk at her, manipulate her arms and legs and shine lights in her eyes. The machines and wires retreat a little and the nurses start to bring cups of things for her to try – thickened liquids that are supposed to be easier to swallow and soups and pureed foods. She still sleeps a lot. Dr Bloom says this is, on balance, a good thing, that this kind of rest is best calculated to aid her recovery. All the same, Jonah can't help thinking that all that dead time alone in a bed must be rather isolating. Surely a world full of nothing but beeps and whirs and the occasional splutterings of other patients can't offer a person much incentive to get well? And so, when there is no one else in the room to hear, he takes ET's hand, leans close and does his best to talk to her.

It is embarrassing at first and he doesn't know what to say. Still, he persists, and with practice he gets better at it. Ideas suggest themselves more readily, and he stumbles less frequently over words. He starts from what she knows: the house, the yard, the field beyond the track. He moves from place to place, talking about his impressions of the things he has found there. He tells her about his feverish time in the storeroom and his notion of what an impressive place it must have been back in the farm's busiest days, before the roof sprung leaks, the ladder lost several of its rungs and the planks in the platform it led to rotted and dropped away. He spends a while talking about the appliances in the kitchen – the fridge of which Aunt Dudu would be so jealous, the primitive yet haughty stove. He has less to say about the room with the big table, where he presumes the majority of the family's eating used to happen, but the piano room sparks a host of reflections. He talks again about hearing ET play on the night he crept into the house to see how she was, and how his own attempts on the keyboard pale in comparison to the sweeping runs and chords she drew from the instrument's belly. From there, it is a short leap to Hattie and her time in the nearby village – their curious relationship that at once seemed to bring them so close and keep them far apart, ending abruptly the morning he arrived at her hut to find the NGO's truck waiting outside and Hattie shoving her belongings into a rucksack. Her time in the village was over, she told him. In a few days a fresh week would be starting at Oxford University, and she had to return to England to attend it. Then she came close to him and looked up into his eyes. She was so grateful to him for all he had taught her, she told him. She would never forget him. He had changed her and enriched her life.

He was frightened for a moment that she might have the boldness to kiss him in full view of everybody. But she didn't. Instead, she swung her bag up on to the truck and climbed into the cab, and he watched as the vehicle jolted off down the track to the sealed road, leaving only dust swirling in the air.

One thing he doesn't touch on is the view of the French coastline, which is often clearly visible from the piano room's big, curved window. Since the afternoon of their shared collapse and ET's strange proffering of the name of that awful last place where he and Amanuel cooked up their ill-fated plan – Dunkirk – he has not trusted himself to venture into those thoughts. He can stop talking at will, as soon as the nurses approach, but tears and trembling would be harder to conceal. So instead he keeps to the bright things and sends his words scudding along the surface of significance: a little motorboat containing just the two of them, unencumbered by the problem of other people.

In many ways what he says is immaterial. It is the talking that is the thing, the holding of ET's hand. Because this is what he has discovered about azungu hospitals: they are lonely places. Full of people, yes, but lonely. They consist of rows of pale bodies in beds separated by rails and curtains, ranks of equipment and machines. And these azungu are tended by people trapped in another sort of loneliness – a busyness that keeps them running from place to place, eyes always darting to the next thing, rarely able to stay long enough with one person to exchange anything more than facts.

At first Jonah finds the calm of the ward reassuring. It is so different to the din and chaos of the district hospital where Abambo would conduct surgical procedures. There the corridors were always packed with clamouring relatives crowding the entrances to consulting rooms, bringing in greasy snacks for their loved ones, and occasionally setting up stalls on the forecourt in flagrant violation of the signs strictly prohibiting hawking. The comparative tranquillity of this place seems to promise care and attention to detail, adequate resources to address everyone's needs.

Yet, as the days slip by, he comes to wonder whether the quiet and apparent order of the hospital don't denote calm after all, but instead a kind of coldness – a machine-like approach to human suffering harbouring a different set of ills to those hampering the lives of his compatriots. In all the hours he has spent on the ward, he has barely seen a single visitor come for the elderly azungu slumped in the other beds. Those that do come say little or sit in silence, turning the pages of books or magazines. Perhaps, like him, they feel self-conscious, and yet he struggles to understand their composure when they are faced with their grandfather, their aunt or their mother lying in the bed in front of them. Why, when his father died… But here he has to shut his thoughts down for fear of the tears that must follow, for fear of – what is that English expression? – making up a scene.

When he is not on the ward he wanders around the hospital. In some waiting rooms they have televisions showing programmes, which usually feature people buying, selling or doing construction work on houses that are bigger than his primary school. He spends some time watching these, repeating the idioms that the participants use under his breath in an effort to commit them to memory – 'down the pan', 'fright of my life', 'I'm made up with that'. Phrases like these will be useful in his future life in England. And in the short-term he hopes they might make his speaking more intelligible to ET. When the news comes on, however, he leaves. The risk of being confronted with images of people foundering in dinghies or staring miserably out from behind the barbed-wire fences of the camps is too great. Moreover, the thought of witnessing them with a gaggle of indifferent azungu is more than he can bear.

It takes him a while to build up the courage to try Gilbert's number again. The sound of his friend's voice when he'd called back and complained about having to buy credit to return Jonah's flashes had been so immediate that it had shaken him. It had been so long since he had spoken to anyone back home – so long since he had heard Chichewa outside his own head – that it was almost as though he had forgotten these people who meant so much to him were as real as he was. In his mind, Amayi, the boys, the twins, Gilbert and Roger have faded like photographs left out in the sun. It was a shock to hear one of them doing anything so robust as telling him off.

Still Gilbert doesn't answer, and Jonah quickly stops expecting that he will. Nevertheless, he keeps calling. He likes the ritual of dialling the number, the sound of the line connecting and the regular tone that announces that the phone is ringing until at last the sound ceases. It pleases him to think that he is making something happen back home – that somewhere, perhaps in the shade of the blue-gum grove or at a table outside the bottle shop or behind the counter of Gilbert's charging stall, he is making a machine produce a sound. He finds the process therapeutic, and at times it is almost mesmeric. As though compelled by a sing'anga's incantation, he stands in front of the hospital payphones dialling and listening, dialling and listening, dialling and listening.

So it is that when a voice comes on the line some time during his fourth day at the hospital, he is at a loss as to what to do.

'Yuh?'

Jonah takes the black plastic receiver from his ear and looks at it. Is he right? Did it just speak?

He puts it back to his head. 'Moni?' he says cautiously. It is so long since he has held a conversation in Chichewa that he wonders for a moment if his mouth retains the trick of framing the words.

'Yuh,' says the voice again – Gilbert, without a doubt. 'What do you want? Why do you keep calling me?'

'Hey, brother,' says Jonah, trying for the casual tone he would have used if he'd simply strolled down to the trading centre and found the G-man sitting in his usual spot. 'It's Jonah. What do you suppose? I'm calling from England, man. I made it all the way here.'

There is a pause. Did he hear that correctly? Was that an intake of breath? Is Gilbert sucking his teeth?

'Ah, Jonah, brother! How's it going?' The sunniness is back. The old Gilbert. He can see him now, stretching out his legs in the shade, sipping on a bottle of Carlsberg Green. Relief floods him.

'Good, good, brother. And yourself?'

'Ah, you know, can't complain. A bit of business here, a bit of business there. Always hustling, not like Roger and the rest of those groovers.'

'Mmn-hmmn.' He does know. He can just imagine he's there now, sitting outside God's Blessings, catching the cool breeze blowing across the mountains from Tanzania!

'But what about you, brother? England, huh? That's big!'

He grins. Yes, it is. He is proud of himself. In spite of everything and all he went through – or maybe because of it as well – he is proud.

'So are you a millionaire yet, brother? Are you best friends with the Queen?'

Jonah laughs and lolls against the plastic screen, eyes searching the foam tiles of the ceiling for a witty anecdote to tell. Ah, he has missed his friend! But then the faces of the others he is missing – Amayi and the boys and the twins – swim before his eyes and urgency takes over. He has no way of knowing how long the phonecard will last him, and he's got to make it do for at least one decent call to his family, if not more.

'Yeah, sure, brother. It's all under way. Just a matter of time. But listen, Gilbert, I need to speak to Amayi, OK? It's been way too long. Can you cycle up there and fix a time for me to call? They can still use your phone, right?'

That pause again. Maybe Gilbert is distracted. It could be that a customer has chosen that moment to come to the stall.

Then Gilbert speaks. 'Yeah, about that. Listen, I don't know if that's going to be so easy. I'm really busy, yeah? Got a lot on and—'

Jonah frowns. What is this? 'Hey, brother. What are you saying? You're too busy to help me speak to my family now?'

On the wall beside the phone someone has stuck up a collection of photographs showing a party in the children's department. In one a mzungu child with a badly shaped head goggles at the camera, its mouth smeared with cake. Something about it makes Jonah feel sick.

'Na, man, it's not that. It's just stuff's happened and—'

'What stuff?' he asks, averting his eyes.

'I think you need to hear it from your family.'

'That's what I'm saying. I'm trying to talk to them.'

'Na, brother. Other family.' From his tone, Jonah knows that Gilbert is sitting with his free hand pinching the skin between his eyes. 'Like, what's that auntie of yours called? Deedee?'

'Dudu.'

'That's it. Talk to her, brother. She'll fill you in.'

His voice is growing distant. He is making to hang up!

'No! Wait! Gilbert!' Jonah shouts into the receiver so loudly that several of the passing azungu turn to stare and shake their heads at the unruly African bellowing in the quiet corridor. He holds up a hand – sorry, sorry, sorry.

'What, brother?' This time there is no denying the reluctance in Gilbert's voice.

'Dudu's number.'

'What about it?'

'I don't have it. I lost everything. My phone. All that stuff. Yours is the only number I memorised.'

'Ah, shame, brother. That's too—'

He grips the receiver. 'Get it for me.'

'How am I supposed to—'

'I don't know. Talk to the pastor or get a phone book or something if you can't get it from Amayi. Wait! No. Aunt Dudu's husband used to work for the national bank in Blantyre. You could call them and—'

'Tch, brother.' An audible yawn. 'It sounds like a lot of effort. Like I said, I've got stuff to do.'

Suddenly, he hates them all – Roger, Gilbert, the rest of them. They used to laugh at him, he knows it. The doctor's son with his airs and graces, thinking he was a big man because he got to stay in the house on the hill. The city boy who was not quite as tough as they were. No matter that he had as many girls as the rest of them, that Gladness said he had the best face of all of them down at the trading centre. When they looked at Jonah, they saw something unfinished and childlike in him, a softness that meant he would never be a proper man. That was what they thought of him. Well, Gilbert is not going to make a fool out of him this time.

Summoning every last indignity, every last jibe, and all the humiliations of the past two years, he growls into the receiver: 'Seriously, brother. Either you tell me what's going on or you get me that number right now. I'm not playing.'

Silence. For a moment he is afraid that Gilbert has hung up, that in his anger he, Jonah, has severed this last link and will never talk to anyone from home again.

Then he hears an intake of breath. 'All right, brother. I'll do that for you. Give me a few days—'

'One hour.'

'One hour!'

'One hour, brother. I don't have time to wait around. I've got pressures this end too.'

Another sigh. 'Well, all right. It's not going to be easy, but I'll see what I can do.'

'I'll call you in one hour.'

'Ndapita.'

'Pitani bwino.'

He puts the receiver back on its hook and leans his head against the wall. When he steps back, the cake-smeared child no longer looks so bad. In fact, it seems to be smiling at him. As well it might. He returns its grin. 'I've got pressures this end too.' Yes. He is proud of the way he said that. He is proud of the way he handled all of it, in fact. The old Jonah would have begged or been taken in by Gilbert's evasions and only started to see their flaws after he'd finished the call. The old Jonah would have been as soft as freshly milled flour. Well, not any more. He is changed. He is different now. He has travelled further than any of them have dared. He is a man of the world. And soon he will prove it to all of them.

*

He half expects Gilbert to ignore his call when he comes back after a period of pacing the corridors and absently running his hands over the soft toys and knitted hats for babies on sale in the hospital shop. But no: the phone is answered after three rings. Clearly his forcefulness has made an impression.

Gilbert is businesslike and comes straight to the point. He has the number. He'll read it out for Jonah to write down. Luckily there is a stubby pencil balanced on top of the body of the telephone and, after glancing around fruitlessly for paper, Jonah opts to scrawl the digits on the bottom of his shirt – one of the thick, rough garments from the wardrobe in the spare bedroom. He suspects ET is past the point where she will mind such damage to her property, and if anyone else notices, well, they can put it down to his odd African ways.

As soon as he has finished copying down the number, he is impatient to end the call and phone his aunt. Gilbert, however, seems inclined to linger.

'Listen, brother: good luck, yeah? I hope it all works out. You're not bad, you know. You deserve a good shot at things. I'm pleased you made it all that way.'

He nods impatiently, his eye on a clock on the wall and his mind scrambling to calculate the time difference. It will be 5 p.m. there now. Aunt Dudu will be home from work and pottering about her kitchen, beginning preparations for dinner. It is a good time to call.

'Yes, yes. Thanks, brother,' he says. 'Go well.'

It is only after he has replaced the receiver that the oddly final tone in Gilbert's voice strikes him. Through the whoosh of the electric doors at the entrance seems to come a whisper that he will not speak to his old friend again. But of course that is nonsense – his head playing more of its tricks. It will settle down when he talks to Amayi.

He dials Aunt Dudu's number. In his mind he sees it: the brick house in the maze of roads near the market. The kitchen table with the ingredients laid out for the evening meal and the stove with its cylinder of Calor Gas nearby. Aunt Dudu bustling around with MBC Radio 2 on, humming along to a gospel song or shaking her head at the latest outrages reported on the news. It's funny. He used to feel awkward in that house – the country cousin forever setting cups down without coasters and eating messily with his hands instead of helping himself to things with spoons and forks. Now he remembers it fondly and it stands smaller in his memory, a quaint place imbued with his aunt's eccentricity, rather than the forbidding monument to city manners it once seemed.

He has grown up at last, he realises. He will be able to talk to Dudu as a man, not as a boy. He is rather looking forward to it. But when an unfamiliar woman answers, his confidence wavers. Has Gilbert tricked him – handing over a random number just to get him off the phone?

He stammers his inquiry foolishly, cheeks aflame.

'Jonah, is that you?'

He blinks. 'Yes. Please. Who is this?' The language is awkward on his tongue – a mouthful of marbles that he is forced to spit out word by word, regardless of the proper order.

A laugh. 'Marie!'

He frowns. Marie? Marie is a scabby little thing who hid behind the door frame and sucked her fingers that awful day that he and Abambo had come to Aunt Dudu's to ask for help paying the St Andrew's school fees. There's no way that this soft-spoken woman could be one and the same with that creature.

'Iwe!' he protests. 'How can that be?'

But then the years spool forward in his mind – a VHS fast-forwarded at film club. Of course: that child would be grown up by now. It is years since the famine, since they had trudged away from Blantyre past the stop for the minibus they could no longer afford to hail, clutching the parcel of mandasi Aunt Dudu had given them for the journey instead of money; years since his father's death.

'Ah! Marie! I'm sorry. I'm forgetting how long it's been. How are you?'

A giggle. She is getting married. To the pastor of the local church. A big man with a house and more shirts than there are days in a month and a gleaming car that he drives between the homes of those in need of spiritual guidance. A Mercedes, no less. Things are going well.

He beams. Well that is wonderful news. Wonderful. He wishes her every happiness.

And as if the words are a gateway, he is back there. Back amid the bustle of preparing for a wedding – the pots of nsima simmering over the fires, the vegetables chopped for relish, the laughter, the drums beating, the Gule Wamkulu gathering on the edge of the village.

All at once he can wait no more. He has to speak to them – his family. He has to know how they are.

'Tell me, Marie. Is my Aunt Dudu, there? I need to talk to her.'

There is a pause. Footsteps. The rustle of the receiver being taken up.

'Yes?' The familiar voice is as strident as ever. Not in the least bit softened by the passage of time. 'Ah, Jonah. So you're calling at last.'

And for all his years and everything his travels have shown him, he is once more the boy in his first pair of long trousers, staring at the implements glinting on the tablecloth in Aunt Dudu's front room.

'Yes, sorry, sorry, sorry, auntie. You see, it's been a difficult journey. I lost my phone and—'

'You should have called sooner.' From seven thousand miles away he can hear her folding her arms. 'Look, unfortunately there's no easy way to say this. I'm afraid your mother's dead. The twins and Elijah too. I'm sorry.'

The day sags. Someone seems to have knocked the image of the hospital around him and all the people strolling through the entrance hall askew.

'What…' he says, clinging on to the receiver as though it is a lifeline that might save him as everything around him lurches and spills. 'How…'

'Diarrhoea. Vomiting. Complications. Some problem with the water supply. They went to the hospital, but by then it was too late. The twins were the first to go. Then Elijah, and finally your mother. I wasn't with her when she died – I had an important meeting about Marie's wedding. Still, they inform me it was a peaceful ending. I contributed to the funeral costs, of course – nothing is too much trouble when family is in the case.'

The walls of the hallway are throbbing at him, shuddering like the boom boxes the groovers always used to play down at the trading centre.

'I'm sorry,' says Aunt Dudu again. Perhaps it is the line, but he thinks he can discern a hint of impatience in her voice.

'What about Daniel?'

'Jonah, you'll have to speak up. I'd have hoped you'd grown out of mumbling by now.'

'What about Daniel? You said about the twins and Elijah, but you didn't mention Daniel. Did he survive?'

A sigh. 'I'm sorry to say it, but he turned out to be a bad one, that boy. I tried my best. I invited him for food three times. Four, in fact. Still, he is one of those who doesn't know how to be grateful. Getting into bad things – drinking, fighting, carrying on with girls all hours of the night.'

'So where is he now?'

'Tch. It is not my responsibility to be the record keeper of everyone's whereabouts. I have enough to do looking after my own daughter. A wedding does not organise itself, as I hope you will one day find out, Jonah. Especially not one involving a pastor with a Mercedes.'

A sob escapes his throat. 'I…'

'Look, I'm sorry, Jonah. I know this is upsetting. I myself am very upset. Don't forget they were my nieces and nephew too. My sister-in-law. But you can hardly be surprised. You know what life is like here. You don't phone all this time, people assume you are dead and then finally when you do call things have happened. That is how life is. Events don't stand still without you. People don't wait at the door for you to return like statues. I am sorry it is sad news, but there is nothing I can do. We have to go on with what we have. That is what your mother did after Jeremiah, and that is what you have to do now. You are young and strong. You have your future. That is more than many people. That is plenty. We all have our troubles. You probably suppose that life is comfortable for us here in the big city. In reality that is not the case. Even with the generous dowry the pastor is paying for Marie we are not as well off as we might be. Really, I should be asking you for help. I should be looking to you for comfort in my old age. Think about that for a change.'

He nods. 'Yes, Auntie.'

'Hmmn. You're a good boy, but you don't consider things properly. That is the problem. When you have lived to my age you will look at life differently. You will see it is not as simple as asking for help and receiving it. There are other factors that have to be taken into account.'

'Yes, Auntie.'

'But of course, if you ever need anything – if you are ever truly in difficulty – you must not hesitate to call me. Nothing is too much trouble when family is in the—'

He replaces the handset and looks around. The hall has righted itself. Everything is just as it was when he dialled the number: the electric doors, the rows of plastic chairs, the reception desk and the people hurrying by. No one looking would know that anything has changed. A wild hope seizes his heart. Perhaps it hasn't happened, then? What if he has imagined the call? It could be that his brain is playing one of its tricks. It could be that someone with evil intent has reached into his head and scrambled his thinking in an effort to prevent him re-establishing contact with his family. Such things are not unknown. Perhaps if he calls again he will find a different story waiting there. Good news. An apprenticeship for Daniel. Some business venture that had enabled Amayi to send Elijah to secondary school. Or how about this? What if, when he calls, it turns out that the family are visiting Aunt Dudu right at that moment and are able to come to the phone, the twins piping with excitement, the boys full of accounts of their exploits on the football field? Surely he ought to take the chance?

But then, behind him, a woman reading a magazine cackles and he crumbles, hunching forward with his face in his hands. Who is he kidding? Why should he imagine the rules of the universe might bend for him? Why should he expect reality to look on him with a kinder face than it had shown to all those thousands of others he saw slumping under sorrow's yoke on his way here? By now he ought to know there are no exceptions.

He leans his head against the plastic telephone cabinet, feeling its rim bite into his skin. So they are gone, then. Amayi, the boys and the twins. Reduced to nothing. Burnt up like maize shoots under the sun. Leaving the landscape of his heart bare.

# 14


'There you are!' A hand grips him and pulls him to stand next to an upended bottle fixed on to the wall to dispense some sort of see-through liquid. He regards the face peering up at him: sharp features, a hungry glint in the eyes. It is the mzungu woman from the other day, Angela.

'I've got it all arranged,' she hisses, glancing up and down the corridor, her words more breath than voice. 'There's a taxi waiting outside. If we're discreet about it, we'll probably be able to take her without a fuss.'

He frowns, his mind swimming, the line from where he pressed his forehead against the telephone cabinet throbbing as though a metal band is being tightened around his head. 'But—'

The woman holds up a claw-like hand. 'Don't worry: you won't get into trouble. It's all above board. Perfectly legal. It's our right to take her whenever we see fit. No one can keep her here.'

He shakes his head, his numb brain unable to make sense of what they are doing, standing there.

'It's all right. I know what you're thinking,' continues Angela. 'That busybody lady doctor won't allow it. Well, that's why we're doing it today. It's the weekend, you see. Different staff. Dr Bloom's off sunning herself, or whatever they do. She won't find out until Monday.'

'Oh.'

Further up the corridor a family of azungu are waddling along, the mother bending to scold the child, who is eating some sort of chocolate sweet – people living their lives just as they did before he made that phone call and discovered the world had ended without him realising. Extraordinary.

'And in case it's money that you're worried about, don't you fret.' Angela contorts her mouth to talk out of the side of it and offers him a grotesque wink. 'If she's not footing the bill for an army of cushion plumpers and bottle washers, or whatever these busybodies take it into their heads to say she needs, there'll be plenty to help with your, er, expenses. When all this is over I'll make it worth your while.'

'I see.' He doesn't, but it is as though his mouth is speaking of its own accord while his mind floats away and hovers somewhere above the vending machine against the opposite wall, staring unthinkingly at everything passing below.

'Good. Well don't just stand there. You go and get her dressed and I'll smooth things over with the harpies on the front desk.'

It takes a moment for the implications of her words to land. When they do he wanders in the direction indicated by her flapping hand, through a doorway and into a room that turns out to be ET's ward. He walks to the old woman's bed. She is lying with her eyes open, staring up at the ceiling, her mouth chewing. Her cardigan is draped over the back of the chair beside it and he picks it up and spends some minutes staring at it, wondering at the way the wool has been crafted into knots and swirls. So much effort lavished on this one insignificant thing.

'Everything all right?' Turning, Jonah finds the Burkinabè man from the pickup-truck ride across the Sahara standing at the end of the bed. He nearly weeps with relief at the sight of his kindly long-lost companion, and is on the point of telling him the terrible news about Amayi, Elijah and the twins when he catches sight of the strange blue overalls the man is wearing. He hesitates, bewildered.

'You seem a little agitated.' The voice is deeper and the language more formal than Jonah was used to from his fellow traveller. 'Still got that nasty cut, I see. I thought I told you to get that looked at.'

The present clouts him, making him reel: he is in the hospital, in England, miles from anyone who could understand.

'Oh, fine,' he says brightly, talking fast to cover his confusion. 'In fact, I am just getting Miss Morley ready to go home.'

A crease appears between the man's eyebrows. 'Go home? Surely not. From what I remember the consultant anticipated keeping her in for several more days at least.'

'Ah, but the woman, the… Angela, Miss Morley's relative, she has decided.'

The doctor shakes his head. 'I think that's very unwise. I distinctly remember Dr Bloom saying she wanted to wait to see how the physiotherapy progressed. And there hasn't been a home assessment yet, has there?'

From the corridor, the sound of Angela's voice, shrill with false good humour, drifts into the room: 'No, it's quite all right. Dr Bloom said she was happy if we were confident to look after dear ET. And we're a very close family. Everyone will be on hand to help…'

'Dr Bloom said she was happy,' says Jonah. 'Everyone will be on their hands to help.'

The doctor gives him a strange look. Jonah blinks at him. Then at the old woman slumped in the bed. Then back at the doctor. He can't think what they are all doing there.

The doctor's mouth is moving, creasing and uncreasing, opening and closing. There is a tuft of black hair on his upper lip that he must have missed that morning when he shaved. Jonah watches that tuft. It jerks up and down, the hairs twitching. Such a small thing. And yet you can bet that if the doctor looks in the mirror later and notices it he will be annoyed. He will think of all the people he's seen that day and wonder if they noticed the flaw in his appearance. And when he gets home he may speak sharply to his wife. Perhaps they will have an argument as a result. Such a small matter. Inconsequential. And yet these are the things that people worry about instead of counting their blessings and holding tight to the ones they love.

The doctor is staring at him now, as though Jonah, too, has a tuft of stray hairs on his face. 'I said, is that all right?'

Jonah shrugs.

'Good. Excellent. I won't be long.'

The doctor walks away and Jonah goes to sit on the chair by the bed. He looks at ET. They have pulled a wooden shelf across her. On it is another of their polystyrene cups containing a gelatinous pink substance and a spoon. Lifting it, he samples the contents. The mixture is bland with a hint of sharpness.

When he turns his gaze back to the bed, the old woman is staring at the cup. He lifts it towards her questioningly and she nods, her tongue protruding, reminding him of a dog that used to hang around the village, begging for scraps.

It occurs to him that he could refuse to give it to her, that he could set it back on the shelf and let her stare at it some more. After all, what difference will it make in the end? She is going to die soon. What does it matter whether or not he grants this trifling request?

But there is nothing to be gained from denying her, and so he loads the spoon and holds it to her mouth. She slurps greedily at it, slavering like a dog so that the pink substance dribbles out of the side of her mouth and runs down her chin. When he blots her neck with a tissue from a box on the side, she belches.

He stares at her in disgust. He has never heard a woman burp before. Back home he, Daniel, Elijah and any visiting uncles always used to observe the custom of eating separately from the women in the family in order to minimise the risk of witnessing or inflicting such indignities. That this English woman – ill though she may be – should behave in such an unseemly manner appals him.

Something is rising in him. He withdraws his hand and clenches his fists, waiting for it to reveal itself. Then he knows what it is: it is rage. Hectic as malaria fever, hot as flame, rage is coursing through him. Rage at this wizened mzungu with her wrinkled chicken skin, lying here guzzling clean water and food, taking for granted her right to have health care and the transport to convey her back and forth, while healthy young people shrivel and die for want of basic necessities. Rage at this world that apportions so much to some and so little to others. Rage at the big men who swing around the cities in their 4x4 VXs, handing out trinkets and fripperies to the starving. Rage at the groovers drinking their dreams away with every carton of Chibuku Shake Shake down at the trading centre. Rage at teachers and books and education for encouraging any of them to dare to hope for more. Rage at the fresh-faced NGO workers coming to his region with their personal crusades and return plane tickets. Rage at Hattie and her cracked keyboard and her worthless gratitude. Rage at chance. Rage at rains that do not come and then pour so hard that they wash livelihoods away. Rage at pastors and the lies they sell about God's love and justice when above them all is nothing but the indifferent sky. Rage so thick he cannot breathe.

'Well, it seems you're right – oh my goodness!'

Hands on his shoulders. The doctor in the blue overalls helping him up. Looking down, he sees he must have flung the cup of pink gloop in ET's face. She is blinking and spluttering and there are splashes of it across her nightgown and down the white sheets.

Eyes on his own, seeking him out. 'Are you all right? Michael?'

He nods, but can't think what to say. He stands looking at the doctor.

In the last camp in Italy, there was a little boy – a Somalian – who used to come to the entrance of Jonah's shelter and stare in at him, sometimes for hours, without saying a word. At the time he had assumed that it was because the boy had been emptied of conversation by the horrors he'd witnessed. Now he sees that the opposite was true: the child had been clogged with words, his throat so jammed with things he needed to say that it was impossible to get them out.

The doctor has been talking again. The tuft of hairs jiggling. A question hangs in the air. Jonah waits for it to resolve itself, the man staring at him strangely all the while. He doesn't care. The doctor can think what he likes. More: he rather hopes he finds out the truth. Let it be now that they discover that he is not a carer, nor any sort of professional, that he has no qualifications of any kind. Let them expose his deception and hold it up to the light. Let them take him away and deal with him, question him, imprison him if they must. It will be a relief to be dealt with for who he really is after spending so long caught in the gaps between other people's lives.

But instead of sirens, officers and the prospect of interrogation by the police, Jonah is led from the ward by the doctor to a little room off the corridor outside, where the man rips a moist tissue from a foil pouch and begins to swab out the cut on his arm.

'I shouldn't be doing this,' mutters the doctor. 'But you're clearly not looking after yourself properly, and I can't risk sending you home with this untended if that woman really will insist on removing the patient. The last thing anyone needs is for you to come down with a roaring infection. Caring is a tough job at the best of times. You need to make sure you give yourself proper attention too.'

Jonah regards the man as he puts a series of tough, adhesive strips across the wound. After so many months of blank faces and indifference, his tenderness is alarming, upsetting even. He doesn't know how to respond. He has forgotten that there can be kindness, that sometimes people help one another without hope of a reward, the way Abambo used to.

Suddenly, he feels an urge to know this man, to build a connection with him. 'Doctor, where are you from?'

'Maidstone.'

Jonah considers this, but no, it is not the answer he is looking for. 'Not now. I mean originally. The place of your birth.'

'Maidstone,' repeats the doctor, but this time with a coldness that is the opposite of the camaraderie Jonah is hoping for. The man finishes tending the wound in silence.

When Jonah gets back to the ward, the nurses have dressed ET in her shirt and blue trousers and put her in a wheelchair, as she is still too unsteady to walk.

The woman, Angela, hovers, overseeing everything with an aggressive smile. The irritation that flashes in her eyes when she sees Jonah quickly gives way to delight when ET beams up at him and murmurs, 'Come to take me home, have you darling? I knew you would.'

Angela nods approvingly, looking round to check that all the nurses have heard, and says loudly: 'Oh yes, you like darling Michael, don't you, ET? He always takes such wonderful care of you. Really, you can't think of anything nicer than darling Michael taking you home to look after you there. Much better than staying here, just as Dr Bloom agreed when I discussed it with her yesterday.'

Jonah says nothing. Taking hold of the chair's handles, he pushes ET from the ward, along the corridor and out to the waiting car.

# 82

He is having one of his difficult times. He is sullen. Brooding. Liable to explode. He is unkind. He shouts. Sometimes – there is no disguising it – he is deliberately cruel. There are moments when she sees his eyes looking at her, cold as a snake's, seeking out the weak places at which to strike.

She hopes when he finally comes back to her, as she knows he always does, regardless of what they say down in the village – the sympathetic glances in Davison's and the rabid whispering behind her back – that all that is behind him. In her daydreams. But of course he cannot be the same Michael if he changes so completely and is sunny every day. And she wants the same Michael, all of him – the smacks and shoves and long periods ignoring her, leaving her alone to watch the sun complete its daily passage along her bedroom wall, as well as the laughter and fun and surprise. For the long years of loneliness teach her that that must be what love is: total acceptance of everything a person has to offer, ungrumbling gladness at their decision to throw in their lot with yours. Not picking fussily over the plate of them and leaving the bits you don't like to one side.

Really, she ought to expect that it is tricky to begin with when at last he comes back. He is such a complicated man – burdened with so much – that things are always unpredictable between them, right from the start. She never knows what she finds when she goes out to the barn to bring him food, water or Father's old clothes: him hunched, leg jittering like a sewing-machine needle; him crouched, ready to spring and attack; him flinging down out of sight, afraid that she is nasty. Spikey – that is the word she uses to describe it to herself in the early days, back when she is still a child. He is on a secret mission. That is what he tells her, that first day she climbs up the ladder to the hayloft and finds him lounging on a hay bale. Well, of course he has to say something, and so he loses no time in explaining. He is on a secret mission, with special instructions from the MoD. He is in communication with the top brass, and they tell him expressly to remain where he is and keep the immediate area and the coastline under surveillance. She must under no circumstances reveal his whereabouts to anyone in the region, not even to Father or Aunt Susan. Especially not to them, in fact. It can put them in danger. Careless talk costs lives and all that. He isn't worried about her – he knows from watching her on the crossing (Operation Dynamo – is she aware that is its code name?) that she is more than capable of coping if she ever gets in a tight spot. But those older ones? No. They are soft. Past it. They need protecting from the truth. So it is down to Edie to be his number two. He requires her to keep him supplied with all the equipment he needs to do his surveillance work: paper, ink and, if she can see her way clear to it, a piece of that rather nice game pie he believes he glimpses through the back door last night.

It strikes her as odd as, to her knowledge, no one comes to the farm since their return. Her bedroom window overlooks the track, and it is rare that anyone passes along it without her noting them down on the list of comings and goings she keeps in her jotter, in case it is useful for the war effort. But then, she is exhausted from the crossing – Operation Dynamo – and so sleeps particularly deeply. And anyway, that is the point of secret missions, isn't it? If everyone knows about them, they lose their value.

In truth, he does seem very much like a spy. Every day he wears a different face – sometimes several in the course of a single afternoon. There are times when she mounts the ladder to find him quiet and maudlin. On other occasions, he's good-humoured and full of jokes, bringing out a parade of accents and having her in such fits of giggles that she has to stuff her fist in her mouth to keep from giving away his position.

Her favourite times are when he forgets about performing and just speaks whatever comes into his mind. Then she hears about his childhood in east London, the way he and his sisters scamper through the streets causing trouble and dodging policemen – the apples they steal from market stalls, the clothes they cut loose from the lines strung between the houses, the schemes they come up with to earn ha'pennies from out-of-towners by taking them on made-up sight-seeing tours.

The stories don't always hang together. Sometimes the sisters are two and four years younger, sometimes three and six, once they are a pair of twins. Michael's mother goes through similar transformations, from washerwoman to nanny for a rich family to barmaid. Meanwhile, his father morphs from dead to absent for long stretches with the merchant navy, to a bus conductor working the number-twenty-three route. She doesn't mind these inconsistencies because she knows there is something deeper in the accounts that is always true – a flavour that is all his own. Whether the surface facts are accurate or not matters little: through telling her these stories, Michael is showing her his true self.

But there are angry periods too – days when the most innocent of comments can have him laughing bitterly or launching into a savage monologue, leaving her edging uneasily towards the hatch. The morning she makes a reference to the British military strategy in France is a case in point.

'Strategy!' he erupts, looking up from the rolling paper he is spreading with a little mound of Player's Navy Cut. 'That's a laugh. Those bastards wouldn't know a strategy if it bit them on the arse.'

She fingers the bottom of her cardigan, shifting from foot to foot. His use of expletives makes her uneasy – she has never heard such words spoken by an adult before. But she reminds herself sternly that she is not a child any longer – she is nearly thirteen and wise to the ways of the world, unlike that snivelling baby Jean. Besides, Michael is a soldier and there are different rules for them.

'Are you saying Mr Churchill doesn't have everything under control?'

Only the day before the new prime minister speaks on the wireless about fighting on the beaches, in the fields and in the streets. She, Father and Aunt Susan sit round listening with tears in their eyes, moved to be led by someone so steadfast and proud in the face of such grave danger.

He spits. 'Pah! Old Bulldog Features? Not bloody likely. The one before him was useless, and I've no doubt he will be as well. Holed up in Westminster with their whisky and cigars. Posh twats, the lot of them. Soft as they come. They don't have a sodding clue what it's like out there. To them it's a game. Moving flags around a map. Packing off Charlies like me to be shot to shit while they pass the port. Give me strength!'

The violence in his words sends tremors through her, but she makes an effort to keep her voice level. 'But don't you think someone has to stay behind to organise things? If everyone went to fight then—'

He jumps to his feet at that, upsetting the contents of the tobacco tin over the boards. 'Organise! You want to know how fucking organised it was? We were left facing Panzers with rifles. Rifles! Ha! They told us .505 bullets would penetrate a tank and bounce around inside picking Jerry off. All the while it was horseshit. Nothing but hot air! There we were, crouched behind a barricade like sitting ducks, firing and firing, and all the while the bastards kept coming. We might as well have been chucking peas.'

She swallows. 'Gosh.'

But he isn't finished. He is striding about the hayloft, but his mind isn't there. It is back in France, crouched behind the barricade, facing the German tanks.

'In the end, there was nothing for it. We had to scarper and make the best of things. Only they found us, of course – Fritz. There weren't many places to hide in that town. It was only small and they checked everywhere, going house to house, room to room. You could hear their voices in the street, the boots pounding up the stairs.'

He is trembling too, now, his voice quavering. He looks down at the heaped tobacco paper he is still holding, then up towards the rafters, high above her head. 'They rounded us up in a field. Took our weapons. They were talking amongst themselves. Then one of our boys who knew the lingo – had a Hun mother or something like that – shouted: "Oh my God! They're taking no prisoners!"'

He sniffs, shakes his head, then continues, his voice hard and lifeless now, like something coming out of a machine. 'They led us to a barn. Once we were all inside, they pointed their rifles at the door and chucked in grenades. The blast must have knocked me out. When I came to, I thought I was dead. I thought all that stuff about hell was true after all and I was in the midst of it. All I could smell was blood and smoke, and there was this awful moaning. But it turned out I was still in the barn and the bellyaching was coming from Jones, who was missing his right leg. Two of the others were helping him – binding up the wound as best they could. I watched them, feeling like none of it was real, like I was dreaming. But when they slung his arms about their shoulders and started lifting him, reality kicked in. No way was I going to be left behind. I called out to them: "Hey, fellas! Fellas! What about me?" They turned and looked. Then one of them, Johnson – I never liked him – said…'

Here, his face crumples and his shoulders slump. She takes a step towards him, but he holds up a hand. 'He said: "Na. Best leave him. Look at him. He's fucked anyway. He'll snuff it in half an hour. We've got enough to do looking after our own." And they went, the bastards. Fucked off and left me to die. Six months together, eating and sleeping in the same billets, sharing booze, smokes and girls, and then Fritz chucks in a grenade or two and you see what really lies beneath it all.'

He snorts. 'Still, it turned out the joke was on them. The blood was nothing to do with me. It came from Smellie, who was lying next to me, minus his guts. I could've helped them carry Jones if they'd only taken the trouble to check me. But they didn't, the shits. Their loss. Fuck 'em. If I believed in it, I'd say I hope they rot in hell.'

His gaze returns to the barn, where she stands, pale and shaking. 'Jesus. Sorry, kiddo. Forgot myself there. This stuff gets into your head and jumbles it all around. You forget where you are – who you are, sometimes. Still, you shouldn't have had to listen to all that.' He takes a step towards her. 'Come on, you're all right, aren't you? Big girl like you?'

She nods, blinking. She is a big girl. Isn't she as good as a boy on the crossing? Doesn't she help Father deliver that two-headed calf last spring without flinching? Even when he takes it off behind the barn and she hears the thwack of the shovel? But oh, the thought of that poor man who loses his leg! And the other one without his guts… That all that can be happening on farms not fifty miles away – just beyond the tilt of the horizon – with no one to stop it. That the world can contain such cruelty and chaos! She shudders and clutches at her arms.

He glances down at the half-rolled cigarette and quickly finishes making it. Sparking it, he hands it over. 'Here. Have a go on that. Good for calming the nerves.'

She puts it to her lips and inhales deeply as she sees him do. The smoke burns her throat on its way down, but she clamps her mouth shut, determined not to cough.

'All right. Go easy, go easy,' he says as her cheeks puff and her eyes begin to water. 'Jesus! What are you trying to do? Kipper yourself? Give it back here!'

But though his tone is stern, there is kindness in his eyes; a joke lurking there. And they laugh then, throwing back their heads and hooting, sending the sparrows in the rafters flapping up in surprise.

That is why she is not worried at his coldness now he is back. Because there is always kindness in there somewhere, even if it is mixed up with a lot of other things. And underneath it all, she knows he is just the same. That same old Michael is in there somewhere, that gentleness, that astounding ability to look through her barriers and really see her. It is only a matter of time until he comes to the fore once again.

# 121

He brings her a drink. It is not well-made – much too thick and a hideous pink colour. She has to have it with a spoon, which he jabs carelessly into her mouth, slopping goop everywhere. Still, she gulps it down, smiling all the while to show how grateful she is, fighting the urge to gag.

Domesticity is never his strong suit, not from right back at the beginning. Even after Father and Aunt Susan finds out about him, he prefers to stay in the barn, rather than sleeping downstairs in the house, for all that they can make him up a bed on the chaise longue.

'Best leave things as they are, kiddo,' he tells her, tapping the side of his nose. 'Easier to keep it hush-hush that way. Besides, some of the work I'm engaged in I have to keep top secret – even from you.'

She still remembers the afternoon of the discovery – the surprise of finding him in the house. Returning from a hack with Dobbin and there is Michael, coming along the hallway to the kitchen in nothing but a pair of Father's corduroys and a vest.

He is adjusting his belt strap, and so doesn't see her immediately. When he looks up a flash of something like terror passes over his face, to be replaced swiftly by his familiar smile.

'Kiddo!' he says, putting on his American drawl. 'Just the gal I wanted to see. Bad news, I'm afraid. The game's up. She's on to us.'

'Who?' breathed Edie. 'Aunt Susan?'

'The very same. The dame's twigged.'

Edie claps her hand to her mouth. 'Oh no! What can we do?'

'Take it easy, kiddo. I've handled it. I've explained the situation and she understands the risks. Truth be told, she was very accommodating. In fact, she's invited me to lunch on Sunday. So, you know, every cloud.'

Then that awful, stilted meal, where she has to pretend that she doesn't know anything about Michael staying in the barn, while Aunt Susan makes cow faces across the table and Father saws into his lamb in silence. And even though she is aware it is a pretence and Michael is doing it deliberately to keep Aunt Susan sweet, she can't help feeling nettled by the way he laughs at the woman's jokes and compliments her cooking and joins in with her digs about Edie's tomboyishness. It gets so bad that she can barely chew the baked apple Aunt Susan serves up for pudding. When Jean appears wearing that awful babyish getup it is more than she can bear.

'In here, dear!'

Oh, the savage delight on Aunt Susan's face at the sight of Jean in her velvet party dress, T-buckled shoes and a large hair bow that makes her look even younger than her ten years. The efforts Edie makes to pin in the waist of her blouse and add a touch of sophistication to her attire with one of Mother's cameo brooches crumble to nothing in the face of this glaring evidence of the immaturity of her friend.

Jean's hand goes to her mouth and she starts to gabble: 'Oh, my goodness. I'm sorry! I didn't realise you'd still be eating. I'm being evacuated to Devon tomorrow, you see, and I wanted to say goodbye to Edie before I go.'

Aunt Susan looks at Father. 'Evacuated, are you? Imagine that.'

It is something they argue about, her and Father, muttering in his bedroom when they think Edie is asleep. Ever since the posters go up in the village calling for children to be sent to safety in light of the growing threat of invasion from the sea, Aunt Susan is doing her best to get Edie sent away. But though he is indifferent on many points, on this Father stands firm: he loses one family member; he will not be parted from any more.

Jean regards them, sucking her fingers, shyness surfacing in her eyes at the presence of the stranger. 'I could come back later if you like.'

Aunt Susan shakes her head and beams. 'We wouldn't hear of it, dear. We're almost finished as it is. Edie, why don't you run along and play with Jean? I'm sure you must have lots of secrets to tell each other before she goes. Leave the grown-ups to round things off here.'

Hot with humiliation, Edie gets up and goes to the door. She cannot look at Michael as she passes behind Aunt Susan's chair, but she knows his gold-green eyes are following her and that she is shrinking in his estimation, becoming more childish and pathetic with each step. She grabs Jean's arm in its silly, lace-frilled sleeve – 'Ow!' protests Jean – and hauls her away upstairs.

'You shouldn't have come, Jean,' she says when at last they are safely out of earshot inside her room. 'I don't know why you did. We're not the kind of friends that have to say hello and goodbye every time they go on a journey.'

Jean looks bewildered. 'But I thought—'

'You thought! The truth is you didn't think, did you Jean? You just came waltzing over here, expecting I'd be pleased to see you.' She is being unkind, but she can't help it. These sentences keep spilling from her mouth. 'You ought to have sent me a postcard. That's what you ought to have done. Or a notice of change of address. That would have been plenty. That would have been quite sufficient…'

The grown-up word ambushes her, bringing tears welling so that she has to shut her eyes and clamp her fists to hold them in. Oh, why does Aunt Susan have to blunder into the barn? What business does she have in there? For the last two weeks Edie lives in fear of what happens if they discover Michael; of the stern words and telephone calls that can ensue. Instead Aunt Susan rushes upstairs to don her blue polka-dot dress and invites him to lunch, and it is much worse than anything Edie imagines.

When she opens her eyes, Jean is sucking her fingers again. 'Do you want me to go?'

Edie shakes her head and sighs. 'You're here now, aren't you? We might as well make the best of things.'

She goes and sits on the bed, patting the counterpane beside her. Jean joins her, and for the next twenty minutes Edie lets her talk excitedly about the farm she is going to in Somerset, where she will be able to watch chicks hatch and learn to milk the goats.

Normally Edie wastes no time in telling Jean that farms aren't what she thinks, that they are hard, cold, smelly places where animals develop diseases that make their eyes clog up with gunk, but today she is distracted. All she can see are his eyes before her – twinkling with secret jokes.

The silence holds the traces of a question.

'Mmn?'

'I said, why aren't you being evacuated? How come you're just staying here?'

She bats the words away. 'Oh, I don't expect it's as dangerous as everyone says. Not if you're brave. Besides, it's not as though we've got anything to worry about. We've got our own military guard.'

Jean looks puzzled. 'What? Him? The darkie?'

She starts at that. Darkie? Is that what Michael is? Surely not. Her mind goes to the copy of *Uncle Tom's Cabin* she receives for her maths work at school prize-giving last year – the story that, with its pitiful account of the sorrows of the good, noble enslaved black man and his friends in America wrings her heart. When she finishes the book she feels heartily sorry for such wronged, gentle creatures and wishes she can take them in her arms and comfort them. But Michael is nothing like that. There is none of Tom's Sunday school meekness about him, for one thing – in fact, she has heard him say some rather rude things about God. Also, he does not talk like a child, all lisping words and charmingly mangled grammar.

Suddenly Roger Allen, the telegram boy from down in the village, appears in her mind. He has a dog, a little black thing that runs after rabbits and gets into church and disgraces itself against the pulpit during a christening. Its name is another word for darkies, one beginning with an N. She never thinks much about it before. When spoken between people in the village the term doesn't seem to hold any significance. It's just another word, like fence, motorcar or tree. And yet, when she thinks about trying to apply it to funny, clever Michael, that word – that dog's name – doesn't seem to fit at all. No. Jean must be mistaken. Michael is not a darkie or any of those other things. He is far too complicated for that.

Only the doubts will not leave her be. There's no denying that Michael's skin is a deeper shade than other people's. Then there are those freckles. And now she comes to think of it, there is a different cast to his features compared to other men's. A hot, sticky suspicion starts to creep up her spine that perhaps her foolish little friend is right.

'Don't say darkie, Jean,' she says crossly. 'It's not nice. And anyway, he's not one of the really dark ones. Just slightly browner than you or I.' She picks at the counterpane – one of the patchwork squares is fraying. 'But since you ask, yes. I do mean Michael. Private Patterson to you. Nothing's official yet, of course, and careless talk costs lives, but between you and me, I wouldn't be surprised if the army doesn't make his posting here permanent.'

It is all making sense. As she says them, the truth of the words unfurls before her, like a picnic blanket shaken open on a sunny day. Of course that's what the army does. What better place to post a soldier than here, right on the cliffs, looking at France? No wonder he's staying put.

Jean wrinkles her nose. 'But won't they want him back at the war?'

'This is the war, Jean. We're in it.'

'Oh.'

'Besides, even if he could leave, I don't suppose he'd want to.'

'Why?'

Edie sighs and kicks her legs back and forth, scuffing another truth up from the floorboards. 'Well, we weren't going to tell anyone, but the truth is Private Patterson and I are lovers.'

Jean's eyes widen. 'You're not!'

'We are, Jean. We are: deeply, thickly in love. Stuck in the middle of it like... flies in jam.'

'Crumbs!'

'I know. So you see, it's inconceivable that he would ever leave or—'

'Have you kissed?'

She looks at the floor. 'Mmn-hmn.' It is not strictly true, but it feels as though it is. They are close to kissing many times. She is sure of it. It is only the fact that he is a gentleman that stands in the way.

'So you'll be getting married. Can I be bridesmaid? Oh, can I, please?' In her excitement, Jean jumps off the bed and whirls round the room, shouting.

A laugh drifts up through the floorboards and Edie is suddenly afraid they might be overheard.

'Ssh! Jean! Not so loud! Listen, whatever you do, you mustn't tell anyone about this. Not even in Somerset. It could be very dangerous for Private Patterson. There are rules about this sort of thing – fraternising in plain sight and whatnot. So you see, you must keep it secret. You must not say a word.'

Jean nods solemnly.

'Cross your heart and hope to die?'

Jean does the actions. 'But afterwards, when everybody knows and you finally do get married, can I be bridesmaid then?'

Edie sighs. 'I expect so, Jean. I expect so.' She puts a harried hand to her head like a busy housewife struggling to make ends meet. 'There's really so much on our plates right at this moment that I can't worry about details like that now.'

'But you'll do your best?'

'I'll try.'

'Goodie!'

They are quiet for a moment. Down in the hall, the grandfather clock chimes the quarter hour.

'Shall we go and see Dobbin?'

Edie likes to go on being in love and harried a while longer, but she sees the younger girl is getting bored and bouncy with it, so she relents.

They clomp down the stairs. As they pass the dining room, she looks in and sees Michael still sitting there with Aunt Susan. He holds up a hand and the look in his eyes is so warm that she knows that everything she has told Jean is true where it counts, true at the core. It is only a matter of time before all that reality sweeps up through the outer layers and bursts to the surface, and the things she says become true all the way down. Not that Jean understands that, silly goose that she is, who thinks that true is a matter of yes or no and doesn't understand that there can be levels in between.

That is why it is best when it is just the two of them, she and him. Because then there is no need to define anything and it can just be what it is. It's for that reason that, to this day, she still thinks of the trip to London as one of their best times together – one of the best of her life, in fact. For all its awkwardness and the trouble that comes after, that day they are themselves purely, Michael and Edie, and hang the rest of the world.

She can go back to it any time she likes. The memory is so vivid that she only has to close her eyes and she is there, reliving that bright, glad morning, when she wakes imagining nothing more adventurous than a gallop along the cliffs and goes out into the yard to find him sitting in the cab of the farm truck, revving the engine.

'Cracked it!' he crows through the open window. 'The fan belt had gone. I borrowed one of your Auntie Susan's stockings off the line to fix it. Here's hoping she doesn't mind!'

He pulls a mock nervous face and she falls about giggling, slapping her jodhpurs and stamping her boots. He is such a joker!

'Fancy taking her for a spin, kiddo?'

'What? Now?'

'There's never any other time, is there?'

She means to muck out. And Aunt Susan asks her to get the washing in before lunch. But – oh, blow it! – a short hop in the truck can't hurt. They only run to the village and back. There isn't petrol for going any further than that.

But when they get to the village, Michael shows no signs of turning round. They pass the school and the church and the hall. At the parade, she sees Jean and her mother emerging from Davison's, her socks at half-mast as usual. The astonishment on the younger girl's face as she looks up and sees her in the cab gives Edie a fierce, pleased, bubbling feeling, much tarter and more delicious than the sherbet dab in Jean's grubby paw. Fighting her grin, she yawns and looks straight ahead, as though it is entirely normal for her to scud about the countryside with a daring, brown-skinned stranger.

But when the last house flashes by and the fields open up before them once more, she says: 'Surely we should be turning back soon? There can't be much petrol, and they've started taking away the tanks from the petrol stations round here. Besides, we haven't any coupons.'

He taps the side of his nose. 'Don't you worry about that. I have an inside line. Here.'

And, reaching into the pocket of Father's old suit jacket, he tosses a paper-wrapped rectangle into her lap. Chocolate!

She does not hold a bar of it in so long that at first she feels quite giddy. Since sugar rationing comes in, Aunt Susan is extremely strict about what they may and may not have in the house. Sweet things must be kept for special occasions and used only for things that really matter – birthdays, visitors and the spoonful of sugar Aunt Susan likes in her tea.

This is different, though. Aunt Susan is not here. They are away from the farm, and with every mile that passes it seems more and more as though they rip a day out of the calendar and suspend the rules, stopping everything except the truck, which bowls gamely on. She unfolds the paper, slits the foil and pops a square of the sweet, yielding goodness on to her tongue. As the last familiar landmark – a little humpbacked bridge – passes from view, she shuts her eyes in bliss.

London. That is where he takes them. The capital. By way of a grubby house on the outskirts where a small, twitchy man runs out to hand over a can of fuel in return for something she can't make out.

Michael grins at her when he jumps back into the cab. 'Necessary pit stop, kiddo. One of those things.'

Within minutes, she forgets all about the grubby house and the man. The prospect of the city marching towards her, building upon building advancing like soldiers massed in rows, is too thrilling. She sticks her head out of the window into the rushing air and whoops with delight. There is so much to see – life and activity everywhere she looks. Market stalls and omnibuses and people bustling.

As they swing into the centre and she catches her first glimpse of the Thames, she barely contains her excitement. The Tower of London! St Paul's Cathedral! Big Ben! All these famous places they pore over pictures of at school, all here and real and bigger and grander than she dreams.

It is a magical day. They wander the streets looking at everything, sampling this, tasting that, doing it all: tea at a Lyons tearoom like a lady in the pictures, where Michael orders far too many cakes and she ends up feeling sicky, a stroll around Trafalgar Square. She gawps up at Nelson's Column, staggered by its height. However, it is the bronze panels on the pedestal that surprise her most – in particular the one depicting the death of Nelson. There, above the inscription 'England expects that every man will do his duty', to the left of the relief, she spies a round-featured man holding a musket, his head a mass of tight curls.

'Oh!' she exclaims, before she stops herself.

'Well waddya know, kiddo?' says Michael. 'Turns out we didn't all step off the banana boat half an hour ago. There were darkies here even then.'

She feels the heat creeping up her neck at that and looks away, ashamed and shy at the idea that he is able to look into her mind so easily and see the colour of her thoughts.

A taxi ride along the Mall soon chases away her awkwardness. The flag is up on Buckingham Palace, so she knows the King is there – he and his big-hatted wife and the two girls not far off her age who wear white frocks and blue ribbons in the photograph above Miss Wright's desk at school. Not that she wants to remember they are similar ages today, of course, she and those children, because today she is a grown-up lady visiting London with her gentleman friend.

As dusk falls, they climb back into the truck. Edie assumes they are driving home, but Michael has other ideas and instead turns off the main thoroughfare as they are passing through the East End on to a cramped side street where he says he knows a place. By the time they park up it is dark and she is hungry again, so he buys her a pot of jellied eels from a street trader flogging off the last of his wares. The gelatinous texture of the stuff makes her gag, but she smiles bravely and finishes the lot. It is such a lovely day, after all, and she is awfully grateful, and besides, as Aunt Susan says, there is a war on and she is to be thankful for everything she gets.

He smokes while she eats, his foot tapping, as though it is in a hurry and anxious to get away. When she is done, he takes the pot from her and hurls it into the gutter. The gesture shocks her, but there is no time to dwell on this, because next he has her hand and is dragging her along the street. She stumbles a little and bumps her knee against an iron railing, but he strides on, oblivious. And even though a little voice in her head whispers that he is being thoughtless, that he ought to stop and see she is all right, she blinks back the tears and hurries to keep up. Because he is Michael – not just anybody – and he is funny and kind and good.

At a post box he turns abruptly and leads her down a little flight of stairs to a dirt-streaked basement door beside some bins. A knock and a muttered word and they are inside.

She assumes from the exterior that this is a sorry sort of place, but it turns out the room beyond is set up for parties. There is a wooden counter with all manner of bottles on the shelves behind it, and there are tables and chairs arranged in little clusters in the corners, just waiting for friends to sit down to laugh and talk. It is almost empty, but at the far end, on a raised platform scattered with musical instruments, a dark-skinned man is sitting at a piano, playing with his eyes closed and nodding his head.

The music is like nothing Edie has heard before – the tune cheeky, almost rude. It whirls around, sticking out its tongue and filling the air with pranks. In the way it bucks and scampers, defying her ears to make sense of it; it seems to be cocking a snook at all the music she knows – the jogtrot tunes of the morris men, the foursquare offerings on the wireless and the reedy warbling of the church choir.

As Michael goes to talk to someone at the bar, a string of sound pulls her towards the stage. When the piece ends with a cascade of notes from top to bottom, she bursts out clapping. But the silence and muttering around the rest of the room make her clamp her arms to her sides and duck her head, willing the piano to embark on another tune and swallow the echo of her applause.

'Hey, you! Yeah, you with the horse trousers.'

Alarmed, she looks up. The piano man is pointing at her, snapping his fingers.

She blinks. 'Me?'

'Who else?'

She glances around. A handful of people who stroll in during the last number are staring at her, smirking.

'What?' she whispers.

'Get up here.'

She points at the stage. 'There?'

'Christ almighty. Where else? Get up here before I change my mind.'

She scrambles up on the platform and rounds the piano. He nods at the space beside him on the stool. 'Sit here. Watch what I do.'

She sits gingerly, nervous of pressing against his body in its stripy suit. But then he starts up a plodding refrain down the far end of the keyboard and she forgets her awkwardness in the effort to make out what he does. In another moment, he leans forward, blocking her view. The fingers of his right hand begin to cavort on the high notes in front of her, and she knows without asking that this is what she is supposed to observe.

The playing makes her smile. The freedom. The recklessness. The sense that his fingers stray where they please as the notes occur to him, rather than following a set path. She likes the unhurriedness of it, too – the way the melody sits back in the saddle of the rhythm so that, if you aren't paying attention, you can dismiss the performance as lazy. But all the while Edie can see this is not the case: there is intention behind every trip and squiggle. She is watching her neighbour's thinking transform itself into sound.

'Now you.' He tilts his head towards the keys.

Her tongue protruding in concentration, Edie places her thumb over the white note the player's finger just leaves. She waits for the bass refrain to come round its wheel, and when it hits the beginning again she starts to play, trotting out the phrase he opens with, pure and unadorned. She tries it again with growing confidence, and on the third time through she dares to add a flourish to the final two notes, such that the melody seems to falter and regain its footing with a smile.

'That's right,' says the piano man softly, nodding.

Emboldened, she tries for more on the next go, only for the reins of the melody to slip through her fingers, throwing a shoe with a sour note that leaves her shaking her head, cheeks aflame.

'Let it go,' mutters her neighbour. 'It won't come back to bite you. Move on.'

And so she does. When the bass comes round its cycle again, she gets back on the horse and returns to the simple melody, letting the refrain develop and grow from there, not trying to force any tricks on it. They play like that for a minute or two, the tune shifting around her as gently as the landscape during a hack with Dobbin, while the low notes plod beneath.

'Keep going,' whispers her companion. And while she plugs away, he brings up his right hand and introduces another layer: rich, scrunchy chords between her and the bass that jump in at odd moments to argue, hustle and plead. At first, she fears the new notes elbow her out, that they edge their way up the keyboard to swallow her feeble tune. But then she realises what is happening: instead of the landscape, her melody is now a bird. The support of the middle registers frees it to wheel and soar.

So this is just what she lets it do. As the man plays, she flings her fingers about the keyboard, daring herself to involve whatever notes present themselves, not minding about the false starts but merely waiting for the bass to work its way back to the start of the sequence, bringing with it the chance to take off again.

In time, it feels as though she really is flying. Her fingers seem to move by themselves, and when a bum note sounds she discovers a way to work it in, so that it seems as though she intends it all along. She gets daring with the rhythm, breaking away from the plod of the bass to trespass on the silences and weak beats along with the middle chords.

'Last time round,' says the piano man, and for an instant she can't think what he means. Surely this is where she lives now? In this daring, bright world of sound? How is there an end?

But then she hears what he is doing down the far end of the piano – how the bass is shifting upwards, the chords intensifying. He is bringing the music to a close, and she must do the same. She hurls herself at the final phrase, risking a swoop and flourish, before the melody spirals into the clouds. As the last chords ring out, she allows herself a few scattered extra notes – feathers falling to earth.

There is silence. Then around the room, people start to clap. Someone whistles. While they are playing, the crowd swells, and now a cluster of faces grins up at her in the semi-darkness. She beams, delighted and also bewildered to find herself back in her body once more.

Flushed, she looks up, exhilarated, eager for the next thing. But over her partner's shoulder she catches sight of the other band members sidling on to the stage, picking up their instruments and readying themselves to play.

'Well done, my friend. Well done,' he says, proffering his hand.

She shakes it, all of a sudden shy to meet his eye. It seems incredible that they just do something so extraordinary together, she and this stranger, with his queer suit and scar zig-zagging across his chin.

She wants to tell him, but instead a clatter from the drums makes her jump off the stage in alarm. She lands amid a forest of jackets and dresses, where hands reach to pat her shoulders and ruffle her hair.

'Well done, chickadee!'

'You're a natural!'

'You sure you haven't tinkled the ivories before, white girl?'

(This last turns her pink: is that how they see her? Is that what she is before everything to them? Pale skin? She never thinks of herself that way before. In her own mind, she is always just Edie.)

They are being kind, these people, only she can't be pleased about it. Because now, as the saxophone guffaws and the drums kick up a fuss and the bodies pressing around her begin to sway to new beats, she is afraid. Where is he? She strains her eyes, looking here, looking there, but she cannot see him. He is not at the bar, offering the serving girl a roguish smile; he is not in that cluster of men around the table in the far corner; none of the heads nodding in time to the music belong to him; and though she spots a passing resemblance in several of the men shucking off their jackets the better to hurl their partners around the dance floor, none of them wears his face.

Anxiety ripples up and down her spine like piano riffs as she moves through the crowd, jostled by elbows, kicked by flying heels, barged by hips flung side to side. Now the voices aren't kind but impatient: 'Watch where you're going!'; 'Get out of it!'; 'This is no place for a child!'

A woman leans down and tries to speak to her, but she shrugs the soft voice off. She doesn't need help. She needs him: Michael, who carries her assured self in his shirt pocket, against his heart, in place of the slab of chocolate. If she can find him all is well once more – she is not a child but the sophisticated young lady of earlier, motoring down to London for a day trip with her gentleman friend.

Oh, where is he? She turns hither and thither with a ferocity that teeters on the brink of tears.

Then, through the jiggling bodies, from the far side of the room, an idea presents itself: a little door marked 'Private', shut tight but seeming to throb, as though pulsing to the rhythm of the drums.

She walks towards it. The handle is sticky, but she grasps it and yanks it down. The door swings open. Beyond lies a tiny room, a store cupboard, judging by the boxes stacked in piles and arranged on flimsy metal shelves. But behind the door there is a desk, and there she discovers two figures: a woman sitting with her head thrown back and her legs akimbo as a man wearing Father's jacket kneels in front of her, his head rooting and butting under her skirt.

The woman opens her eyes lazily. 'Well, if it isn't our little pianist.'

There is a sharp movement under the skirt and Michael's face appears, mouth glistening. 'Edie! I didn't realise you'd finished. If you just give me a minute—'

But now the drums are throbbing through her and the room seems to be concertinaing in and out, as though one of the musicians on stage picks it up and is using it as a squeeze-box. She cannot breathe and her chest is tight. Clutch at the shelves as she might, wheel round, flail, there is nothing she can do to keep herself from tipping down into blackness, at the end of this, the very best day.

# 7

A horrid dream. She is in her bed, in her room. Only it is not her room as she knows it: the lace on the cushion covers is faded to a sickly yellow, the pretty forget-me-not walls are a patchy grey and there is dust furring every surface.

She doesn't feel well, so she calls out. But no one comes. Not Mummy, not Daddy, not even Aunt Susan. The house has a dead feel, and she is certain that if she went from room to room she would find no one there.

Still, she tries to get up. Only, what's this? Her body, usually lithe and capable, leaping up so spryly on to Dobbin's back and taking the stairs two at a time, is crabbed and painful. Where her fingers usually encounter smooth flesh, they find sagging and dimpling, a thinness to the skin, which is creased all over like crumpled paper that has been flattened with a tea towel and a hot iron. Her bones seem nearer to the surface, and when she moves her tendons protest and feel liable to snap.

With an effort she pulls open the covers, but more horrors lie beneath: the bed is soiled. Her nightgown too. Her body crusted and stinking.

When at last she gets her feet to the floor, her legs are unable to bear her weight. There is a disagreement between them. One refuses to keep up its end of the bargain and she slants sideways, tumbling on to the rug. Fresh pain floods her and she shudders in misery.

Wake up! she urges herself. Wake up into real life! Wake up now!

But her mind remains stubbornly locked in the nightmare, trapped on the rug in a body drained of all its do.

A happy memory, a good then – that's what she needs to jolt her brain back on to its customary tracks. She casts about for something sturdy enough. At last, she has it: the day the piano came.

When she hears the van pulling into the yard, she resolves not to bother to go down. It cannot be anything interesting – some foolish order Aunt Susan places, no doubt. Fabric from the haberdasher in Totwith or a flimsy bit of furniture that looks quite ridiculous beside the solid oak hand-me-downs from Father's family.

When Aunt Susan shouts up for her from the hall, she rolls her eyes. Why can't the silly woman leave her alone? Doesn't she already have her triumph by sending Michael away and pulling the plug from Edie's existence, emptying it of all joy?

For years afterwards the memory makes her cringe. That awful night after she and Michael get back from London to find the farmhouse lights blazing, regardless of the blackout. The indignity of being banished to her room like a baby. Lying in bed, straining her ears to make sense of the mutters and rumbles coming from below. The horrid conversation when Edie slips down the following morning in search of him: Aunt Susan waiting in the kitchen to force a congealing fried egg on her, trapping her into sitting down and suffering an interrogation over whether Michael involves her in any 'fun and games – you know, rude things – of the body' during his stay. Susan! Who shuffles out of Father's room in the middle of the night to use that disgusting porcelain device with the rubber tube that she keeps hidden under the bathroom sink and imagines Edie knows nothing about.

The sad goodbye in the yard – his gold-green eyes flitting repeatedly to the doorstep, where Susan lurks. The knowledge that he says so much more if they are alone. His joke about her Aunt Pittypat fainting routine making her splutter with laughter and tears all in one go. Her vigorous shaking of her head that of course she won't forget him – how could she? Why would she? The sight of him walking away down the track once more, this time in Father's clothes.

And then the days shrinking in on themselves. Everything – even rides with Dobbin – becoming pointless. Life limp and lacklustre, a dishcloth from which someone has wrung all the good. The summer going stale and browning round the edges. Good times rationed, along with cooking fats and tea. Surly, silent meals. Hours lying on her bed watching specks of sunlight shift across the ceiling, heedless of exhortations to pull her finger out and help around the farm. Aunt Susan bursting in one afternoon brandishing her pink, pompommed slipper, only to catch Edie's eye and retreat wordlessly.

And every now and then the memory drifts to the surface: the throbbing door, the cackle of the instruments and the two figures at the desk. She examines it sidelong for as long as she dares, two responses squabbling within her. There is disgust at the way he buts and roots like a lamb at its mother's teat, along with the stomach-bubbling thought that maybe the woman is going to the toilet in his mouth and he is drinking it straight from her. But there is also the shameful knowledge – admitted to herself with her eyes clenched shut and her fingers jammed in her mouth, sour with the taste of herself – that if he comes back when she is older and wants to do the same thing to her she allows it. More: that if he asked her to, she sits on the altar of St Stephen's with her legs spread wide and lets him and lets him and lets him.

For the most part, though, she does not think at all. Those weeks after his going, that first time, her brain seems as misty as the Channel in autumn – so much so that she wonders sometimes if she might not in fact be dead. In odd moments it occurs to her that there is an accident on the road back from London and that she is a ghost haunting the farm. Most mornings, she feels as insubstantial as a spirit – and as weak.

As a result, the day the marvellous thing arrives she can barely find the will to get up.

'They won't let me sign for it,' says Aunt Susan when Edie finally slouches down the staircase. 'They say they have instructions to deliver it to you. I hope you haven't been ordering anything foolish, young lady. Your father isn't made of money, you know.'

Ignoring the remark, she goes to the back door. A russet-faced man with a large moustache is standing on the step holding a Shannon Arch File half full of papers. Behind him, two youths loll about the open rear doors of a yellow delivery van, the contents of which she cannot see.

'Miss Edith Morley? Delivery for you. Sign here, please.'

'What on earth can it be?' she says as she scrawls her name.

The man fetches up an envelope from his jacket pocket and hands it over. 'No doubt that'll explain matters.'

As the youths begin setting up a ramp down from the back of the van, Edith rips open the flap. Her heart quickens when she sees that it contains a picture postcard of the River Thames and the dome of St Paul's against the sky. On the other side, there is a message printed in an ungainly hand: 'Hey, kiddo. Sorry for the hassle. Thought you could make use of this to keep you entertained. I saw you up on that stage playing that Joanna. You were good. Learn something to play me next time I call. Yours, M.'

'Well, who's it from?' says Aunt Susan, nosing over her shoulder.

She turns to shield the postcard from view. 'A friend.'

'Don't give me that!' blazes Aunt Susan. 'It's him, isn't it? Let me see!'

She reaches out to take the card, and Edie jumps off the step to prevent her. She is about to sprint across the yard when – 'Oh my goodness!' – she sees a grand piano trundling down the ramp on to the cobbles. The scuffle forgotten, she and Aunt Susan stare open-mouthed at the instrument. It is black and glossy and it gleams in the mid-morning sun; quite the most handsome object Edie ever sees.

'We'll have to take it round the front to get it in – there's no way we'll manage to angle it through there,' says the delivery man, indicating the back door.

Aunt Susan lurches forward, hands raised. 'Now wait a minute. I'm afraid there's been some mistake. We never said we were accepting this. We've no place to put it. I'm awfully sorry, but I'm afraid you'll have to take it back.'

The delivery man shakes his head. 'No can do, I'm afraid, madam. The young lady's signed for it, you see. Fair and square. That makes it your responsibility. Unless you want to pay the cost of transporting it all the way back to London, of course.'

Aunt Susan opens and closes her mouth like a ventriloquist's doll. 'I—'

Edith grins. 'Of course we're keeping it. It can go in the drawing room, in the bay window, looking out over the sea. That'll be the perfect place.'

The delivery man winks at her. 'That's the right idea, young lady. Don't look a gift horse in the mouth. If you run along and open up, me and the lads'll bring it round.'

It isn't easy. The front door isn't open in years – not since Mummy's funeral, in fact. When Edie eventually finds the key, it takes several minutes of pushing and shoving to get it to budge. Furthermore, the route around the house proves trickier than expected, and there are several points at which the movers have to tilt the piano in order to get it past the bushes. Once it is over the drawing-room threshold, there is the business of moving the sea chest and the oak chairs out of the bay and then waiting while Aunt Susan insists on sweeping every inch of the floor before the men are able to move it into position.

All the bother only makes Edie love the piano more. She smiles to herself at the grunts and groans, at Aunt Susan's tutting and head-shaking. It is so like him: too big, too loud – too much. In the half hour since its arrival, it causes all manner of inconvenience, and yet it doesn't care. It remains proud and stylish, standing boldly by the window, proclaiming its promise for all to see: I return.

# 0

He has forgotten the dank feel of the air in the kitchen. He has forgotten the dust that clogs the surfaces and floats in the air, dancing in the breeze through the broken kitchen window, irritating his nostrils and congesting his throat – not fine, fresh dust kicked up by the wind racing across the bush, but the stale accumulation of years of neglect. He has forgotten the noises – the way the house creaks and groans, its pipes gurgling, belching and clearing their throats. Back home there were noises too – the rustle of termites in the roof beams, the cackle of hyenas in the dead of night. But those sounds were not mechanical and dead like these, they spoke of life, of nature, of the world beyond. They were not born of enclosure, of shutting oneself up behind walls and doors.

When they pull into the yard and the driver gets out to wrestle ET's wheelchair from the boot, Jonah stares up at the peeling paintwork and dingy windows of the house with resentment. And when he has to lift the old woman out of the car and she reaches up, clutching and clawing at his neck, her mouth gaping, it is all he can do to prevent himself from hurling her to the cobblestones and running off down the track.

Inside, the place is just as they left it: the unwashed crockery from the most recent round of tea drinking sits by the sink, the pile of letters on the windowsill. Only there is a heaviness that he did not sense before, as though the weight of this great structure, with its two floors and many rooms, is pressing directly on his head.

When they reach the hallway, he realises the cause: the last time he was here he thought of this place as a refuge, a piece of luck, a stepping stone on the route to fulfilling his ambitions and rescuing his family. Now he sees it is a trap. The longer he stays, the more the fiction of him being ET's carer hardens into fact. That story is setting around him like concrete, becoming more robust with every passing day. He saw it happening at the hospital as one after another the nurses, doctors, that sharp-faced woman and Jeans accepted the untruth which he had expected to be dug out and exposed. They did so, he realises now, as he looks about the cluttered, stinking space, because it was convenient to them, because it felt better than the reality. The idea that ET is provided for absolves them of the need to give the situation further thought.

He has encountered such thinking before, and he knows how dangerous it can be. Years ago, back in the November after the rains came late, word went round that President Muluzi would visit the local town. Though everyone was suffering by that stage, boiling up green mangoes and pumpkin leaves to bulk out the last pails of gaga selling in the trading centre for ten times the usual price, excitement swept through the villages. Here at last was Muluzi, the first freely elected ruler in the history of the nation, venturing forth to meet his people and commune with their troubles. Now, surely, all would be well. The grain stores would be opened and the prices subsidised so that everyone would have the wherewithal to make it through to the ripening of the succulent dowe cobs and the blessed bounty of the harvest six weeks or so after that.

For all their difficulties, the community made every effort to celebrate the president's coming. A stage was erected and what they couldn't provide in food they made up for with music, hauling every drum each village boasted on the backs of ox carts and bicycles, ready to play until sundown. The women wore their brightest chitenje, and masked and feathered Gule Wamkulu appeared to strut, shudder and writhe in the streets. Hungry though he was, Jonah had been excited and had started out on the fifteen-kilometre cycle ride before the sun was up, eager to get a good spot from which to watch the president rescue the district.

The great man arrived several hours after he was expected, but his cavalcade was every bit as impressive as anyone could have imagined when at last it appeared. It included a truck laden with speakers blaring reggae, which made the drummers largely redundant. No one cared, however, for when President Muluzi emerged from his Mercedes Benz limousine looking sleek as a gecko in rainy season, an enormous cheer went up and everyone pressed towards the stage, eager to hear what the great man would say. They didn't have to wait long. The leader's words were many and grand. He lavished praise on the people of the district and the enthusiasm with which they had received him. He talked about the greatness of the nation and his pride at leading such a rich and wonderful land. Then he turned to the things he knew they were most eager to hear about: his plans for the district. Well. He was delighted to say that in the spirit of taking the region from strength to strength, he had signed off on the development of not one but three new toilet blocks to be built within the next five years. That was not all. In addition, he had given his assent to a scheme to provide wells in eight of the local villages. Just think of that. Think of the time that would save all the women and children each day! But most importantly of all, because he was a forward-thinking president who knew the key to his people's long-term happiness was in growing the economy, he had approved a raft of packages, tax breaks and financial incentives that would tempt the finest, most successful businessmen in Southern Africa, if not the world, to start ventures here, ensuring employment and prosperity for many generations to come.

The crowd roared its approval. The drums thundered. The noise was so overwhelming that Jonah was unable to resist joining in and shouting along with the rest.

After that, there was a series of speeches from local dignitaries in praise of President Muluzi and his bountiful provision for his people's needs. The enthusiasm of those listening knew no bounds. Cheering and jumping up and down with them, he felt his whole body suffused with a wild, dizzy joy. But towards the end, a solemn-looking man stepped forward. He was chief of a village in the extreme south of the district, where the food shortages had been felt first. He took the microphone and wiped a quaking hand across his brow. He was grateful to President Muluzi for his munificence (more cheers; a clatter from the drums), but he had a few concerns he would like the ruler to address. People were hungry, sir. More: they were starving. Since the harvest had failed they had been living on reserves of maize, and now these were nearly gone, with six months until the next harvest could be expected. Unless they received relief it would not be long – indeed, he feared it may already have happened in remote places – before some of them died. Couldn't the president in his great wisdom and bounteous solicitude for the people of the region open up some of the national stores of grain they had heard were at the government's disposal and supplement the local stocks until then?

There was silence after the chief finished speaking. When he shuffled off the stage the microphone whined. People's heads turned, looking here and there, seeking the appropriate response. At length, the next chief in line to speak began to approach the podium. But as he reached the lectern bearing its garland-bordered photograph of the president, the great man himself stepped forward and waved him aside.

The crowd held its breath as he opened his mouth and looked around the gathering, sunglasses glinting. A guinea fowl screeched on the road leading out to the bush. Then the president laughed. You know, it was funny, he said, to hear suggestions of food shortages and starvation in the district because – rack his brains as he might – he couldn't recall a single instance of a person ever dying of hunger in the nation. Not one. Malaria, yes. Cholera, yes. But hunger? No. Never. Such things did not happen here. This was a great country. Strong and stable. All its people had enough. Any talk to the contrary was surely the work of the nation's enemies, those who wished to destabilise the country by distracting its government from getting on with the job. Project Fear. So it puzzled him to hear his esteemed friend make such assertions. Knowing him to be an ardent patriot, he could only assume that the worthy chief must have made a mistake. Ah, well. Such things were not unknown. They were all only human after all – even him. (Laughter at this; thundering from the drums.) Even so, as a show of his solidarity with the people, and because this district was particularly dear to his heart, he was prepared to make one further commitment: in addition to the toilet blocks and wells he had already approved, he would sign off on a new health centre for the town, subject to securing money from the Global Fund. Never let it be said that he was a man who didn't care for his people. He cared passionately. Deeply. What could matter more to him than their well-being? (More cheers and the crowd stamping its feet.) So now: on with the festivities! Dancing for as long as they could stand!

The people roared and flung themselves into impromptu writhing to the accompaniment of music blaring from the speaker truck. Standing three feet from the stage, Jonah raised his arms to join them, but the impulse died. He stared at the rapturous faces around him and could find no echo of their fervour in his breast. Instead of the thumping music, he heard the static of a badly tuned radio, and where joy should be he found only emptiness and a creeping feeling that something was terribly wrong. When a gap opened up behind him, he ducked through it and walked away to where his bicycle waited in front of a Western Union shop.

The streets were deserted as he left town, but as he drew level with the last of the buildings a scuffle in an alleyway caught his attention: a group of young men were beating and kicking a figure curled up on the ground. As one of them stepped back to take aim, the prone man craned his neck towards the road and locked eyes briefly with Jonah. It was the chief from the southern village, his face slick now with sweat and blood.

When he got back to the farm, Jonah told his parents nothing about any of this – not the chief's speech, nor the way people had shuffled uneasily, nor the beating he had glimpsed. Instead, he found himself talking enthusiastically about the toilet blocks and the wells and the possible new health centre, as though his very mouth had become the property of the president and was being pressed into public service.

Thinking back on that performed enthusiasm and the way the crowd had whooped and danced rather than confront the terrible truth, he sees how similar what the azungu are doing now is. Though ET's thing-filled house here in grey old England seems utterly different to the sparsely furnished huts of the villagers, the same desire for something other than the facts to be true was pressing down upon this place. And just as it did then, that pressure is warping his behaviour once more. Under the weight of their expectations, he is becoming the thing these white people want him to be, conforming to their version of events. He does it almost automatically – so much so that when he shoulders the old woman like a maize sack up the stairs to her room, he finds himself adopting the bright tone of the hospital nurses.

'There,' he proclaims as he dumps her – slippers, trousers, cardigan and all – into the bed.

'There,' she echoes gamely as he pats the covers down. And in spite of the heaviness weighing on him, he gives her a smile. It is not her fault, after all, this blinking little bird of a woman. She did not ask for her brain to burst. Nor did she commission Death to snatch his dreams.

But eeeh…! And here he turns away, biting his hand, that she might not witness his sadness and ape it back at him the way he has seen her mirror the expressions of others around her hospital bed.

'Darling!' she calls.

But he doesn't respond, and instead goes down to the piano room to stand in the bay window and stare out at the mindless sea.

When the gold of the afternoon has silvered into evening, the squirming of his stomach prompts Jonah to think about food. He goes to the kitchen. The familiar spread greets him: the tins, the cartons, the bread now blotched with blue and green. He yanks out a couple of slices, rips them into pieces and stuffs them in his mouth, heedless of the mould or the crumbs that shower the floor.

Once more the bloating, heavy feeling from the wheat spreads through him. How do the azungu live like this? Even in the hospital cafeteria, where there was at least hot food and meat to choose from (including one dish that he had thought for a brief, glad moment comprised nsima, only to discover when he'd purchased it and plunged his fingers into the fluffy mound on the side of the plate that it was some sort of mashed root vegetable), the emphasis had been so much on bread that he had found it hard to avoid eating several slices a day. As a consequence, his guts seized up, sending him doubled-over and groaning to the cubicles in the men's toilets. He had used to think of bread as a treat – a luxury item consumed only on special occasions. Now he can't stand the stuff. It is an evil, bland, dry concoction that the world has made too much of. If the azungu didn't eat it, you could bet no one would give it a second thought.

Still, it serves to stave off the worst of his hunger pangs. Once these have died down he goes back to the piano room and stretches out on the lopsided couch, hoping to lose himself for a time in sleep.

Only his mind won't let him. As the cares of the day begin to recede, a fresh preoccupation gets to its feet and starts to address him: oughtn't he to take ET something to eat?

He dismisses the thought and turns on to his side. Iwe! She'll be fine for tonight. Doesn't he know from personal experience that it's possible to go without food for several days without suffering any long-term effects? Besides, she is not a vigorous, growing boy as he was when the first famine struck. She does not have to rise before dawn to hoe the fields with an empty belly. She is not obliged to walk five kilometres to school and sit, head swimming, trying to copy sums from the blackboard. She is an old woman doing nothing but sitting in her bed, sleeping, farting and muttering the odd bit of nonsense. She'll be fine until morning. Probably she'd be fine until the next evening, or the following day. Even the day after that. The amount he saw her guzzling in that hospital! Barely an hour seemed to go by when there wasn't someone approaching the bed with a pot of some mixture to be spooned into ET's mouth. Well, then. He'll leave her tonight and get some rest. Tomorrow will be soon enough to tend to her. Besides, hadn't they said at the hospital that further improvements were entirely possible as the swelling in her brain continued to reduce? Wasn't there every chance that here, back in her own surroundings, she might regain the knack of fending for herself? In all likelihood, it was unwise to rush to do too many things for her. Such well-meaning interference might rob her of the capacity to take care of things after he is gone. And let's face it, he will be gone soon. This is not how his life is going to be. He is destined for greater things. He is going to the big city, to London, to earn a fortune, to give Amayi and the children everything that they—

The memory of what has happened ambushes him anew, every bit as violent as the first time he heard Aunt Dudu speak the news. Sorrow rips through his guts and he curls himself around the pain, gasping. Sobs shake him, putting him in mind of the way he sobbed once before in this room – those selfish, naïve tears for the hardships he had undergone. Pah! He had been a baby then! Thinking he was the only one to suffer – a child throwing a tantrum over a game of bawo, while back home its parents wasted with slimming disease. He had come all this way with his smart and proud dreams, confident that the world would treat him justly and reward his effort, thinking he was a man when really he had been an infant in his knowledge of the ways of grief. How life could take you apart. He presses his face into the hard, frilled pillow on the couch, heedless of the dust that puffs up to clog his nose and throat, hoping only for oblivion – not to see, hear, think or feel.

*

The morning sun slits open his eyes. He sits up, blinking. Thirsty. His tongue pasted to the roof of his mouth. Stumbles to the kitchen. Drinks one helping of water out of a dirty cup – the dregs of tea making it bitter – then another.

Outside, the field running up from behind the storeroom. It's early, so the diggers are not yet working, and stand instead like sleeping flamingos, their heads tucked down by their breasts. He wonders what they are doing, what it will be, this big venture – the grid of trenches spreading through the grass. Some moneymaking concern, no doubt. A luxury hotel like Sunbird Mount Soche in the centre of Blantyre, with palm trees at the entrance and a thick-necked guard, watching for anyone who was not either mzungu or rich (preferably both), trying to get inside. Or maybe a night-club like the one on the outskirts of the town run by the wrinkled mzungu, who everyone said had earned his money from diamonds made of blood – Cadillac Clive's. Some sort of glamorous place, at any rate. And it would be well done. You could be certain of that. Everything thought out efficiently. The plans followed to the letter to maximise the utility of the project, and the profit. Not like the school Hattie's NGO had come to his village to build – situated in the sunlight with a corrugated-iron roof guaranteed to make the place swelter by mid-morning. Iwe! There'd be no mistakes of that kind here, you could bet a million kwacha that—

The knock on the door is firm and businesslike, rattling the glass. The woman on the step gives him a cold smile when he opens it. Behind her stands a little blue car.

'Ah, hello, uh…' she checks a clipboard. 'Michael, isn't it? I'm Clare from social services. I've been sent to do a needs assessment for Edith Morley, who I understand self-discharged from St Luke's yesterday afternoon.'

Jonah's thoughts fly to ET in the bed upstairs. How long has he left her alone? Certainly all night and – Jesus have mercy! – the whole afternoon before that. She must be in need of food by now.

She must be thirsty. Surely he ought to have at least taken her one of those thick pink drinks they gave him the powders for at the hospital? Guilt punches him the chest. Then he looks at the visitor, who is craning her neck to see past him into the kitchen, and panic follows through. Who knows what the azungu laws will have to say about this kind of misdoing?

He holds up his hands, scrabbling on a smile. Oh yes, of course. How nice to meet her. Clare, did she say? He was hoping she – or someone like her (not her specifically, of course: he doesn't know her) – would come. Only, the thing is they haven't had time to get organised for visitors yet.

Clare narrows her eyes and tilts her head to look past him once more, taking in the piles of dirty pots and pans on the kitchen table. 'All the same, if I could just get in and take a look around… It won't take long. Miss Morley will hardly know I'm here.'

The steeliness that flashes beneath her politeness chills him. His brain whirs, mouth gabbling. He wishes that were possible, really he does. Only, the thing is, Miss Morley is asleep. He didn't say it at first because he was worried Clare might disapprove of the old lady being in bed so late in the morning. Sorry, sorry, sorry. But there it is. Miss Morley is tired out. She didn't get much rest in the hospital, what with all the beeping and buzzing, so now she is making up for lost time. She is exhausted after all the excitement of yesterday and the big meal when they got home to celebrate. So really, it would be best if she came back later.

Clare jerks her head and checks the clipboard again. 'Big meal? I thought she was on fluids and Pure-As only?'

Jonah swallows. Yes, of course. That was what he meant. Not a big meal. A big Pure-A. Sorry, sorry. His head is flustered. He, too, is a little – what is the English expression – knackered. Not dangerously so, of course. Not to the level of being incapable of caring for Miss Morley properly. It's simply that it has been a difficult few days. The family have been very demanding and—

Something gives in the woman's face. She smiles wearily. 'Oh yes, families can be the worst, can't they? Honestly, my workload would be half the size if I didn't have to deal with relatives.' Then she sighs and checks her watch. 'All right. You win. I'll come back on Monday. But you'll have to let me in then.'

Jonah nods enthusiastically. Monday. No problem! Of course.

He watches until she drives out of the gate. Then he goes inside and closes the door. Trembling with relief, he leans against the glass. That was lucky. That was blessed. Who was to say what might have happened if he had let that woman in to wander around the house, noting things down? Perhaps he would already have been on his way to the police station by now to answer charges of performing neglect on an old person or something similar.

He thinks of ET and his cheeks grow hot with shame. He ought to have taken better care of her. Even if he was awkward and embarrassed about doing things for her because back home the intimate side of looking after sick people was women's responsibility, he still should have made sure she was comfortable. At the very least he should have taken her a drink. His dismissive words of the previous evening echo in his ears – the self-serving things he had told himself about how there would be no issue with the old woman going without food for several days just so that he wouldn't have to go and see to her. In the morning light he feels ashamed of his callousness. It is one thing to starve out of necessity, but quite another to go hungry while only a few feet away there is a kitchen full of things to eat. And anyway, what if it isn't true? It could be that the old woman can't manage without eating regularly. In the hospital they had made much of sticking to a schedule and monitoring ET's intake to be sure she was getting enough nourishment. From what he had observed, it seemed conceivable that azungu stomachs were more delicate than he was used to. You only had to look at the amount of food with which they surrounded themselves. The hospital cafeteria had been stuffed full of choices – surely far more types of sandwiches and wraps and salads and soups and main options than the people coming through its doors could consume. And as for that boxing shop in the local town – Spar – well, its shelves were packed. On his first visit he had counted no fewer than twenty kinds of breakfast cereal jostling for his attention. Of course, he was familiar with the notion of similar foodstuffs being produced by rival makers. Back home you had Prestige Margarine and Blue Band; Carlsberg, Kuche Kuche, Chibuku Shake Shake and the occasional bottle of Nigerian Guinness brought by traders passing through. But that was nothing compared to the plethora of products available to the British shopper. It almost felt panicky – that massive spread of slightly different versions of the same thing stretching for aisle after aisle – as though people were afraid of what would happen if there wasn't enough to choose from or if supplies ran low even for a few hours. Maybe they had good reason to worry. Couldn't it be the case that generations of good living and regular meals had stripped British azungu of the ability to survive periods of deprivation? Perhaps if they didn't eat a variety of foodstuffs several times each day there was a serious risk they might die. Who knows? The next time that woman, Clare, appears, he may have a murder charge on his hands.

He bolts up the stairs, seizes the handle of ET's bedroom door and rushes in. The first thing that hits him is the smell. A fetid, sour stench that thickens the air. He hurries to the bed. She is lying where he left her, her head twisted towards the window and her right arm stretching out as though beckoning for something out of reach. Her eyes are closed and she is breathing. She is breathing! He groans in relief.

Her eyes flutter open. She regards him for a moment, her face warming up to a smile.

'Hello, darling,' she mumbles at length. 'Why don't you get in and join me? Father won't be back for hours.'

And with that, she pulls back the covers, revealing a brown stain spreading out from her trousers and releasing another wave of stink into the room.

Jonah gags and claps his hands to his mouth. But the urge to vomit is too strong and sends him hurtling along the corridor to the bathroom. There he bends over the toilet bowl, disgorging chewed-up bread, water and bile until his stomach aches.

When at last he straightens up, he catches sight of himself in the spotted mirror above the sink. His face is lean – the cheekbones straining against the skin, the jaw sharp. His eyes are red at the edges and oddly sunken, as though they are trying to retreat from examining the world too closely. He looks ill. He looks – the thought makes his heart thud – like one of the waganyu he used to see trudging the roads back home, petitioning plantation owners for day work in the hopes of earning enough to see them through until the next morning.

Is that what he has travelled all this way to become? A slave to circumstance? A pitiful creature forced to drift through his life, begging for menial tasks to help him accrue just enough money to keep him alive but never more than that – never anything that would allow him to save or plan or look further ahead than the next few days?

Anger collars him once more. No. He won't succumb to that. He will not be a fool. He will not stay here washing, feeding and clearing up the shit of this fortunate mzungu in her enormous house stuffed with possessions, this crumbling person who has probably never known an hour of real suffering. He will not waste another moment here doing woman's work while his life ticks away and opportunities flower and wither beyond his reach.

Blasting out of the bathroom, he charges down the stairs. He makes for the door that leads out of the kitchen, but as his fingers close on the handle, he turns and catches sight of the drawer at the end of the row of cabinets.

Yes. Why not? Why shouldn't he? Others would. Gilbert would. Roger, too. They wouldn't think twice. They would see it as an opportunity – something they would be foolish to ignore. Time and again life had kicked sand in his face. If he took the money, would he really be doing anything more than accepting a bit of good luck for a change? It is doing nothing here, sitting in that drawer. Why should the old woman have it when he needs it so much more? Besides, if she misses it, it would be nothing more than justice – a taste for her of the evil fortune that Jonah and his ilk have been facing their whole lives. OK, Amayi wouldn't like it if she knew. Neither would Abambo. They would say it was un-Christian. Not how God intended human beings to live in the world. But where had that kind of attitude got them? Amayi and Abambo are dead. They all are. The whole family. There is no one left to hold him to the standards of who he used to be. And as for God? Pah! A fairy story. A grown-up version of the yarns about ghost trucks and nfiti curses he and Gilbert used to scare Daniel with or the tales Grandma would tell about the days when the forest encircled the villages and ran its creepers through people's minds. A con – that was the point. A trick to scare gullible people into handing over money and living miserable lives without complaining, into dancing, cheering and beating drums while their children starved.

Well, fuck it, as he'd heard a man shambling past in the hospital spit into his mobile phone. That wouldn't be Jonah. Not any more. No more meekness. No more – what was it they said in the films? Ah yes – no more Mr Pleasant Guy. Yes. No more of him. Pleasantness only left you sitting stupidly in the corner, smiling while the focused people elbowed past to help themselves to the things that should be yours. It is time he became more like them, time he served himself a portion from the selfishness pot.

He runs to the drawer, drags it open and begins stuffing the money into the pockets of the green jacket with the brown ribbed fabric on the collar from the wardrobe upstairs. There are so many rolls of notes that it is a struggle to cram them all in. Still, he persists, snatching up every scrap. When at last it is done, he rattles the compartment closed and leaves the house for good.

He walks quickly, arms and legs jerking, driven by furious determination. Track. Road. Village. Soon he is through them all and out into the countryside beyond, passing a little arched bridge. Then comes another town – a bigger place, with buildings rearing up to the height of four or five storeys, multi-lane roads clogged with cars, and other parts where the pavement seems to spill across the whole street. In his bewilderment, he steps in front of a bus and receives a vicious horn blast that sends him staggering backwards just in time to avoid being decapitated by its side mirror. Panting, he dusts himself down, fighting a feeling of foolishness and an odd surge of tears. It is all right, he tells himself. It is all right. He will learn how this all works soon enough, and by this time next year he will be as British as they come, striding around London, hailing taxis and ordering cups of tea, a mobile phone clamped to his ear.

Speaking of which… across the road is a phone shop. Why not take the first step on the road to that vision now? He has done without that basic tool of civilised society long enough.

Checking carefully, he crosses the street and enters the bright, rectangular space. There is a chemical smell and a faint flickering among the white lights that makes him narrow his eyes. Around the walls are hundreds of rectangular phones in plastic cases. He scans the labels, looking for the most expensive. When he finds it, he goes to take it off the wall, only it is attached to the perforated backing by some sort of plastic wire and in attempting to yank it free he triggers an alarm. A woman hurries over, mouth smiling, eyes wide with concern, behind her a spindly man with owlish glasses who eyes Jonah's jeans, mismatched jacket and battered trainers.

The fuss renders him awkward and sullen, and he sits through the purchase process at one of the little tables in the middle of the room hardly saying a word. There is a bit of difficulty when the sales assistant wants to take his address, but the money soon smooths it over, and within twenty minutes or so they have settled a deal. The final number on the piece of paper makes his stomach contract. It is a massive sum. Bigger than Mount Mulanje. He daren't even attempt to convert it into kwacha, but he suspects that if he did it would be at least enough to buy Roger's family fertiliser for the next ten years. Guilt walks its fingers up his spine. Perhaps he ought to stop the purchase, say he's changed his mind and walk right out of there. What does he want with a phone like that, anyway? Who has he got to call? A cheap Chinese version will do well enough. There are places that sell such things. He has already seen several – little booths set into the shopfronts of other stores that remind him a bit of Gilbert's stall.

Yes. He should apologise, say he's changed his mind – let them think he's silly in the head if they must – and leave the shop. Such excesses as this are not for the likes of him.

But then he remembers the resolution he made in ET's kitchen to be more like the focused people, to look after number one. This is exactly the sort of weak thinking that runs counter to that. This is the insidious pleasantness he needs to force from his mind if he is ever to succeed, the same you-firstness that caused Abambo's death. Why shouldn't he have an expensive phone? Isn't he every bit as good as the azungu strolling up and down the pavement outside, stuffing their mouths with snacks and drinks, their eyes fixed on glowing screens? That woman there, rubbing the back of her hand across her mouth and wrinkling her nose like a snuffling pig – doesn't he deserve as much from life as she gets? What about that man eating crisps on the bright-red plastic bench shaped to look like lips in the square across the way – isn't Jonah his equal? And what about those teenagers with their baggy clothes and furtive glances at the girls walking by – underneath their designer labels aren't they just the same as he, Gilbert and Roger were in the days when they used to hang around God's Blessings barbershop trying to look cool?

The apology dies on his lips. He looks the sales assistant square in the eye and hands over the money – both delighted and appalled to find that it requires only a handful of notes peeled off one of the rolls secreted about his person to settle the account. She hands him the box that contains his new phone in a plastic bag, and he takes it like a real British customer – haughty and slightly bored-looking, as though he conducts these sorts of transactions every day of the week.

Once he is outside the shop, however, he cannot contain his eagerness. He rips through the packaging, liberating his purchase from a nest of cardboard and plastic ties that bite into his fingers when he tries to break them. There it is at last: his phone. Smooth, thin and gleaming, its screen protected with a layer of film. Quite the most beautiful thing he has ever seen. He is in love with it. Just wait until he calls Gilbert and tells him about it! Just wait until Daniel and Elijah—

Once again the memory descends on him. Once more, his heart contracts. He gasps and hunches in on himself. Eeeh! Eeh, eeh, eeh! When will his mind make the adjustment? Why must it keep attempting to carry on as normal, lumbering up again and again like a stupid person outnumbered in a fight, who fails to recognise that lying still and accepting the beating is the only sensible course?

He trembles as tears threaten and feels his throat shaping a moan. But no, he will not give in to his grief. Not here in this grey street with the crisp-packet man on the lips bench staring at him.

He looks again at the phone in his palm, seeking something in its sleek lines to sustain him. The solution comes at last: this costly piece of technology is a promise to himself, a down payment on his future. Although it is next to useless to him now, alone as he is, there will come a time when its contact book is full of the numbers of friends and associates. The fact that he has bought it proves that he has faith in himself and is determined to achieve his dreams. It shows he is a man of action who will not be beaten down by the cruel things that life has thrown at him. What was it Gilbert always used to say? That's the spirit.

'That's the spirit, brother,' Jonah whispers to himself, gripping the phone. As if in answer, its blank screen flickers on, drawing him into a bright world of wonders as the day fades, the shops close and the town empties itself of life.

# 0

It is dark when they wake him and he is lying on the lip-shaped bench in the square. The first he knows of it is a warm sensation and an unpleasant, fishy smell. He becomes aware that his face is wet and when he opens his eyes, he sees that a mzungu is leaning over him, with one hand on the back of the bench. The other is between the man's legs, holding what Jonah in his drowsy state takes for a piece of sausage, until another jet of liquid spurts from it, forcing him to clamp his eyes and mouth closed.

'What's the matter, you fucking monkey?' says the man, shaking the last drops from his penis and pushing it back into his trousers. 'Don't you like the taste of my piss?' He glances behind him. 'Come on, Rigsy. Your turn. Get him while he's still half asleep.'

Another figure in a white tracksuit lurches forward. Jonah holds up his hands in protest, letting fly a volley of Chichewa.

The first man regards him with disgust. 'And he's one of those foreign niggers too. A fucking scrounger. Not even home-grown.' He looks round. 'Come on, Rigs. What's keeping you?'

The figure in the tracksuit glances at Jonah. 'Nah, you're all right. I went before we left Spoons.'

'Pussy!' spits the first man. He looks back at Jonah. 'Enjoy that, did you, monkey? First wash you've had in a while, I'll bet. Maybe it'll teach you to piss off back to where you came from. Ha!' Then he yawns. 'All right, let's go and get a kebab.' And the pair stagger off in the direction of a road leading out of the square, where a streetlamp blinks in disbelief.

Jonah lurches up, retching, his mouth sour with the man's urine. He dashes to a water fountain and wrenches the handle, splashing handfuls of liquid over his head, spitting again and again. But it is no good, the smell remains: the man has wet his T-shirt and jacket too, soaking Jonah with his stench.

The next few hours are miserable. He spends them shivering, gagging and holding his breath, waiting outside a public toilet that a sign promises will be unlocked at 6 a.m. By the time an official arrives to open it, Jonah is slumped on the steps drifting in and out of sleep.

'It's all right, son, I'm not going to hit you,' says the man, reaching over and fitting a key into the lock as Jonah raises his hands to shield himself. 'Only, you shouldn't be here. Sleeping out's not allowed in this area. Council's orders. There's a homeless shelter two streets over. You ought to go and put your name down there.'

Jonah gets to his feet, squinting in the dawn light. 'Ah. Sorry, sir, sorry. I'm not homeless. I'm…' But then he can't think what he is, so instead of saying anything further, he nods at the man and pushes through the door. The toilet is dank and cold. There is a sour smell and the sound of dripping. But there is at least running water and synthetic-smelling soap in dispensers placed at intervals below a long, cracked mirror. He goes to one of the sinks and yanks off the jacket and T-shirt. He empties the pockets of the rolls of money, piling them on the side, and holds the garments under the cold tap for several minutes, before rubbing in handfuls of the lurid pink soap. He rinses and repeats, rinses and repeats, scrubbing the fabric until his fingers are sore and there can be no trace of the mzungu's urine on the clothes. Then he stands back and looks at his reflection.

The voice of the man with the keys drifts back to him: homeless. Is that what he has become? Blundering around like mad old Musaiwale, dependent on the charity of others.

And now comes the other voice, the harsh, cruel one from the middle of the night and those names it had spat at him: monkey, scrounger, nigger. Odd terms. Almost funny-sounding. That last one is something he'd heard now and then in the American rap music blaring from the T-shirt stall in the trading centre where Daniel hung around sometimes, trying to look tough. But in that white man's mouth last night it had taken on a different complexion. It had been ugly, filthy, slick with loathing. Though the man had been the disgusting one with what he did, it was Jonah who was left feeling dirty.

Monkey. He ran his hands up his scrawny chest, feeling his ribs jutting under his fingers like piano keys. Is that what they all think of him here? Is that what he is doomed to be? Is that what coming to this place of white people has made him? An object of hatred rather than a man. An animal. All skin?

A great loneliness rises up around him, like a wall. He pulls the phone out of his back pocket and stares at the bright screen. It is early morning there too, but he can't help himself. Though he is certain Gilbert won't answer, he plugs in the only number he knows. The international dialling tone sounds, low and haunting, like the horn of a big ship signalling its presence in darkness. He listens to it until it dies, picturing his former friend lifting himself from his sleep mat to check the number before tossing the phone aside. When it is finished he calls again. Then once more. He ought to leave it there, but instead he forges on, using the national code to dial other numbers at random. Sometimes the long ring tone goes unanswered. On other occasions, it clicks on to an answering service. But when he gets his first human response and hears Chichewa coming down the line, something cracks in Jonah and he gasps in relief. The sound of the familiar rhythms and cadences robs him of his own language so that he can do nothing but listen as the man speaks and waits, speaks and waits, becoming increasingly indignant until at last he ends the call. As the daylight strengthens outside, he leans against the hand-dryer and dials number after number, drinking in cascades of Chichewa, Shona, English, Lomwe, Yao and other tongues he cannot name. When at last his credit is spent, he drags on the soggy T-shirt and jacket. Emerging from the toilet, he feels hunger begin to stir once more. It has lain dormant in him since yesterday, but he knows from experience that it won't be long before it renews its assault, hollowing out his insides bit by bit.

He looks around for something to assuage it, but the town still seems to be asleep. There is only one place that shows any sign of activity – a grand building on the right-hand side that yesterday in his bewilderment he took for some sort of palace. Today the doors are open and figures are passing through them – mostly hunched old women who enter alone. Jonah frowns. What can the wealthy person who lives there want with all these wizened azungu? Surely he is far too important to concern himself with such humble individuals? Then he sees the cross. Sense drops into place. Of course: it is Sunday and the grand palace is a church.

Food forgotten for a moment, he walks towards it. It has been days since he tried to talk to God; months since he's really prayed. When the old woman took the silver cross, it was as though she relieved him of the last of his faith too. These days, on the rare occasions he tries to close his eyes and form an intention, he finds his mind roofed over. His thoughts hit a blank ceiling instead of zooming upwards into light as they'd always seemed to do during Pastor MacDonald's services back home. Perhaps here, in this impressive building, that channel might open again, allowing Father God to be a lamp to his feet once more.

He ventures into the gloom. Some sort of service is under way in the main part of the building – a priest in rich robes is extending his arms to a small number of kneeling figures. But Jonah is afraid of interrupting, and so he turns left and makes for another, smaller space beyond a wooden screen, where an altar is set up behind rows of burning candles. He sits down and tries to concentrate, but it is no good. There is no way he can find God here. The place is too solemn, too formal, too polite. The mzungu Jesus over the altar bows his head almost apologetically over the neat little trickle of blood streaking his side, as if embarrassed to have betrayed even that much of his physicality. Everywhere Jonah looks, there is cold stone and polished metal – precious things arranged forbiddingly, not to be touched. Nowhere does he see the joy and the passion that always swept him along in the lot behind the trading centre. This is not a place to feel your heart on fire.

And yet, beneath it all, there is something. Not the ebullient, powerful force he is used to, not the guiding voice, but a sense of expectation: a great ear listening, an eye watching, an active silence. Below the muttering and shuffling of the priest and the women, behind the cold marble and glittering forms, a being is observing him with a dispassionate eye. For a second, the camera swivels and it is as though he is looking through the being's lens at himself: a skinny, dirty figure leeching off others, a coward who left an old woman in need, stole her money and ran away.

He leaps up, alarmed, sending his chair clattering backwards. In the main part of the church heads turn, but now he doesn't care. He didn't come here for this. He came here for comfort, love and guidance – not to be scrutinised, stripped bare and coldly known. He is the one who has suffered. He is the one who has had everything taken from him. He is the one who must do everything he can to survive.

But still the ear listens and the eye watches until he can stand it no longer and he runs from there, upsetting a stand of leaflets in his haste. On the steps he bends with his hands on his knees as the images of the last twenty-four hours wheel about his mind: the phone shop, the drunk mzungu, the man with the keys. He screws up his eyes and tries to think. Hunger – that is the problem. It is hoeing furrows through his brain and sowing it with foolish thoughts. He knows its tricks of old. He just needs to eat something and all will be right again. That impression of the eye watching, the ear listening – that will recede, and he will be able to make sense of things once more. He will go to that café across the square where the man is setting out tables and buy—

And then he remembers: the rolls of money! He left them on the side in that public toilet! He bolts across the square, the loose sole of his right trainer slapping the paving stones. A man is just emerging from the entrance and Jonah barges past him, earning an 'Oi!' His eyes go to the countertop. It is not there. None of it. Not a single note.

When he walks out into the street the eye is watching him again, staring down from the clouds and up from the pavement and peering out at him from each of the windows above the shops opposite. Looking through it at himself once more, he sees what he has to do. He turns up the high street and begins to trudge back the way he came.

# 1

The first thing that hits him is the smell. The stench that had emanated from the soiled sheets in the bedroom has spread through the house, bringing with it a cloud of flies that assault him as he opens the door.

She is dead. She must be. He has left her too long. Two days, three days – it's too much for an old woman. A strong ache starts up in his chest, a compound of responses searing their way into him. Guilt – yes, that. Sorrow – indeed (for he had liked her, the weird old thing). But also – he can't deny it – relief that he won't have to assume responsibility for her again, that this cup has passed.

When the flies let up enough for him to look around, Jonah realises the reason for the stink. The place is smeared with faeces. There are brown streaks up the walls, on gaping cupboards and across the heaps of objects that have been tumbled on to the table and floor. One of the stove doors is open, revealing the charred remains of what seems to be a heap of clothing. And everywhere he turns there is disorder – spilt milk, half-opened tins, butter turning rancid. Each of them adding their own sour note to the air.

As he raises his hand to his nose and mouth to contain a gag, he notices something moving out in the hallway. Stepping towards it, over shards of crockery, mouldy pieces of bread and upended pans, he sees a small, hunched figure scoot past and into the eating room. For an instant he is back in Tripoli, creeping through rubble and pressing himself flat against the walls of ruined homes to escape the notice of the hard-faced children who dart through the streets clutching AK47s. He casts about for something to defend himself with, and his fingers find the handle of a heavy frying pan. Gripping this, he tiptoes towards the eating-room door, poised to strike.

Luckily, the clouds of the vision thin just enough for him to recognise his mistake. The scuttling figure is ET. For all that the doctors at the hospital said she may not walk again, she is walking now, albeit in a lopsided fashion, lurching and gripping pieces of furniture for support. She has changed her clothes, too – even if, his nose tells him, she hasn't washed – and is now fantastically attired in a clash of colours, as gaudy as a bird of paradise flower. Her chest is heaped with strings of beads – red, green, purple and pearl – through which flashes of gold and silver shimmer. Under this, a red and white-spotted dress with a heart-shaped neck line leaves much of her chest bare, revealing the tops of her shrunken breasts and the swirl of blue veins over her bones. Her legs are bare too, but on her feet are fluffy pink slippers that must have traipsed through the debris in the kitchen numerous times, for they are daubed with every hue.

ET giggles delightedly as he walks into the room, and lollops towards him. Taking the frying pan from him, as though it is a precious gift, she ushers him to a chair at the table and presses him to sit down. Four places have been set, each featuring a different arrangement of crockery, glasses and silverware. In front of Jonah, two plates jostle with a handful of forks and a teaspoon with a picture of a flower on its handle. To his right, a bowl contains an upturned wine glass, while anyone who sat at the end of the table would be greeted by three knives balanced in an oddly impressive pyramid formation over a small crystal bowl. Beside ET's place (three glasses standing guard around a small, silver dish containing salt), a pot brims with a rank-smelling stew. Picking it up proudly, ET rounds the table and attempts to spoon the concoction on to one of his plates. The stink is unbearable, and what Jonah glimpses in the pot – bits of bone, scraps of rag and clots of paper all swimming in a foul sauce – turns his stomach.

'No!' he protests, instinctively shooting out his hands and blocking the pot so that the noxious mixture slops down ET's dress.

Thunder gathers in the old woman's face. Her features crumple like those of a toddler brewing a tantrum. With a howl, she hurls the pot at the far wall, spattering the evil stew across the room. Then, grasping the skirt of her soiled dress, she lurches out, leaving Jonah sitting at the table with his head in his hands.

When at last he can bring himself to go and look for her, he experiences a profound shock. The house has been turned on its head. In every room, furniture has been upset and the boxes and stacks of papers – all those newspapers and unfinished letters – have been scattered every which way, ripped and trampled as though a monstrous rat has rampaged through the building, shredding its contents to make a nest. In the hallway, the grandfather clock lies on its side with its door open, eviscerated of its pendulum. And in the piano room clumps of cushion stuffing festoon the chairs and floor, while the ivory keys of the proud instrument in the bay window have been smeared brown, red and black. Upstairs it is even worse: every drawer has been emptied, every cupboard ransacked. The bathroom mirror is a spiderweb of cracks; the floor of the spare bedroom a sea of smashed ornaments. At the door of ET's room, Jonah pauses, wary of what he will find. He opens it slowly, braced for chaos and for the frenzied figure of the little woman, who he half expects to come flying out at him. But when he finally peers inside, things are not as he imagines: the room has barely been touched since he was last in it. Although the smell of excrement lingers, the bed has been made and the covers smoothed of wrinkles. The window is open and a light breeze is making the gauze curtain billow inwards above the low desk with the mirrors, upon which the bottles of make-up and perfume stand in their orderly rows.

Jonah is so surprised at the contrast between this room and the rest of the house that it only strikes him belatedly that he has not found ET. Turning in haste, as anxiety floods him again, his foot strikes an object lying on the floor. He looks down and sees that it is a small floral-patterned book. Initially he assumes it is the notebook he found when he first arrived, containing ET's list of instructions about her likes and dislikes, but on closer inspection he sees it is a finer piece of work than that: covered in cloth and bound like a real book. It is older, too. The pages are yellowed, and when he holds it close to his face he catches a scent that reminds him of the mouldering textbooks he used to share between three during his brief time at St Andrew's.

The spine is cracked, and the book falls open in his hand to reveal a block of writing scrawled in jagged capitals:

I hate him! I hate him! I hate him! I don't care if black people were forced into slavery and we have to be kind to them because of that. Maybe they deserved it. Maybe they aren't sensible enough to manage things on their own. Maybe they need white people to tell them what to do and that really is the best way to organise things. Oh, why does he have to be so cross and rude and make me feel so uncomfortable all the time?

A few pages earlier, he finds this:

I went out for a hack with Dobbin today, but before we were past the headland I remembered I'd forgotten my sandwiches, so I rode back to the house. He must have expected everyone would be out for a while, for he was in the kitchen, not in the barn, and when I came in he jerked round hurriedly as though he was doing something wrong and didn't want to be caught. The stove door was open, and he scrambled to push it shut but too late. I saw what he was doing: he was burning his uniform. The muddy green sleeve of the jacket stood out on the coals. When I said, 'You're burning your uniform,' he laughed. Said it was orders from the higher-ups on account of flying beneath the radar and throwing Jerry off the trail. But there was a guilty look about his eyes, like Jean got the time she wet herself and tried to pretend it was water from washing her hands. What can it mean?

And later in the book, the following paragraph catches his eye:

And if that wasn't bad enough, I have to contend with all these awful letters from Jean. Real stinkers. Spelt wrong and everything, like you'd expect. But that's not the worst of it. The way she goes on about this boy, this farmhand – Mallett. Anyone can tell by reading between the lines that he must be the most awful oaf. Anyone can tell that he's one of those with dirty fingernails who smells of manure and eats peas with his knife. But Jean doesn't see it. She just moons on and on about how handsome he is, how dreamy, how gallant. She uses lines from films about him as if I won't realise. 'It comes to you, this love of the land,' she wrote the other week, as if we hadn't all seen *Gone with the Wind*. She forgets we have a cinema in Totwith too. In her head it is like Somerset is the centre of the world and she is the only person ever to fall in love. Well, won't she get a surprise when everyone here is proved wrong and Michael comes back!

Sitting down on the end of the bed, Jonah turns to the first page of the little book and begins to read.

*

He doesn't understand it all. For one thing, the handwriting is too erratic to make out at certain points. It degenerates into scribbles when the writer gets agitated and some pages are almost scored through where the pencil has pressed too hard. Then there is the matter of the idioms and words he simply doesn't know, as well as the author's eccentric habit of breaking the rules and writing incomplete sentences without the correct quota of verbs, subjects and objects. Most puzzling. Jonah is sure Mr Mapanje would have given a very low mark for such careless composition.

The first three or four sides contain nothing but complaints about someone called Aunt Susan, who it seems has just arrived. Aunt Susan is nosey. Aunt Susan is jealous when it is just the writer and

Daddy. She doesn't like the two of them going off to do things together. She tells the writer that she (it is a she, he realises fairly early on from references to dresses and the unsuitableness of the writer's short hair) ought to be spending more time doing ladylike things rather than gallivanting off along the clifftops with 'that horse'. She over-boils the vegetables. She saves up things that the author has done wrong and repeats them to Daddy with a triumphant look in her eye. She makes the writer sing in the church choir and go to all the Sunday services while she stays at home lounging in bed. She thinks she can be another Mummy when there was only one of those. Her hair stinks of…

Bewildered, Jonah flicks through the pages, until his eyes light on a date: Tuesday the 14th of May 1940. So it is old, this notebook. He had suspected as much from the yellowed paper, except that odd modern words like 'wireless' had jumped out at him from the opening section, giving him the uneasy feeling that he might be reading something written much more recently and making him worry that the document might have been smuggled into the house by someone who had looked around, seen the mess and smelt the smell.

Tuesday the 14th of May 1940 – he calculates, running through numbers on his fingers. Almost seventy-five years ago. A generous lifetime. He stares at the page:

*Tuesday 14th May 1940*

Well, this is a turn up for the books! Who would have thought it? Today the BBC put out an appeal on the wireless for all owners of self-propelled pleasure craft measuring between 30′ and 100′ to register them with the Admiralty within fourteen days. '*Bessie's Delight* is one of those, isn't she?' I said, nearly swallowing my boiled egg down the wrong way, I was so surprised. 'Oughtn't we to let the Admiralty know about her?' You could see Father was thinking about it, but at that moment Aunt Susan leapt in, fluffing her hair in that hoity-toity way she has and declaring that what I'd said was ridiculous and there was no chance the Admiralty would be interested in an old wreck like Bessie. 'But didn't it say "order"?' I said. 'Doesn't that mean it's the law?' Aunt Susan rolled her eyes and told me with a pinched smile that some things were more complicated than they sounded and this was one of those things. But from the way she blushed under her powder, I could see that it wasn't complicated at all. It was very simple: she doesn't want Father sailing again after what happened with Mother. But it should be him who decides, and not her. One bad thing shouldn't spoil a whole life. Well, she has miscalculated, that flibbertigibbet (I heard them calling her that in Davison's when they didn't realise I was behind the tinned peaches). I have seen the posters. BRITAIN EXPECTS THAT YOU TOO, THIS DAY, WILL DO YOUR DUTY. That's what they say. I shall work on Father until he does the right thing. Don't think I won't do it, dear heart.

Dear heart. Suddenly he has it: the book is the work of ET. ET long ago. He recognises her in the writing, young and naïve though it is. There is a certain confidence and fearlessness that he saw in her before the hospital trip. A defiance, if that is the right word. A ribbon of steel running through the writings of this young person and on through the decades into the old woman he saw briefly, striding around the house, sitting at the piano, sturdy and resolute. This is ET's diary from when she was young, her story, written in her words. Tuesday the 14th of May 1940. Yes, that would be right. If ET is eighty-seven, as the doctors said at the hospital, she would have been a child back then. She would have been twelve. It is an odd thought, but he is holding ET's young life in his hands.

Intrigued, Jonah turns the page, only to meet with frustration. The next few sides are covered in a near-illegible scrawl bristling with exclamation marks. After this, the young ET seems to take a dive into fiction writing, for there is a long and wild account about a boat trip and soldiers and a coastline in flames and planes shooting.

He loses patience and skips forward until the word 'Michael' snags his eye. Struck by the appearance of the name ET sometimes calls him, he turns his attention to the entry dated the 6th of June 1940:

Today he told me his name: Michael. It was not what I'd expected. Not something heroic and dashing like Clarke or Cary, which I half imagined because of the American accent he sometimes does when he's putting me on. Michael. A solid name. An ordinary name. The sort of name that might belong to the postman or someone at school. And in a way I like it more for that. It feels real and rooted. It feels like an anchor holding him in place when he bobs about in one of his wild times. Somehow knowing it makes me less afraid that he will do something bad (not that I really think he would hurt me, only he gets so upset sometimes that it feels like all the rules are cancelled and everything could explode). And I am happy that he has trusted me with it, because it shows he sees me for who I really am. It makes me feel important and grown-up, which I am, if only certain people. Not that it matters, because I have got the better of her. I simply knot bedsheets together and climb down from my window, and she doesn't even know I've left the house, let alone suspect a thing about our visitor and the top-secret work going on in the barn. Sometimes it's all I can do to keep myself from laughing in her face.

Jonah chuckles to himself. So she was in love, then, young ET. And fully in the grip of physical passion, by the sound of things, scrambling out of her window on a rope of bedsheets to visit the object of her desire. For what else can the idiom 'putting her on' mean? Also 'top-secret work' – the significance of that is fairly obvious. It is strange that the man in question, this Michael, felt the need to use an American accent during the process, but Jonah has seen boys do many unusual things to impress the opposite sex. The first time he went with a girl, when he was ten or eleven, he had tried to seem experienced by looking serious the whole way through.

Afterwards he heard that she, Gloria, had assumed he was angry with her, and so never came near him again. Probably this young man, Michael, had been caught up in a similar idea.

All the same, he doesn't like what ET says about being afraid. There seems to be a hardness and unpredictability about this Michael that makes Jonah uneasy. The words she uses – that thing about the rules being cancelled – make him think again of the desperate strangers who used to come to the door during the food crisis before his family's own supplies ran out. Simpering and cringing, they would peddle all manner of stories while their eyes shot wolfishly to the storeroom door. Peering up at them from behind his father's shoulder, he had seen need – naked and ugly – in their faces and known with a shiver that if their bodies hadn't already been so wasted, these beggars would have had no hesitation in taking his family's supplies by force. It was not their fault, these walking skeletons with savage eyes. They did not want to inflict harm. It was simply that their ability to think of others' needs had wasted with their bodies to the limit of their own want.

This Michael man was not starving in the physical sense, as far as Jonah can tell, but there was a ravenousness about him. Something in him had been denied or blocked. The lack was perhaps not in his body so much as in his heart or mind. But it was there, all the same, making him dangerous because he was so bruised that he did not have the scope to consider that it lay within his power to cause another pain.

He flicks on, past the jagged entry in capitals; past the paragraph complaining about the letters from Jean (Jean, he notes, not Jeans – not like the trousers, after all); past a long, rambling account that is so riddled with scribbles and crossings-out that he can make nothing of it beyond the mention of a trip to London.

There is more furious writing about Aunt Susan – the pencil has scored through the paper in many places here. Then the book starts to race forward. Long gaps of time open up between entries, and there is nothing much of interest or sense to read, apart from a rather strange account of the time that two dogs started a fight above the house – Jonah can't imagine how. According to the notebook, ET went out into the yard to watch, even though her father advised against it – she was strong-headed, this English girl. But then a plane dropped like a plum out of the sky into the sea, leaving a parachute drifting down to the ditch beyond the top field. ET had run to meet it, her heart beating as loud as thunder. Even though she knew Michael wasn't a pilot and it took years for people to train for such roles, she was certain she would find him there. She thought it would be just like him to make such a grand reappearance. As she came around the hedgerow and caught sight of the silk canopy and ropes splayed on the ground that reminded her of one of the jellyfish that sometimes washed up down in the cove, she felt hope expanding her chest, stretching her until she thought she might burst with the effort to contain the possibility of all that might be about to happen. His smile. His fingers on her cheek. Some witty remark. 'Hey, kiddo. Fancy seeing you here. What are the chances?'

But she was wrong, of course. When she got to the ditch, Michael was nowhere to be seen. And the thing at the end of the parachute thrown down by the dogs… Well, it was not a man – not a body, even – but a charred lump, an object that lurked on the fringes of her vision for weeks afterwards and dragged itself through her dreams.

At last the book runs out of words. Jonah is on the point of closing it and laying it aside when he turns a final page and finds himself confronted by what seems to be a different, more mature hand, inked instead of pencilled. At first he thinks that someone else must have taken over – maybe this is the work of the mysterious Aunt Susan? But when he peers at the lines he sees that there are traces of twelve-year-old ET's script among the letters: the tails on the ys are the same, and each word still ends with an upwards swoop, as though its author is tired of writing it and impatient to get away. The date heading up the block of text supports the impression that this entry is also ET's work: it was written in 1945, a whole five years after the previous set of sections, when ET would have been – what? – seventeen.

*Tuesday 8th May 1945*

Funny to find this old thing tucked at the back of the wardrobe. I was looking for my red slingbacks and there it was, hiding behind the shoebox. I'm so distracted today that at first I couldn't for the life of me remember what this notebook was. But then I opened it and read through some of the entries and it all came flooding back – the excitement of that summer, how caught up I was in Michael hiding out in the barn. I was so hopeful then. So certain we would be friends for ever. Sad, really. I'm not much older now – some people would say I'm still a child (Aunt Susan certainly would if she hadn't run off with the haberdasher in Totwith) – and yet I feel as though I've aged centuries since I wrote those things. I'm certainly nowhere as naïve as I was then. If I ran into another Michael now, I'd spot him a mile off and know him for what he was: a chancer, a good-for-nothing, someone liable to say and do whatever was required to get what he wanted, a person who promises to keep in touch and then goes back on his word.

Thinking about it now, it's probably for the best. Although I was too young to realise it at the time, he put us at risk by doing what he did. Father could have got six months in prison for harbouring a deserter if anyone had found out. Because that's what he was, of course. A deserter. Not a spy or a war hero sent to watch over us. A common criminal. So yes, it's best he never came back to hear me play that wretched piano. Even if it did mean that waiting and hoping made the dreary last few years, well, bloody terrible, if I'm honest, we're well shot of him.

And now, with the end of the war and a new peace beckoning, it's time to look to the future, to think of 'the toil and efforts that lie ahead', as Mr Churchill said in his speech on the wireless today. Which brings me to the reason I was looking for the shoes. There's a VE Day dance at the village hall. Normally I wouldn't get excited about such things. I've never been much of a one for all that spinning and contorting to music – it beats me how people can remember the steps. Left to myself, I probably wouldn't go.

Only I'm not left to myself these days. I haven't been for a while. And this morning, as I was coming in from mucking out Dobbin, I bumped into him – Roger – walking down the hallway in a shirt and tie. Though it was early, the smell of cigar smoke curled out of the drawing room and, through the open door, I saw Father's foot jutting out from where he was sitting on the chaise longue. That was when I knew: tonight, Roger Allen is going to ask me the question.

I suppose I ought to feel excited. If I were one of the girls down in the village, I'd no doubt be running about the house staining my legs with tea and setting my hair in victory rolls. But the truth is I mostly feel nothing at all. I will say yes, of course. Roger is a decent sort of man. Polite. Tall. And if he can be a little awkward and does have a nasty habit of sucking his peas off the end of his knife, he is thoughtful. When we go to the Totwith Odeon, he always buys me popcorn from the Butterkist machine without me having to ask. Also, he has a steady job. Although it might not set the world on fire, being a postman is not to be sniffed at. What most people don't seem to realise amidst all the VE Day excitement is that it's not all going to be plain sailing from now on. There will be lots of men coming back from the war looking for employment and precious few openings for them. A guaranteed income from a reputable employer – that's a serious advantage. Of course, it's not romantic. It's not like Humphrey Bogart and Lauren Bacall in *To Have and Have Not*. But I've never been one to think that life ought to be the same as in the pictures. I'm not like Jean with her mooning descriptions of that farmhand, Mallett, filled with phrases straight off the silver screen. Being sensible, that's the thing. Being realistic. Applying the same logic Father uses when he goes to look at a new milking machine: does it work, and will it be useful? By that reckoning, the answer as far as Roger is concerned is absolutely yes. And I ought to pull myself together and stop sitting here wasting time and go and get ready for him to pick me up.

None of this makes much sense to Jonah, and the next entry does little to clear up his confusion. In fact, it is barely legible:

He came back! So happy I can hardly breathe! Will write the full story later but for now oh my God I feel as though I could fly!

Then a few lines later, there is this:

*Saturday 12th May 1945*

I said before that I felt centuries older than when I wrote the entries at the start of this book, but I have aged a million years since then. And not in a bad way. Blossomed. Grown. To think it was only four days ago that I wrote all that nonsense – all that stuff about love being like buying a new milking machine and real life being nothing like the pictures. What rot! It is exactly like the pictures. It is every bit as good. Better! And those who don't know that are just children or half asleep.

But before I get carried away and waste all the time that Michael's in the bath writing about how wonderful I feel, I want to set how it happened down – every last instant of it – so that when I am an old lady I can look back and remember it exactly as it was.

We went to the dance, Roger and I. He picked me up just after seven o'clock. Oh God, he was wearing this awful blazer – striped pink and white like a stick of rock – that he clearly thought made him look the bee's knees. I had to spend the whole of the walk there trying to ignore it and attempting to convince myself that it probably was fashionable in certain circles, and if I didn't like it, it was down to my bad taste. (Crumbs – I was an idiot, wasn't I? Just imagine if Michael hadn't turned up and Roger had asked the question and I'd said yes! It doesn't bear thinking about.)

There were all there, all the usual gang – Dolly, Sissy, Mags and Sue. All tricked out in their VE Day finest – peep toes and lipstick and the predictable victory rolls. Mags had even used an eyeliner to draw seams up the back of her legs to make it look as though she was wearing nylons, but the lines weren't straight, and besides, it was mentioned as one of the thrift tips in a free copy of *Woman's Weekly* that came through the door only last month, so she wasn't fooling anybody.

The hall was tricked out, too – all bunting and streamers. Cakes everywhere you turned. Little Mary Beasley serving everyone punch. As we walked in I caught the odd snide expression and saw them whispering among themselves about how some people might have helped more. I didn't care. I was too nervous thinking about what the evening held and trying not to wince at Roger squeezing my arm. (Oh, I can't keep from giggling now. I had no idea, did I? No idea at all.)

When the band struck up, Roger pulled me on to the dance floor and started doing an awkward jitterbug, all elbows and knees. You could tell he'd been practising, for his tongue poked out between his lips in concentration as he moved. When I saw that, it somehow made me awfully sad, and a terrible urge came over me to run out of the hall there and then. I forced myself to make the best of it, however, and gamely jived along. A slower number came next, and that was better. And when Roger smiled at me, I began to think that perhaps we could find a way to be happy together after all.

But then, just as the band was making a start on 'Boogie Woogie Bugle Boy', the hall door banged open. The band stopped playing and everybody's heads turned to see the figure standing there, like a scene in a John Wayne film.

At first I didn't recognise him. With the sunset behind him he might have been anybody. But then he sniffed and rolled his shoulders and I knew. I couldn't help myself. 'Michael!' I called out.

He turned to look at me in that lazy way he has. 'Well, hey there, kiddo,' he said, and then I saw him do a double-take and it seemed to jerk my heart on a string.

He walked towards me as people turned back to their conversations and the band picked up the threads. I could feel Roger tugging at my arm, trying to pull me away, but I couldn't give two hoots. I could only stand there and watch him walking across the floor towards me. The hall seemed to empty and there was no room for anything else.

He gave a low whistle as he reached me. 'Well, well,' he said. 'Someone grew up.'

Jonah grits his teeth. He knows this tone. He has seen it employed on his few visits to Mangochi by the traders who hang around the beaches and bars, keen to capitalise on the azungu women who come to the place to sample a bit of local sugar – as Gilbert would call it – and aren't afraid to spend money in the process. It is throwaway talk. It means nothing. 'Step away from him, ET!' he wants to shout. 'Remember what you wrote about life not being like a picture. Go off with Roger and answer your question and live your slightly happy life! This man is no good.'

But of course the ET of seventy years previously can't hear, locked behind the wall of already-been.

We stood there talking. I don't know how long. I don't know what we said. I could only look at him, at his gold-green eyes and the Michael that lived inside them, and burn with gladness. All the years of waiting melted away and I found none of it mattered any more – not the long dreary afternoons staring out to sea, not the dead hours, not the questions. Because he was here. Michael was here. And that answered everything.

Of course, Roger didn't like it one bit. When tugging at my arm didn't work, he put his hand round my shoulders in an effort to steer me away. That was when Michael told him to sling his hook.

It didn't go down well. Roger started spluttering. Then he shoved me aside and strutted up to Michael so that their faces were only a few inches apart. 'Now look here, I'll have none of your lip!' he shouted in a queer, plummy voice, as though some old-fashioned aristocrat had taken over his head and was speaking through his mouth. 'You barge in here, taking over, muscling in. Well, I won't stand for it. You might be in the army or whatever else, but you don't scare me. You don't cycle a ten-mile post round six days a week without learning a thing or two about how to look after yourself, let me tell you.'

And I know it was awful of me, but he looked so ridiculous standing there with his furious red face and jutting chin and talking in that odd, pinched voice that I couldn't help myself. I started to laugh. Michael, too. Both of us doubled over like a pair of schoolchildren.

Well, you can imagine how that went down. 'Yes, that's right!' shouted Roger, so loudly that the band stopped playing once again. 'You people think you can march in here and have it all your own way. Well, it doesn't work like that. It's not one rule for you and another for everyone else. You've got to wait your turn. And the sooner people like you learn that, the better for everyone concerned.'

There was silence. Michael rolled his shoulders. 'People like what?'

Roger took a deep breath. And I saw it coming before he said it. That appalling dog's name rushing up his throat. And I couldn't bear it, the thought of hearing it, the thought of seeing that slur applied to my Michael.

'Don't!' I cried.

But too late. Roger's lips were already forming the word: 'Niggers.'

Jonah stares at the page. For a second he seems to see face of the man from the town square rearing up through it, mouth contorted into a snarl. Then the image fades and ET's writing takes its place once more.

I looked around at them all standing there, Dolly, Sissy, Mags and Sue, all listening, clutching their glasses of punch and fingering their victory curls, approval glinting in their eyes. And that was when I realised: they saw nothing wrong in what was happening. They thought such labels were part of life. They didn't recognise how a word like that squashes everybody.

I couldn't stand to be there a moment longer. 'How dare you!' I shouted. It was directed at Roger, but I meant it for all of them, really, all of those smug, satisfied sods. But it didn't hit home. They looked back at me with a strange kind of fascination, as though I were a horse that had just started walking around on its hind legs. A curiosity that had no bearing on their lives. Another species. I saw then that it would always be that way: them cosy in their certainties and me shut outside.

'Come on,' I said, seizing Michael's wrist. 'Let's get out of here.'

In spite of himself, Jonah can't help smiling when he reads this. His pleasure doesn't last long, however, for the following pages contain a description of what followed – the long walk ET and Michael took that night over the cliffs and the obviously made-up story he told her about his reasons for going away and not contacting her. Apparently it had nothing with her father being angry about the trip to London. Instead it was because, quite out of the blue, Aunt Susan had fallen in love with him and tried to persuade him to run away with her. Given what happened with the haberdasher, this made perfect sense to ET. For her part, she told him about the years of waiting and her time at the piano and how horrible everyone in the village was (this last point had only occurred to her that evening, but she saw now that it was entirely right). Finally, as it started to get light, they came back to the farm. And as the first rays of morning broke on the horizon, something happened in the hayloft of that storeroom-barn that hurt ET but also made her proud and glad, although precisely what this process involved is unclear, as the language here in the book becomes so idiomatic and strange that Jonah can barely make sense of it at all. He supposes it might be some sort of azungu betrothal rite. He hopes that is the case after ET so recklessly passed up her opportunity of a comfortable life with the postman. This is never confirmed, however, for there is only one entry left in the book – a sad, undated little cluster of words:

They came to arrest him. They took him away in a van. It was that bastard postman who tipped them off. It had to be. The whole village was watching as they drove him down the track – the vicar, the women from church, Jean. After everyone had gone I went up to the hayloft and cried and cried. I shall never—

A banging jerks him away from ET's words so abruptly that for a moment Jonah cannot remember where he is. Time swirls around him – now, then, here, there, home, away, past, present. Bewildered, he staggers to his feet and goes to the window. He sees the track and the storeroom and the yard, where a little blue car is parked. In front of it, stepping back to peer up at the house, is a mzungu woman holding a clipboard – the official from that services organisation, Clare.

Horrified, Jonah steps behind the curtain, hoping he hasn't been seen. His first thought is that he won't open the door, in the hope the woman goes away, but when he peeps down once more he sees her heading back to the kitchen door and trying to peer through the glass. It will surely only be a matter of time before she tries the handle, discovers it is unlocked and ventures in.

The thought of her walking through the filthy house as he gabbles excuses is terrifying.

Heart pounding, Jonah runs down the stairs.

'Hello!' he cries, anxiety making his voice oddly jolly as he opens the door and pulls it hurriedly closed behind him to prevent Clare seeing the mess inside. 'Well, isn't this a lovely surprise!'

The woman frowns and checks her clipboard. 'I don't see why it should be a surprise, uh, Michael,' she says. 'We arranged that I would come back on Monday to perform the needs assessment for Miss Morley, and it's Monday. Here I am.'

'Ha!' he bellows, beaming as though the mzungu woman has made a hilarious joke. 'Of course!'

She looks at the door. 'Well, then. Can I come in?'

Jonah smacks a hand to his forehead. 'Eeeh! That's just the thing, you see. It's difficult.'

Clare frowns. 'Difficult how?'

'Difficult in the sense of problematic. Complicated.'

Clare rolls her eyes. 'I know what difficult means. I'm asking for the reason.'

Jonah claps his hands, grasping for words. 'The reason. Yes. Well. You see, the problem is Miss Morley is not available at the moment.'

'Not available?' She takes a step towards Jonah. Even though she is half a head shorter than him and he is standing on the step, she manages to be menacing.

'Yes, not available.' And all of a sudden it hits him, the awful truth that his confusion and the diary have made him forget: he doesn't know where ET is. He couldn't take the woman to her even if he wanted to.

'Well, that's all right,' says Clare, coming closer still. 'I don't need her present to perform the assessment. We normally do them before the patient comes home.'

Jonah waves his hands as panic thickens the air so that he has the sensation he is suffocating. His mind flails.

'It's not possible.'

'Not possible?'

He pinches the skin between his eyebrows, as if by doing so he can keep the English words from falling out of his mind. 'I mean, not necessary.'

'What do you mean, not necessary?'

Slavishly, his mind reaches for the definition – but of course this is not what she wants. His mouth, however, keeps speaking, and he listens – half-fascinated, half-appalled by what it might say. 'She's not here.'

The woman jerks and looks insulted. 'Not here?'

His head is fogged with alarm, but his mouth talks on, all those hours sitting around swapping stories down at the trading centre finally starting to pay off. 'That's right. She's back in the hospital. There has been another...' – what was the word that mzungu doctor used? – '...episode.'

The woman glances at her clipboard. 'It doesn't say anything here about—'

'That's because it's a very new thing. The ambulance left only half an hour ago.' He nods, confidence building. 'So I'm very sorry, madam, but we won't be needing your sociable services today.'

The woman blinks and flicks on a smile, and it is as though a different personality has dropped into her head. 'Well, of course. It's the last thing you want to be bothered with. Oh, I am sorry to hear that. I'll contact the office and get them to update the file.'

And so saying, she walks to her car and gets in. Starting the engine, she gives him a cheery wave. He returns it and watches until the little blue vehicle pulls out of the gate and away down the track. Then his gaze swings to the door creaking back and forth in the breeze across the yard. The words from the notebook drift into his mind and, all at once, he knows where ET is.

He goes to the storeroom, or barn, as she called it in her writing. The ground floor contains nothing except the few bales he used to sleep on and the wisps of straw stirring on the floor. Doubt flutters at him. Perhaps he is wrong after all?

Then he glances up. Through the gaps between the boards of the platform – the hayloft, as ET called it – he sees her: a small form curled by the edge of a jagged hole. His stomach lurches. But he knows what he must do. And though it makes him tremble, he goes to what's left of the ladder and climbs its remaining rungs. When he reaches the top and steps on to the platform, the barn seems to sigh. Through the cracks and gaps, the floor lies far below him, its cobblestones tiny – much further down than he imagined. He feels as though he is higher than he has ever been, anywhere in the world. It gets worse when he starts to move towards ET. The boards moan and creak, and there is a sagging feeling underfoot. He is certain that if he ventures more than another metre he will crash through the rotten wood.

He pauses and takes a deep breath, trying to still his shaking and find the focus to think. His mind presents all sorts of outlandish solutions – ropes, pulleys, phone calls to the village, piling up a heap of the soiled bedding and cushions from the house on the floor below, waking ET and coaxing her to walk back to the ladder by herself – but he rejects them all. Too risky, too time-consuming, too liable to create other problems. He has to generate the solution by himself.

Finally, he knows what he will do. There is a thick beam running all the way from one end of the barn to the other. It passes under the middle of the platform, showing through in the patches where the boards have splintered away. If he edges along this, it ought to bear his weight, and he should be able to get close enough to ET to lift her.

He sets out along it towards the slumbering woman, placing one foot in front of the other, keeping rigidly to the line of the beam. He takes it slowly, pressing down the thin, cracked soles of his trainers once, twice, three times before he commits his weight to each step; listening intently for the faintest creak. His breathing sounds like gale-force gusts in his ears, and he assumes the workmen in the adjacent field have begun hammering something before he realises he is listening to the thudding of his own pulse.

At last, he is level with ET. He crouches down and stretches out his arms. But it is no good – he can barely touch her with his fingertips. He will have to venture on to the boards. Shuddering, he edges forward, sliding his feet. Is it his imagination, or are the boards beneath him bending? Is that ticking the start of a splintering sound? He tries to keep these questions at bay, but when he reaches ET panic overwhelms him, and he bends quickly to snatch her up and bear them both back to the relative safety of the beam. She starts awake at his touch, and he hears a crack. Now he has another fear: that in her alarm she will jerk backwards and tumble down the hole behind her on to the stone floor.

'It's all right, ET, it's all right,' he says, trying for a reassuring tone when all he wants to do is scream. 'It's me, Michael. There's no reason to be afraid.'

She looks up at him, her cheeks stained with streaks of salt, her lashes clotted with dried tears. He feels the moment sway with the floor beneath them, everything dependent on whether the rafters of her thought processes will hold under the weight he is asking them to bear.

She watches him a moment. Then her face creases into a smile.

'Hello, darling,' she says, and holds out her arms for him to scoop her up.

He does not allow himself to think until he has borne her down the last rung of the ladder and is standing on the floor. When he looks up he nearly vomits. The platform is as flimsy as an orange crate. What's more, between the space where ET was lying and the central beam, he spots the blond zigzag of a fresh fracture. He quivers so violently at that that he almost drops the old woman.

Luckily, she remains oblivious to his distress. Reaching up to stroke his cheek, she offers him a toothy grin. 'Come on, dear one, won't you take me to bed?'

And so, carrying her into the house and up the stairs, he takes her to the dishevelled but clean spare-room bed and tucks her in. Then he goes next door and starts to clear up, stripping the filthy sheets from her bed. As he lifts the pillows, a shiny object slides out and slithers to the floor. It is the silver cross.

# 2

It is not easy looking after another person's body. Washing and dressing them. Wiping away saliva and shit. Anticipating the needs that will become urgent. Feeding them and cleaning up the results. Dealing with the body's products and the filth that flocks to it, accumulating in folds and wrinkles, and trapping itself between teeth.

Neither is it easy being another person's keeper. Monitoring their movements. Accommodating their habits, frustrations and their flights of fancy. Seeking always the line between asking too much and expecting too little, both of which lead to fury and tears.

This is what Jonah learns in his first days back at Cliff's Edge – long days where hours drift as he follows ET's tottering figure from room to room, holding half-finished drinks, spoonfuls of food, items of clothing and towels. At first the intimacy of what he has to do shocks him. It is improper for a man to handle the flesh of a female who is not his wife – officially, at least, and certainly in the manner in which ET's care requires. Also – though he struggles to admit it – her body shocks him. It is less wizened and weathered than her hands and face, retaining more of the memory of its youthful lines and curves. Breasts still jut from its ribcage and the mound at the base of its belly protrudes defiantly under its cloud of hair, as though hinting that its possibilities are not quite exhausted.

These things make Jonah uncomfortable. He had expected to find the old lady's naked body alien and repulsive; instead, it is closer to a young woman's form than he would like. As a result, he starts out tentatively, leaving her alone in the bathroom with sinkfuls of warm water and bundles of clothes in the hopes that she will be able to attend to these private matters for herself. But after he shuts her in the lavatory only to come back ten minutes later to the sight of her standing in a puddle, chattering at the toilet as though it is a friend who has come to visit, he realises he will have to be more hands-on. With the help of the notebook of instructions – which he finds stuffed in the door of the fridge – he sets to work tending to ET's needs as best he can.

Often she doesn't appreciate it. There are times when she slaps at his hands and screams in his face and runs off along the corridor from the bathroom, pale buttocks twinkling. Once, after he leaves her in the bedroom while he runs the bath, he has to sprint down to the yard and wrestle her naked form into a towel under the amused eyes of the workmen, who are beginning to lay lines of bricks in the field across the track. On that occasion, she scratches him, raking a line down his cheek. Thereafter he makes a point of coming at her with the nail clippers before attempting anything more ambitious than a flannel to her face and neck.

While it is rare that looking after ET becomes a physical battle, the mental toll and the relentlessness of the task is wearing. She approaches him with objects – tea towels, jewellery boxes, items of clothing – and an expectant look. If he does not take them and use them as she sees fit, her face crumples and she lets out a wail, sometimes slumping to the floor and beating the boards with her fists as he has seen small children do. After that, she can be inconsolable for several hours.

When the item with which she presents him is a letter or a newspaper, things are easier, initially. He has grasped that she generally intends him to read the document aloud, while she nods sagely, staring into space. The problem comes when he has done so several times and tries to stop. That often heralds the start of a fury that can only be assuaged by several of the yellow, custardy biscuits he keeps finding in packets stashed in odd drawers and cupboards.

The house is equally grudging in the face of his attempts to care for it. Though he lavishes hours on picking up the scattered letters and newspapers, sweeping up dust balls, scrubbing the foul stew and faeces from the walls and floor, and running damp cloths along grimy surfaces, it shows little evidence of his attentions. It retains its musty smell. Stains linger. Cobwebs redraw themselves minutes after he removes them. And though he does his best to arrange the contents of the drawers and shelves as neatly as possible, he can't shake the suspicion that he is merely reordering the mess. He frequently feels overwhelmed by the sheer volume of things in the place, and spends many an hour muttering long monologues in Chichewa about the azungu obsession with belongings. There are times when it seems the place is deliberately trying to frustrate his efforts. Cupboards burst open, spewing a welter of objects. Handles snap. Windows unlatch themselves and crash wide, admitting gusts of rain, leaves and, once, a small brown-and-grey bird, which flew round and round the piano room, speckling the furniture with white.

When health officials come he admits them, watching nervously from the doorway for signs that they have found something amiss. He does his best to smile, answer their questions correctly and accommodate their suggestions, but it is a frightful effort that invariably sees him slumping trembling on to one of the chairs at the kitchen table after they're gone. Luckily the visits rarely last long: ET seems to like these intruders as little as he does, and usually kicks up a tantrum when they try to touch her, so that they hurry through the queries on their forms and back out to their cars without ever looking Jonah in the eye.

For all that, though, there are moments of calm. Times when ET smiles up at him with a warmth that makes him certain she understands something of the efforts he is making; hours when they sit together in the piano room, watching the light shift out at sea while he fumbles his way through Hattie's tunes at the keyboard. On these occasions he feels he knows her. He sees how it must have been to sit alone in this house year after year, and that a life of unchosen silence and solitude contains its own kind of pain, regardless of how comfortable its trappings might be. And while he can go a day without being able to pick an intelligible word out of her slurred mutterings, there are points at which he seems to glimpse the meaning beneath them, as well as other moments when, with startling clarity, she pronounces something so emphatically that it is impossible she can't intend some sense by it. One afternoon, the television flares into life of its own accord, delivering the sight of a babbling, purple cartoon bird into the room. 'What a load of poppycock!' she blurts in her old, confident tones. They look at each other in surprise and laugh. He doesn't know what the phrase means or how much she understands of the oddness of what has just happened, or indeed whether her chuckles are merely an automatic reaction to an unexpected event – something wired in below the level of conscious thought – but it doesn't matter. For those few minutes, the two of them are united in their mirth, relishing the joy of laughter's release.

Another time, when he is helping her in the bath, kneeling by the tub and soaping her with the loofah, she grips his wrist and looks up into his eyes.

'You were in a war, weren't you?' she says, staring up at him intently.

He returns her gaze, searching her face for the key to her words. Her eyes gleam with a strange kind of intelligence. Is she back in the present? Could she possibly be trying to talk to him, Jonah, rather than Michael or some other figure superimposed on his body by her wandering mind?

He opens his mouth to correct her, to say that his homeland is a tranquil place, that conflict was not why he left. But then he considers. In a way, it had been war. Not a war with guns. Not the pure violence that rampaged through Tripoli, smashing buildings and laying waste to businesses, exploding lives in showers of gristle, blood and bone. But a battle, nevertheless. A struggle against seeing your future trickle away like maize grains from a rotten sack, against having your energy, ease, fun and fire diminished – choked by injustices and misfortunes, but smothered most of all by those who came with their cavalcades blasting reggae and their cracked keyboards and upside-down maps to decide what you ought to be, where you ought to stay, to put boundaries on your imagination and tell you that you were small and helpless, incapable of doing without their clumsy, self-serving intervention, doomed for ever to live a broken, piecemeal life.

He nods, sniffing as a tear drops from his cheek into the bathwater. Yes, it has been a war. A bitter, remorseless fight to the death. Really, it is a miracle he has survived.

He presses his hands to his face and in the darkness of his sightlessness it comes to him once more: the vision of Amanuel's eyes as they grabbed him and hauled him back on to the boat, the way the boy had searched for a glimpse of Jonah bobbing beyond the reach of the torch beams. Sobs shake him. Only this time he is crying not from guilt, but from sadness. For the pity of it. For the cruel circumstances that put them there and the irresistible forces that obliged him to twist himself into the shape of a person who would abandon his friend.

When he opens his eyes, ET pats the back of his hand clumsily and reaches up to claw away his tears. 'War does hurt,' she says.

As the days pass, Jonah feels increasingly protective of his charge. When a woman from the hospital comes and wants to spend time moving ET's arms and legs, he can't help feeling secretly triumphant when she spits in the visitor's face. He knows that the treatment is for the best, that it will make ET sturdier on her feet and help her regain more independence. All the same, he can see how the professional's brisk manner must appear through ET's eyes – how frightening it must be to be approached and gripped by this stranger with her quick eyes, muscular hands and comments about traffic on the M20.

And when the visitor starts to ask questions, Jonah becomes irritated. None of the inquiries are quite right. They simultaneously make too much and too little of ET's needs. Though she is surprising them all with her quick return to walking, her mind is still fogged, the occasional fitting sentence notwithstanding. And yet, given patience and space, she can often work out more than you'd think. Many's the time he's spent ages looking for something only to turn and find her standing next to him holding it out. She doesn't deserve the slow, yet faintly impatient tone the woman uses to address her. She needs understanding and patience, not tickboxes and forms; kind people around her who accept what she is able to offer, rather than seeming perpetually poised to catch her out. He can't help thinking that the guarded look in ET's eyes owes more to annoyance than it does to confusion, to irritation at the failure of her fellow human beings to appreciate that often compassion consists in meeting someone in their reality rather than insisting on dragging them into yours.

Perhaps this is the reason that, when Jean appears later that day, Jonah lies. He is sitting at the piano, absent-mindedly running his fingers over the keys during ET's nap, when he hears the car pull into the yard. By the time he comes through to the kitchen, Jean is on the threshold.

'Coo— Oh. There you are.' She looks around the room. 'Having a clear out, I see. Very sensible. It will make things easier… later on.'

He follows her gaze. He is not clearing out. This is how the kitchen is these days – the pots and plates piled on the surfaces wherever he can find space, alongside ET's tins and the odd other things he brings back from the Spar shop, seduced by bright packaging or the impression that a product is like something he remembers from home, usually to be disappointed. Perhaps it is not as neat as it could be, but at least he knows where everything is and can reach it easily in the event of an emergency. And it's not as though ET minds. Occasionally he comes in to find her standing at one of the counters murmuring to herself as she runs her hands over the assorted objects, but there is always a friendly tone to her voice, even when the words are out of reach. He never gets the sense that she is troubled by where things are.

Still, he nods at Jean. Let her think what she likes about the state of the house.

'And how is she?' says Jean, in the quivering voice she always uses to talk about ET's well-being.

The truth is, ET has been tired and fractious since the woman from the hospital left. She threw her bowl of Ambrosia on the floor at lunchtime, spattering yellow goo all over the piano-room rug, and when he tried to take her to the lavatory later she refused to respond to his suggestion that she ought to sit down and instead urinated where she stood, glaring furiously at him all the while.

Still, he is loath to confess all this to Jean. It would feel like a betrayal, particularly after he gave away so much in response to the hospital woman's cold, practical questions.

So instead, he smiles and says: 'Very well. Better every day. There was a woman here earlier from the hospital, and she was amazed by the progress.'

'Oh good!' exclaims Jean, clasping her hands under the knot of her headscarf as though she is a woman in a musical film on the point of breaking into song. 'That is wonderful news.'

He nods again.

'I don't suppose she's—'

'She's sleeping now,' he says quickly.

Jean nods eagerly. 'Of course. Sleep is the best medicine.'

Her eyes drift to the window, the ceiling. 'I'm sorry it's been such a while since I popped by. Maisie was up for half-term, as you know, and then, what with one thing and another – Derek's anniversary and organising all the blow heaters for this charity concert up at the church… Which reminds me, I brought a flyer round for it a while ago, but just in case, here's another.' She pulls an orange leaflet featuring a black-and-white picture of a candle and someone's hands on a piano out of her bag, and passes it over. 'Piano by Candlelight,' reads the large, looping text. 'A classical recital by Harriet Grover in aid of the Rotham WI Migrants Relief Fund.'

'I thought ET might not be up to it,' continues Jean, 'but as she seems to be making such strides…'

He stares at her. ET does not walk in strides. She shuffles from room to room gripping on to doorposts and the backs of chairs, resolutely refusing to use the metal frame provided by the hospital.

Doubt flits across Jean's face. 'Unless, of course, you think she might not be well enough.'

He shakes his head vigorously. ET is well. She will be perfectly fine to listen to this Harriet Grover reciting. He will make sure.

Jean's smile flicks on like a light. 'Oh good. Well in that case, I'll pick you both up at seven on Saturday. Don't hesitate to let me know in the mean time if you need anything, will you? Bye-bye, now.'

As the back door closes behind Jean, he turns to find ET on the kitchen threshold.

'What did that bitch want?'

At the sound of his laughter, she breaks into smiles. She comes forward, holding out an envelope. 'This, please.'

He stares at her. It is so rare that two complete sentences come together that for a moment he is a little alarmed and has to fight the suspicion that the old ET has somehow walked back into Cliff's Edge and resumed her existence. But her eyes are on the envelope, watching it with the intentness of a dog anticipating a scrap of fried goatskin, and it is clear from the way her fingers twitch and worry at the air that she is not her old self.

He looks down at the envelope. Unlike the other documents she has brought him, it is sealed. It is crisp to the touch and unfaded; the flamboyant handwriting spelling out ET's address still looks black and fresh in contrast to the purpling ink on most of the letters he found heaped along the hall and up the stairs. In another moment, he recognises it. It is from the pile of post that used to lie on the kitchen windowsill – the pile that Jean suggested he might go through with ET when she was well enough.

He glances at the old woman, seeking her approval to open it, but she is oblivious, keeping her eyes on his hands, twitching impatiently. So he slits the thick, creamy paper and pulls the contents free.

'It's from him, isn't it?' she blurts, and then gasps, as if surprised by her own voice.

Jonah looks at the page, with its neat blocks of typed text and the green logo at the top, then at ET, then back at the page. He is on the point of telling her that no, of course the letter is not from Michael. But then he thinks of the diary lying in the bedroom upstairs and the years of loneliness its blank spaces and crossings-out contain.

'Yes,' he says slowly.

She nods and opens her mouth to say more. Only this time, the words aren't where she wants them. She stirs the air urgently with her hand. The meaning is just as plain as if she had spoken it. So, having guided her to one of the wooden chairs at the table, he sits down himself and begins.

'Dear kiddo,' he says, and looks up to check her response.

There is a dreamy smile on her face, and her eyes are far away, following the drift of clouds beyond the window.

He takes this as a sign that he should continue. 'You must think it is exquisitely rude that I did not write to you all these years.'

A frown appears on her face. He thinks fast, trying to work out what in the words might have upset her. He glances at the paper, as if it can help him, but of course there is no answer there. Exquisitely. Perhaps that was the problem. Perhaps it struck too fussy a note. He pretends to frown at the letter.

'Eeeh! Sorry, sorry, sorry. I have made a mistake. It's actually "very". "Very rude" is what he wrote.'

ET's frown intensifies and distress begins to gather in her eyes. He hurries on.

'But the truth is, kiddo, after I was in prison I was ashamed. I did not think I could contact you. I did not see how I could come back here and be in front of everyone, the whole village. What with all the poppycock people talk.'

The smile is back on her lips.

'They are all nonsense people, those customers. They think they are doing kindnesses, but in truth it is all about themselves. You knew that even when you were very young, kiddo. You were always wise in that way, even if you didn't realise that what I said about Aunt Susan coming after me all the time I was in the barn wasn't the total truth, because I did encourage her a little bit, even though she wasn't as nice as you for sleeping with. I am only a man, after all, don't forget.'

He looks at her again. Her eyes are threatening tears, her mouth framing a wail.

'But that's enough about things that are long finished,' he says quickly. 'The main thing is that you must know I loved you. That is the essential point. That is why I am writing this letter. And all these years I have never forgotten you. You must know that too.'

Jonah coughs. His head is beginning to ache with the effort of this reading. It would be best if the letter didn't go on too much longer.

He clears his throat. 'I am an old man now. I am almost dead. I doubt I will ever see you again. In fact, I am far away in a place you wouldn't recognise. So it is unlikely. If you must know, I am in Africa.' She jerks. 'Sorry. America. I am in America. That is the truth.'

He coughs again. 'Anyway, like I said, I am an old man. There are many things I would like to tell you about my life, but tragically that cannot be. I would like to know your secrets too. Ah well. If God allows it…'

He glances up to check the effect of the words. Despite all that he has come to know about her, he is uncertain of her religious views. She has never mentioned faith, and it occurs to him that she might be one of those azungu to whom God is not a welcome prospect. He remembers coming across several such in the camps – charity workers whose smiles wavered when they saw his cross. Perhaps Michael had been such a person too.

ET's face is impassive, however. The reference appears to have made no impression.

He picks up the thread. 'If God allows it, perhaps we will meet one day in the life after this. Then there will be some stories to tell and some pleasures to attend to. My goodness, won't we make the walls of heaven shake! But until then, there must be only silence and memories. I hope life has been nice for you. Yours favourably, Michael.'

He looks up. She is still staring out of the window, only now her eyes are wet. But he sees from the calm on her face that these are not the thunderous tears of fury, door banging and screeching, nor the precursor to the heartbroken sobs of the child she sometimes becomes. Instead these are gentle tears, kind tears, soft like the good rain that washes the fertiliser into the soil and makes the maize shoots grow.

# MANY

Morning. Must be. Sunlight through the curtains. So yes. Sun means day. And those flying things singing. Feathers. Yes. Nice in the house. Comfortable. Mmn.

The man coming in with a… one of those… well, those things you drink. Hot. You can tell by the stuff coming off it. Smoke.

And here is the round thing with the tasty stuff. Sweet and sloppy. Smooth in the mouth. Smile up gratefully. Lucky girl. Treats every day. Please sir, can I have some more? Yes you can, you good thing. As much as you wish for. And no Aunt Susan to make a smash about it. She is in the other room, resting. One of her heads.

He is nice, the man. Some people would call him names. Brownie. Digger. But not her. She is not like that. She knows bigger than that. More world and how it goes. More than the people here with their pork-chop faces.

Yes. He is nice, the man. For all that he is… painful about the eyes. Something sore in him. Something… snipped. Her reminds her. Oh yes. He reminds her.

He is not him, that other one, Michael. But also he is. And many other things. And that is the wonderful of it all – the ssh! that people don't understand. Moments don't go one then the next like people waiting by a stick for one of those… things that travel you about. Time happens in a rush, a whip, a whee! Giddier than a twizzle-whizzle at the fair. Toffee apples. Dental floss. Things that you buy from a grubby hand stretching over a counter to hand you

244

your difference. But not eels in gloop. Crap! We don't like those. Hurly heave. Chug chug.

Oops. Blobules on the blanket. Brown hand wiping with a manual.

But she had something there. Of the thinking persuasion. Yes! It is about everything coming together. Minutes in one go. Like louds on a Joanna. A rope – no – a chord. Or one of those sound-ribbons where the first bit comes and then another bit says it again lower down or higher up and then it comes overmuch, and before you know it, it is a merry tangle, but all making sense. A fug.

Not that she diddled that kind of music in her Joanna days. It was too smart for her. Too Sunday best. She liked the messy. The can-you-guess. The let's-see-what-comes-next.

But moments. That's different. Those you can fug around with all you like. Those you can chord to your heart's content. It makes the meaning stronger.

Only sometimes there are no moments, and it is the quiet between the louds. And nothing comes. And suddenly it's later.

Like now. Now she is underneath in the drawing room and it is middling in the day. The sun peeping under the top of the window frame like a gigantic come to nosy in. Glinting on the Joanna. The water grey as Jerry uniforms out there. Perhaps they will come today. Rowing over stealthily. Faces evil under their hatments. She has watched many times, ready to run and give the alert. She is ready now. Fight them in their breaches. Yes, Mr Bulldog. Too right she will.

But what's this? Some person in blue come to fidget her arms about while he watches, the traitor? Not ruddy likely. Per-cha! How do you like that? Flobber in your face! Oh, you want the legs too, do you? There's leg for you. And there! And there!

Stumbling away. Nose clutching.

Sniffs. Well. Not a bit sorry. The incontinence of it! Good riddance.

A door whams open in her mind on to a dizzying emptiness. Fearful. Something terribly, terribly wrong. But she bangs it shut and carries on being correct. They are all idiots. That is the problem. Even him.

Blink and the day jerks forward again. Or perhaps it is another opening altogether, time shuffled like a pack of… what magicians use. Darkness swilling now. Owl toot. And then the rumbling of a doing machine coming into the yard. A driver. That's it. Click, clack, voices. Hello!

Someone she ought to know smiling down. Face full of expectation of a friend. Bring out the jolly phrases. How nice to see you! How are you? So thoughtful of you to come. How nice to see you!

Upgetting. This way. This way. They push a thing in front of her that is like a metal gate. Thrust it aside! Can't they see it's unhappy?

Out in the yard, the driver waiting. Its engine ticking. Broom broom. Beep beep! Smash, bash, bang! Whizz over the humpback bridge as fast as you can! But no. Not this time. This time, sensible and slow. The young man in the back, she in the front and off we go.

Ah, it's that place. With the men in dresses. Little children craning their necks up for the high notes. Stories coming out of a big book of olden times and far away. Not been here since ever, but it is just the same. The smell: candle wax and censure mixed with a faint note of wee-wee. It could be any time. It could be the young Oxford graduate organ player with the thick glasses and knuckly hands coming down the aisle to see if she'll reconsider leaving the choir. But no, she'll tell him. No. She has been through all that. She has seen through all that. She has unpacked life to the bottom of the box and knows there is nothing there.

Not the organ player with his lozenge breath, however, but a man with face fur and a round laugh standing by the door. 'Edith! How wonderful you could make it. Great to see you up and about.'

She opens her mouth for a hit back. Fiddling around for a bonbon. A bon mot. A bon voyage. No good. Too much hardness. The man smiles like a post box, flurries them inside. God, he is a penis.

So across the aisle to one of the long chairs. A pugil? A hugh? Something of that frock. Sitting down. Jeans, her, him. Someone handing her a gulp in a plastic cup. Glug glug. Scrunch the face. Not nice, but there we are.

'Finished already? You must have been thirsty.'

Blank face. As if she would answer such a toilet-paper remark.

Time happening all at once again. Jean running down the aisle giggling, her hair in bibs. But Jean also here, next to her, fat and creased. Michael on the other side. But not Michael too.

A notice in her hand with a show-me on it – the mouth of a Joanna, fiddlers and a name that sounds like chariots. And also hats. So this is what this business is about. She might have known. The haberdasher'll have a hand in it somewhere. You mark my card.

And then, as if to play a jape, the vestry door spits out a woman with orange hair, the audience raps and the Joanna begins to play. And it is one of those spidery pieces stalking all over the louds, a sound-ribbon going from one highance to the next. Fuggish.

Only she can't hear it properly, because there is some blasted blaster blasting at the end of the long seat, throwing hot air at them.

She turns to not-Michael to get him to stop it. But there is queerness about him, his eyes round as marbles, staring at the flimsy at the front.

After years and in a minute, the music stops. More rapping. New balls, please. People getting up to poo. But what is this? Everyone coming at them. Speaks asking. What about this matter? And this? And this? That little-boy-grown-bulbous doing his best with his waistcoat and his head to seem destructible.

Not-Michael turning here, turning there. Buts bursting like balloons.

Voices high and low. Gobble gobble. Gabble gabble. Hatracks turning to see. Not-Michael vacuuming, hands wretched. Clitter-clatter, a stool flopped. Then a blare and a smash and now whoops of worry.

One of the askers leaping around in a jig, slapping at her back bit. Fire crinkling up her legs. The face-fur man coming forward with a red thing attached to a snake. Blurt! Blurt! Foam like a snow scene all around. Now more people snap to their feet, some for the exits and others beavering up the aisle to the asker's allowance, tugging not-Michael away. As their voices spiral upwards, shouts and plantations pickling with the sound of running footsteps, the forest of people rises around her so that she can no longer see. She tries to speak, to no-say, to hold them back, telling that this is not it, that they are missing something vital, they have misunderstood, they have got the wrong end of the biscuit. But her voice is lost in the slurry, which washes around her, battering the pillars of the instant; smashing away the masonry of what is; sluicing out now with before. Until the rafters of the present tremble, crack and fall, crashing down on her thinker, knocking away all knowing.

# PHEW

They will keep on. One voice then another. Many mouths squiggling. Chat, chat, chat. Standing by the piano, clubbing it with their hands. 'The point is' – that's a favourite wheeze of theirs. 'We have to be realistic' – there's another. 'In everyone's best interests.' All very serious, as though they imagine they are delicatessens arranged around a big shiny table doing the ordering.

There's a... thing that has happened. Only, when she tries to look it in the peeper it wriggles away, sniggling. That is why they are here with their funeral faces. That is why they are being helpful. The fat women. Jean. The sir with the waistcoat who makes people take off their clothes in his office and keeps writtens about them in metal drawers. But, oh fuck! Doesn't she wish they'd go? Go away and let her get back to being... even. If they'd just give her room!

But they won't. They will keep going on about the young man – the boy, they call him. The not-Michael. The him. They will keep going on. He has done something. Been something unrespectable. And now they want his guts for gizzards. They have trapped him like a wasp under a thing you drink with in the bedroom upstairs while they parade around making sandwiches. The rogers!

The thought of it braises her. All that sad stabled up when he was meaning to be kind. He's a soldier. Can't they see? He's been in a war. She and Father collected him from the burning. Didn't they ought to gentle him like one of those midgets they are always canvassing money for?

They advance, cooing, leaning over her where she sits on the wonky couch. Poor Edith. Poor girl. Poor thing. How gravely she's been masticated! The boy is not any of those nicenesses. He's a stickler. That's the fact of the matter. He has taken her for a giddy-up. He isn't a sorry person. He isn't from a war zone. He hasn't fled hideousnesses. Quite the reverse. He is from Malawi, a small, quiet patch of earth where there hasn't been a shindig in decades. They even have bicycles there. Luxury by the standards of boom and blast. Money. That is what has brought him here. Pure and simple. Greed. A desire for easy gets. Sorry to say it, but he is one of those they always gobble about in the black-and-whites – parasites shimmying their way in to leech off the system, giving real-needers a bad name (that documentary last night: the Syrians. Awful, wasn't it? The little baby at the end).

She shakes her head. Not true. Not true. Not true. Not true. Until she can't remember what she is not-truing about and it seems life is stuck for ever in this intimation, like a record scratched and jumping on the gramophone, playing the same hiddle-diddle roundly.

There are people talking. The fat women. Jean. The sir with the waistcoat who makes people take off their clothes in his office and keeps writtens about them in metal drawers. There is a to-do they are saying about, some cacophony in the church last night. (Edie laughs. She malingers it: she hasn't been inside that church in seventy years. But go on, go on.) Not-Michael causing a ransack. Pedalling bicycles (they have them in Malawi, did she know? Luxury by the standards of boom and blast.) How about this for a ding-dong: he told a woman from the sociable services that the hospital had come to get her. That was wickedness. And his name isn't even Michael: it's Jonah. What stink can she make of that? Also, just look what he did to poor Ruth, bullying her into the blaster. Her leg is like a ham. Clearly, he is an understudy. A potwasher. It doesn't take a genius to unlatch it.

Edie narrows her eyes. Jonah? Oh yes. She sees what they are trying to do. Coddling on about the church and such. They are trying to be Christian with her. They are trying to do her into godding again. Well, toodle-pip and all that. Her father's house has many rooms. She won't sit here to be lectured like a lemon.

She tries to rise, but they thrust her down. Hands on her shoulders. Smiles flashing like firemen.

Words bat between them. 'That is the trouble with these cross-cultural schemes…'

'Of course, it's a lovely idea to behave as though everybody's the same…'

'Have you seen the way he's kept the house? The state of the oven! It looks as though he's been conducting some sort of ritual in there…'

'I'm not saying they're animals…'

She closes her eyes and opens them again, and there are people above her, talking. The fat women. Jeans. The sir with the waistcoat who makes people take off their clothes in his office and keeps writtens about them in metal drawers.

The thing is, someone's kept the house in an offish manner. The thing is, what does she eat? The thing is, someone saw a person crouched on a sitter in the houses place, stuffing bread into his mouth, bold as brass. The thing is, where's her spend, that's what they'd like to know.

They carry on saying, but she's ballooned if she knows what it means. Her attention keeps being distracted by the sinister lines of the black van waiting outside the window, its back doors open, revealing the bare bench and the Poohsticks creamed to the inside of the window halfway along its flank. A Black Mary. No, not quite. Odd that they should have brought it round there, next to the cliff, clambering over growers and greens. And yet there it is, its engine bubbling, doors yawning, attending.

They are tugging the sleeve of her cardigan, bringing her back to this-here. Sorry, Edith, they know it's upsetting, but it would help – really it would – if she could try to pay the waiter so that they can get everything straight. She nods. Someone hereabouts is wearing a flower pong. Lily of the valley. Too much of it. It's making her head ache.

And then there is the van, still out there on the other side of the window, belching. They ought to have asked before they brought that round, boggling her box hedges. They did really.

Sorry, Edith, but could she look? They know it's delicate – sorry again – but they have to ask. It's important. Does she keep large amounts of lovely about the place? The how's-your-father from the business in the field. Purely for her own sake, could she tell them how she'd been managing things? Did she give any to the antelope? Is it possible he might have snaffled in the trough?

She flaps a hand impatiently. (How she wishes someone would offswitch the van.) Yes, of course there's money. Dollops of it. All neatly tucked away in the kitchen dressing table. The one on the end with the broken hold-me. What do they imagine? That she is a poor old sausage who doesn't know which up is down any more?

Glances scatter-gun. Someone hurries.

All of a sudden, her heart is a-scamper. The suspicion comes that they are not friends. Impostors marched here to unseed her. Jerries in disguise, crept up from the cliff foot with their rifles jerk-angled up their trouser legs. She puts her hands to her cheeks and readies for a screech.

A woman titters back into the room. Daughter of the man at the chip shop who is supposed to have died of chest expansion when really everyone knows it was the slurp.

'It's all gone!' she splurges triumphantly. 'Not a sou.'

They turn back to her. Fat smiles. Oh dear, Edith. This isn't good news. This really is starting to look rather strict.

Oh, they are eggs! She is sick of them. She wants them gone. Who told them they could come here? Who said they could bring that wretched van?

But they close in on her, brandishing their heads. Oh dear. It is exactly as they feared. This is what they were rowing at all those weeks ago when they sent those sirs to have a quiet speak with her. They were concerned she was valuable and that some unscrupulous person might take umbrage. But would she listen? Stubborn old seawart! Well, thank goodness they've squinted in time. And just as well he's still up in the bedroom. Just as well Martha had the moxy to turn the key. When the police get here, it should be a simple matter of undoctoring the evil and putting everything back the right way.

It is all getting bitty now. Words flying flintwise. Scents scattering. She is finding it tired.

But then one of them shifts and a new rampant breaks in. For there in the space between their fiddling bodies is the friend, the old one, Jean, sitting in the wicker chair, teeth worrying at the dry skin on her lips. Time slots in puzzle over puzzle, and she sees the same face on a young girl, standing on the track, watching as a black van drives away. All because he is a pudding. A desert. A tut-tut. It gasps her. All this time she has been certain it was Roger Allen who did the filthy, calling up the hard hats to come and take Michael off to the banger. But all the while it had actually been…

'You! It was you! You piglet! You snot!'

She is standing now, bellyaching. Finger jabbing. Piercing frightened into friend Jean's eyes.

They clutch her back – hands on her shoulders, voices muttering in her ears. It isn't what she supposes. No one is acting slenderly. They are all in agreement that involving the calamities is the right thing to do.

But she won't listen. Not this now. She won't be held back with wizeneds about justice and duty and no one being above law. She is no longer a fluff who can be kept off the land by scarecrows. She has lived and she has felt and she has pained. After seventy years of good girl, she is going to make a smell!

All at once the Black Mary outside the window becomes sensible. She knows what she has to do. She shrugs off their grasp and ping-pongs from the room, glancing left and right: the runway, the stairs, the door to the dining room.

'Michael! Michael!' She has to find him. She cannot let them rob him this time.

She jogs to the kitchen – empty, but for the usual cosies – and out of the back door. They come after, they try to refuse her. Only she is too Hovis for them. Ha!

But out in the yard, what's this? Another van. White, this time, with blues and yellows on the side. Men in uniforms officiating.

'Excuse me, madam? We're here about the—'

She waves them aside. No fish today, thank you. Off across the cobblestones.

'Michael! Michael? You've got to get away! They're coming to invest you!'

Of course, the barn. He'll be in there. The doorway gallumphing. The sweet sniff inside. The hay starting to rot. Make a scribble to order more for Dobbin's stall. Soon. Another time.

'Michael? Michael?'

She looks around. Only the bare walls. No sign of him, nor his kit bag. No dazzler glinting up from amid the wisps. No pack of Player's Navy Cut.

They come barrelling in after her, the women and the fishmongers, clutching their caps. Fear shoots through her that they will slab her before she is able to find him and lead her away, forcing her to knuckle under.

But then she sees it: the highway to the hayloft. Of course! How could she forget? The place where the do was done. Up there.

She seizes the stiles and begins to monkey. Scurry at first, worried of hands. But then she sees them standing in a circle, mouthing up, too lumpish for that. And so unbends she and takes her time, sure of seeing the wonder any moment, almost longing it for the fun. His face, his smile, the heavy of him.

Oh, it has been too much! To think she let them scarf him from her all these years!

'Michael?'

Blankness booming when she puts her head through, but no daunt. She grins as the climber squeaks a giggle. Some game here, no doubt. She knows him.

'Michael?'

She takes a step and the floor seagulls in reply.

'For pity's sake, Edith,' snips from below. 'Please come down. It's not safe up there.'

Odd, but the floor has a window in it. A jagged pond that looks straight down. And there they all are, peering up through the waters, necks bobbing like squawks.

The look makes her smile. How she is Queen of them! How further ahead of their stock-cube lives. She feels triumphant. She feels velvet. She rides to the wonder on a ploughshare of stars. It is all coming to harvest now, and she is waiting with a giant spoon.

She takes a step forward, gladness at the ready. 'Michael?'

Across the yard, a dark figure slippers round the side of the house and runs towards the gate. It is beyond their looking, but she sees it mumly through the open door. She hugs a pleased. Yes, let it go like that. There ought to be bananas for everybody.

She telegraphs back down to where they are, those others, frogging up at her. And now she spots it all. There he is, smash bang among them, her Michael, her special. There all along, his mouth spread like butter, his arms held wide. Today he is his midsummer self, the shadows blinded. And now the sense of the van is unfolded. She sighs happily. He has come at last, as she knew he would. He is waiting for her to join him. The roof sighs with her. The floor groans with delight. There is a crack and a slither. And here she goes – nothing can stop her this time – tipping, tilting, tumbling, rushing everwards into his arms.

# ONE

It is raining when he gets off the bus, washing away the dregs of the afternoon. Even in the sunshine, however, the place would be ugly: concrete houses and towers huddling either side of a road with a metal barrier running down the middle. Everything stinking of traffic fumes; empty crisp packets and drinks cans twitching as the cars speed past. It reminds him of a motorway he slept beside once, shivering under the bushes.

Much of London is like this, he has learnt in the days since he arrived here. The images you saw in the books – St Paul's, Trafalgar Square, Buckingham Palace. All that was big talk. Sunday best. This is where real people live.

At first, trudging through street after street of grime-smeared houses until he found the one with the sign in the window – ROOMS TO LET. UNQUIRE WITHIN – he had been disappointed. This was not the London he had imagined, the bright, grand place where he would settle to work in a handsome office with a view of the Thames. But when he banged on the door and saw the woman's face soften as he got out the one crinkled roll of ET's notes that he had discovered zipped in the inside pocket of the old jacket, he had felt more comfortable. Hers was an expression he had witnessed a hundred times in the trading centre when the kwacha started to flow again. He understands it. It is better this way than what he had imagined. He can find his path through this.

He gets out his phone and checks the map. He is in the right place. There is the star at the entrance to the patch of green. Not far to go now. A five-minute walk, maybe. Along this road, then a right, then a left.

He starts off along the pavement, pulling his jacket tighter as the rain intensifies. His muscles are aching, still adjusting to the lodging-house bed. He hadn't fancied stretching out on the rough carpet, which caked the soles of his feet with crumbs and flecks of dust and dirt when he walked across it. And it was time, he decided, looking out through the dingy gauze curtain that hung over the window as night welled up, to adjust to the way people lived here. He couldn't sleep beside beds for ever.

The thought had occurred to him first as he crouched in the bedroom at ET's house, listening to the voices coming up through the floorboards. High ones, low ones, the gabble of Jean, the rumble of the man in the waistcoat – as varied as the bodies from which they proceeded and yet all soaked in the same, grave tone. Now and then he heard ET's interjections, fluttering and frail like the calls of the caged birds he used to see for sale on stalls at the trading centre. But these had come less and less frequently as time went by.

He wasn't sure how many of them had stayed in the house that night. When they had brought her back after the abrupt break-up of the concert, it had seemed likely that they would phone for an ambulance and send her to hospital. Only the large man in the waistcoat, who seemed to be some sort of doctor, had given his opinion that it would be better if she rested quietly at home. (He had half wondered if they might call some sort of vehicle to cart him away, too, but after the initial flurry of outrage when, in his confusion, he had been unable to come up with a satisfactory answer to their questions about what he had told that sociable worker, Clare, most people seemed to have forgotten him. ET's illness and that woman tripping over the heater and injuring her leg had conveniently eclipsed him. He had slunk into Jean's car and accompanied them back to the house without anyone appearing to give him much thought.)

Thereafter, they had apparently made it their mission to force ET to do everything but rest. They had fussed around her, bringing plates of food and mugs of tea – heedless of her preference for the small china cups – and they had stood awkwardly outside the bathroom, trying to direct her through the door, oblivious to her confusion, her preference for using the lavatory before brushing her teeth at night and the way she liked to be wrapped in her towel. In an effort to be useful, he had emerged with her notebook of instructions and tried to press it into the hands of one of the women, but she waved it away as if it was nothing and fixed him with a furious glare.

'You get back in there!' she said, gesturing to the spare bedroom. 'We're perfectly capable of looking after dear Etith without further input from you. If you're wanted, you'll be called for.' And she'd pushed him back into the bedroom. A little while afterwards he'd heard the key scraping in the lock.

Dear Etith. Only, from the way they were speaking to her, she didn't sound particularly dear to them, especially not that morning. There was a sternness to their manner that reminded him of the voice of the headmaster of St Andrew's on the morning he had announced in assembly that any boy arriving for class without a receipt for his school fees would be turned away. It was the rigidity of yes or no, a shutter rattling down, a way of deciding things that left no room for the possibility that life might prove to be more complicated than either-or allowed.

Of course, he didn't blame them for being angry with him. His behaviour had been erratic, and he must have seemed very strange. It was just that when he had looked up and seemed to see the Hattie who had come to his village all those years ago sitting at the piano in place of the stranger he was expecting, he had forgotten where he was. The years had fallen away, and it was as though he was back there, sitting in the shade of the shelter with the prospect of a stroll down to the trading centre later to hear about Gilbert's next business idea or the latest love cheats to fall victims to the sing'anga's sticking-together curse, while Amayi and the twins prepared nsima for the evening meal. It was only when the large woman toppled into the heater and he looked around to see horror inscribed on the rows of pale faces stretching back into the gloom that he remembered he was in the church, in England.

Even so, the seriousness of the situation did not strike him until the following morning, when he heard ET shouting, urging him to run. At the sound, his mind – sluggish from hours of staring at the locked door – lurched into action. He would not sit there to be caught. He glanced feverishly around the room – walls, ceiling, floor. Then his gaze caught on the old floral notebook, ET's diary. In a flash, it was back in his mind: her description of how she used to escape her room without Aunt Susan noticing – tying bedsheets together and climbing out of the window. He lost no time in following suit, shrugging on the jacket and letting himself down into a flower bed just beyond the piano-room window. Rounding the corner of the house, the sight of the police van nearly sent him reeling, but he held himself together and crept across the yard behind it, dodging the eyes of the cluster of grey-haired figures gathered in the barn. Luckily, they appeared to be engrossed in something, staring up towards the roof. Slipping down the track, he passed the new sign proclaiming the coming of a cliff-top jazz bar and restaurant in the adjacent field, and away to the road.

The traffic rumbles past him on the grey London street. He takes a right turn off, then goes left into a leafy street lined with large, rambling houses. There are the gates in front of him, just as he expected. His pride at finding the place is short-lived, however, quickly displaced by the realisation that the big gates are closed. Perhaps he has come all this way – taken the two buses, walked through that sinister underpass – for nothing. Disconsolate, he walks up to the entrance and pushes his nose through the bars.

He takes out the piece of paper and checks the address. No doubt about it: he is in the right place.

The great, conical, shrubs and bushes stare back at him, flanking the forked drive that leads off to expanses of green stippled with stone sculptures glimpsed here and there through their trunks. A cold, formal place.

'Coming in, are you?' A man in what looks a bit like a bus conductor's uniform emerges from a small hut beside the gate. Lifting a latch, he swings open a smaller rectangle that Jonah hasn't noticed in the metalwork and beckons him inside.

'Shuts in forty-five minutes, so you'll have to be sharp about it,' says the man, clanging the gate to.

'Yes, sir,' says Jonah. He takes a few steps and hesitates, gazing at the two roads leading off between the trees.

The gatekeeper sighs. 'Need help? Here, let me see that.'

Jonah hands him the piece of paper and he nods. 'You'll find the old pauper graves over by the far fence. Goes by year. Probably won't have a headstone, mind.'

Nodding his thanks, Jonah sets off along the right fork to the far patch of gravestones, a meaner, more regimented collection than the rest, lacking the elaborate tombs of the older sections and the heaps of flowers and soft toys evident among the lines of newer monuments.

He finds the part where the graves from the 1940s begin and works his way along the rows as the years mount – 1943, 1944. Many are unmarked – just mounds with paths running in between. Some have little wooden crosses jutting from one end, weathered and rotting with the years. Where there are headstones they give little away. Most of them hold only the name of the person and their dates. Occasionally the engraver has added 'R.I.P.' There is nothing else. It seems that the families and villagers of these people have not given much towards the cost of putting them in the earth. Shivering in the drizzle, Jonah reflects that a Malawian would be ashamed to leave a family member to meet his maker in this condition.

1945. 1946. Ah, here it is: 1947. And, look: a small stone. Neville Brown, 3.10.29–7.8.47. He checks the letter, the same creamy slip of paper from which he pretended to read to ET in the kitchen:

Dear Miss Morley,

Firstly, apologies for the long delay in responding to your inquiry. The advertising campaign we ran in the newspapers back in 2010 was far more successful than we could have expected, with the result that there is a backlog of correspondence, much of which is only now being processed.

I do not know if you are still at this address or, indeed, interested to know the answer to your query after all this time. But in the event that you are, I can tell you the following.

It seems the military authorities were correct when they told you there was no record of a Private Michael Patterson answering the description you gave. However, as it was not unusual for soldiers who went AWOL in those times to assume aliases, I took the liberty of looking up the arrests for desertion on the date in July 1945 you mentioned.

There were two that day. One in Liverpool, which I think we can safely discount, and one on the south coast. From the details you mention in your letter, I strongly suspect that this is our man, not least because the arresting officer's report describes the suspect as being 'of negroid extraction' (apologies if this seems insensitive – these were less enlightened times).

The man's real name was Neville Brown, and he was sentenced to serve three years in HMS Pentonville, where, I am sorry to say, he died in August 1947. The records give the cause as 'unexplained' (sadly a common shorthand for foul play in those days, or, sorry to say it, suicide). As there were no next-of-kin listed in his papers, he was buried in a pauper's grave in a London cemetery. I enclose a printout of the details, should you wish to visit. It is likely that his remains are still there, although the precise resting place may not be marked, and it is possible that the body may have been moved to make way for others in the intervening years (again, less enlightened times).

I am sorry not to be able to be the bearer of better news, but hope that after all this time the knowledge of what happened to Neville may at least afford you and your family some peace, or 'closure' as the Americans say.

With kind regards,

Yours sincerely,

Wilfred Jameson

PS: Should you feel inclined, we are always grateful for donations to help fund our research. Where Are They Now? is a small charity run almost entirely by myself. We accept cash, cheques and bank transfers made out to the details above, but please not postal orders – the last one caused no end of trouble. Thank you for your consideration.

Jonah folds the letter and slides it back into his jacket. So, here he is. ET's friend. Michael. Neville.

He stands and stares at the little grey stone. He doesn't know what he had expected to feel, but he had anticipated it would be more than this. Perhaps he had thought there would be sadness. Or the sort of clicking-shut sensation that used to come when one of Grandma's fireside tales came to an end. Maybe he had imagined he might feel a sense of kinship with this man who had died all those decades before, yet whose name he had worn briefly and whose story had become oddly entwined with his own.

Instead he feels only the cold wind, blowing moisture into his face, and the sensation that the man at the gate is watching him, glancing now and then at the clock in his cabin counting down the minutes until the cemetery closes.

He wonders if he should say a prayer. The old urge to get out the silver cross surges through him briefly before he remembers that he no longer has it. He left it behind when he lowered himself down from the bedroom window at Cliff's Edge. He only realised it was gone when he was on the bus to London. After the initial pang, he decided it didn't matter: he didn't need it any more. God, whatever it was, did not live in that object. He or she was a much more diffuse, nebulous force than that, rushing in at odd moments and then receding like the tide. Gusting up unexpectedly to interrupt the scurry of life. A great, queer, awkward kindness, shining through the scuffed, dirty pane of human affairs, glancing sometimes off faces and the acts of strangers.

No. He cannot pray for Michael, and so instead he thinks about ET. He hopes she is happy and that they are looking after her. That whoever is with her can find a way to interpret her needs. His eyes drift to the horizon and the collection of tall buildings glittering there – the financial district that he walked round on his second day in the city, with its strange collection of maritime station names. Canary Wharf. Surrey Quays. West India Docks. Perhaps one day when he is successful and has an office in such a tower, he will go back and visit ET. Maybe then he will be able to return all the money that he took and lost. He would like to do that.

The gatekeeper is approaching. It must be nearing closing time. He takes a last look at the reticent little stone. And in that moment he makes a vow: whatever the future brings him he will not allow himself to end in such a lonely manner, unknown and unremarked. He will matter. He will make connections and involve himself in things that last. He will look this chilly country, this indifferent world, in the eye and make them respect him. He will not sit alone as the years go by, waiting for things to change. He owes them all that – ET, Amayi, Elijah and the twins, Abambo and all the people he watched fall on the journey. He will live if it kills him. Yes, God, if you are listening, he will live.

'Find it?'

He nods.

The man whistles. 'Lucky. They didn't always take great care in them days.'

He nods again – 'Thanks' – and, raising a hand, walks away through the trees.

He will get the buses back to the lodging house. Perhaps he'll treat himself to a takeaway from the fried-chicken shop nearby. Tomorrow he will make a plan.

But as he reaches the main road, his pocket starts to buzz. Taking out the phone, he sees a number on the screen, starting with a familiar code. But before he can answer, the call ends. Someone has flashed him.

He clicks the button to phone back. 'Hello?'

'Muli bwanji, brother?'

He frowns and looks about him as though the person might be standing nearby. 'I'm sorry. Who is this?'

'Daniel, man. Who else?'

His eyes flit to and fro, trying to read the sense of what he is hearing in the cracks of the pavement.

'Daniel?'

'Yes, achimwene!'

'How did you get this number?'

'You flashed Gilbert. He passed it on. Knew it was you because of the UK code.'

'Daniel. Where did you…? I thought you were…'

'Listen, man. I don't have much battery. I just wanted to let you know I'm coming.'

'What do you mean, you're coming?'

'The back route, man. Like you did.'

He staggers in disbelief, causing a car pulling off the road into one of the driveways that run across the pavement to sound its horn.

'I've got it all arranged. Gilbert's out of the game now – you probably know that – but there's this new guy who knows all the shortcuts. Ten thousand kwacha and I'm on the truck.'

Jonah waves absently to the driver and steps aside as the wheels rev crossly up the curb. Is this really Daniel? This swaggering youth with the big man's voice? Daniel? That little boy he'd left kicking the tied-up plastic bag around the dirt pitch only two years before?

'So get prepared, brother,' the man's voice is saying. 'Two or three months, I'll be there.'

He shakes his head. 'Look, man, I don't know if it's a good idea... It's not as easy as you think. The journey... it's tough. People die. You might not make it.'

He can almost hear the shrug. 'People die here. What's the difference? Besides, things are getting a little... hot round here for me, brother. You understand? It would be better if I went away. And with my brother being the big man in the UK, in London, no less, what better place to head?'

Jonah can't help smiling. Even so, a frown follows quickly. 'I don't know, Daniel. It's dangerous. It changes you. You see things. You won't be the same when you get here. You won't be you. That's something you have to consider.'

'Well who will I be, then? Who are you?'

Jonah shrugs. 'I... I don't know.'

'Honestly, brother. A few months in the UK and you're already talking like some mzungu hippy. Look, my battery's nearly dead. I'm coming, OK? It's all arranged. Expect me.'

The road seems different when he slides the phone back into his pocket and looks up. The street lights are flickering on, making haloes in the mist, and the last of the daylight is throwing pink into the sky.

He is about to turn in the direction of the bus stop when his eye snags on something in the row of buildings next to him: a brightly lit shop amid a row of dark façades. Inside a group of men are standing around or lounging in black swivel chairs, drinking beers and watching a match from the Africa Cup of Nations playing on the screen suspended in the far corner. 'Head Doctors', reads the sign. 'Specialists in Afro Hair.'

Jonah laughs in disbelief. So Gilbert hadn't been making everything up, then? What he'd said about the African barbershops in London had contained a kernel of truth. Or perhaps it was just chance. Maybe among all the nonsense his former friend talked it was inevitable that something would prove genuine. It isn't important. But neither is the bus ride home nor the fried-chicken dinner. Not any more. Smiling to himself, Jonah walks up to the shopfront, pushes the door and goes inside.

# AUTHOR'S NOTE

I wrote *Crossing Over* in 2017, shortly after I had moved to the Kent coast. At that time, the number of small boats attempting to cross the English Channel was very low – the Migrant Crisis, as the media was calling it, was mostly still in the Mediterranean and on mainland Europe. As a result, the events in this novel were largely speculative, a vision of what could happen if and when more people started making the trip from France.

Back then, the prevailing attitude was that there ought to be a distinction between the way the UK treated refugees and economic migrants. Genuine asylum seekers, many pundits and politicians claimed, should be welcomed, while those purely seeking a better life should be sent away. This stark categorisation bothered me: it seemed to me that such a line was difficult, and even dangerous to draw when for many the trip was clearly about survival, regardless of the precise nature of the challenges they had left behind. It also seemed to me to ignore the fact that moving is part of being human – a freedom that many of us raised in historically dominant cultures take for granted. Consequently, I set out to create a character who challenged this distinction, making Jonah the son of a farmer whose family had been devastated by the 2002 famine in Malawi, and who had faced a level of suffering comparable to that of many victims of war. This was the version that came out as an audiobook, published by Audible, in 2019.

In the five years since I wrote the original manuscript, things have changed. The number of people crossing the Channel annually is now in the tens of thousands, while at least 150 have died making the attempt since 2016. In November 2021, I attended a vigil on a local beach in solidarity with the twenty-seven people who drowned in a single incident that month, a few miles from my front door. I have also had the privilege of working with some of those who have arrived recently, thanks to the support of the Royal Literary Fund and collaborations with local charities including the Kent Refugee Action Network (KRAN) and Samphire. Meanwhile, government policy has hardened towards those trying to come to the UK by this route: the distinction between refugee and economic migrant has collapsed into general suspicion, if not outright hostility, with navy boats and helicopters patrolling the coastline, far-right groups picketing asylum seekers' accommodation, and flights planned to Rwanda. At the same time, there have been many important discussions about the portrayal of African characters in British literature, and the damaging perpetuation of certain stereotypes and dynamics – stereotypes and dynamics that I attempted to subvert in my first version by having Jonah effectively become ET's saviour, but which I felt I could do more to tackle.

With all this in mind, I decided to revisit Jonah's circumstances for the print edition. Instead of the son of a farmer, in this new version Jonah is the son of a clinical officer – a medical professional who performs the role of doctor, albeit with less formal training, in many parts of Malawi to this day. Although a lot of the changes are subtle and may not be immediately obvious, they do, I hope, present a richer, more complex picture. In this version, Jonah comes from a relatively affluent, educated family background. His prospects, at least as a young child, were good. Yet he still finds himself compelled to leave his home and family in search of a better life, travelling across the world, just as human beings have done throughout history and will no doubt continue to do.

# ACKNOWLEDGEMENTS

It's been a long journey getting *Crossing Over* into print. And it would have been much harder without a stalwart group of early readers who believed in this project from the start. These include Caroline Hardman, Thérèse Coen, Oliver Jones and Emily Bullock. Thanks, too, to Harriet Poland and the team at Audible for giving this story a life in audio four years before it made it on to the page. And a special thank you to Adjoa Andoh for doing a phenomenal job with the narration.

The ethics and pitfalls of writing cross-cultural narratives have rightly been the subject of much debate in recent years. As someone working from a dominant culture, I was conscious of a duty to be particularly diligent and sensitive in Jonah's creation. As such, I am grateful to very many people who read early drafts and answered questions to help me bring his story alive, in particular Antonia Windsor, Shyne Phiri, Melissa Eveleigh, Ben Mankhamba, Rhoberto Magasa and Joshua Mwalweni. I am also thankful to the many brilliant writers whose work continues to inform and challenge my thinking on these issues, among them Reni Eddo-Lodge, Nanjala Nyabola, Michael Holding, David Olusoga and Sathnam Sanghera, along with the scores of fabulous authors I have encountered through A Year of Reading the World, some of whom I am privileged to call friends.

Similarly, I am grateful to poet Denise Saul for lending her expertise on aphasia and brain trauma to help shape my development of Edie, and to my parents, Pat and Richard, for providing medical insights into Edie's care and the progression of her illness. A large number of books on ageing and dementia also informed her creation, chief among them John Bayley's brilliant memoir, *Iris*. Any mistakes, false notes or biases clouding either character's story are my own.

Without a publisher, a book is nothing but a manuscript. *Crossing Over* might have continued in this limbo state had it not been for Will Dady and Renard Press. Your enthusiasm, ingenuity and energy are hugely inspiring. I have long said that indie presses are the heroes of the publishing world; now I have experienced this first-hand too.

Thanks, too, to Steve Cook and the Royal Literary Fund, which is an unstinting source of support, camaraderie and wonderful opportunities to build connections and use my storytelling skills in fulfilling and enriching ways.

Finally, a big thank you as always to Steve and Dil. *Crossing Over* was written while I was pregnant with Dil, and as such she is perhaps its co-author. At any rate, I can well believe a lot of its hopefulness, warmth and humanity comes from her.

# ABOUT THE AUTHOR

ANN MORGAN is an author, speaker and editor based in Folkestone. Ann's writing has been published widely, including in the *Guardian*, *Independent* and *Financial Times*, and by the BBC. In 2012, she set herself the challenge of reading a book from every country in a year – a project that led to a TED talk and to the non-fiction book *Reading the World: How I Read a Book from Every Country*. Her debut novel, *Beside Myself*, has been translated into eight languages. *Crossing Over*, her latest novel, draws on her experience living just a few minutes from where many of the small boats crossing the Channel land. She is Literary Explorer in Residence of the Cheltenham Literature Festival for 2022 and 2023.

ANNMORGAN.ME 🌐 🐦 @A_B_MORGAN

WWW.RENARDPRESS.COM